Praise for "Feasty-Fe

MW01047790

"A unique, creepy delight." –
and Bestseller Michaelbrent Collings

"'Feasty-Feast' is one of the best horror shorts I have ever read.
Michael Darling is a talent, a master of perspective and playful
horror." – *Johnny Worthen, Award Winning Author of WHAT
IMMORTAL HAND*

"'Feasty-Feast' is a rare blend of enchanting and ghoulish. I adored
it from the very first read!" – *Caryn Larrinaga, award-winning author of
DONN'S HILL and editor of THE HUNGER*

Praise for "The Hollow"

"The ultimate haunted house ride."   – *Michael R. Collings*

Praise for "Spera Angelorum"

"Harry Houdini and Charles Dickens cross swords of wit, debate
sociology, and team up on the stage in a technological hereafter. I
can't tell which part of that I like the most! Then there are the
demon manacles..." – Derick William Dalton, author of
SPACEBOOTS

Praise for the *Sailing on the Tides of Burning Sand* Short Story Collection

"This anthology of short stories provides a variety of fictional
genres sure to please any reader, from sci-fi to horror to fantasy.
The reader can find beautiful imagery in the title story, 'Sailing on
the Tides of Burning Sand,' and shivering horror in both 'The
Hollow' and 'Feasty-Feast.' My favorite story was 'Grandmother
Who Breaks the Sky,' with its nod to Ray Bradbury. But there is
also fun in the eternal competition between Charles Dickens and
Houdini in 'Spera Angelorum.' And lastly, this anthology provides
a taste of the author's Behindbeyond Tales with three short
stories…just enough to whet one's whistle. All told twelve
delightful stories to pass the time." – Linda Kuzminczuk on
Goodreads.

Read Michael Darling's #1 Bestselling *Tales from the Behindbeyond* Series

Got Luck – Book One from the Behindbeyond

> "Got Luck is the private detective Harry Dresden would hire to solve a murder. Highly Recommended." – *Paul Genesse, author of the bestselling Iron Dragon series.*

Got Hope – Book Two from the Behindbeyond

> "Darling's surprising and inventive prose, powerful characters, and exemplary attention to Celtic details make this book as intriguing as it is action packed." – *Mikki Kells, author of the Ace of Hearts series.*

Got Lost – Book Three from the Behindbeyond

> "The Behindbeyond series is a pinnacle of urban fantasy. Got Lost reaches new heights of excellence and takes the series that much closer to the status of fantasy classic." — *Kevin L. Nielsen, author of the Sharani Series*

> "Great plot. Wonderful visuals. Witty humor, often contained in Got's internal dialog. I plan on going back to the beginning and re-reading the entire series again. Michael Darling earns a hat-trick of top ratings for his Behindbeyond series from me. I give *Got Lost* a resounding five stars and look forward to more from this brilliant and imaginative author extraordinaire." – *Nicholas P. Adams*

Read the Outstanding Sci-Fi Novel *Hollowfall*

"If you're a cyberpunk science fiction fan with a love for the unexpected, then *Hollowfall* sets everything apart, leaving you wanting more after each chapter. The pace is phenomenal, keeping you at a razor's edge." – *Nick Defina, Playingoffline and Workincomics*

More by Michael Darling

Tales from the Behindbeyond

Got Luck
Got Hope
Got Lost

Master of Wills

Hollowfall

Sailing on the Tides of Burning Sand

and Other Stories

Sailing on the Tides of Burning Sand and Other Stories

Text © 2020
Cover art © 2020
All rights reserved

Cover art by François Vaillancourt
www.francois-art.com

A Lucky Darling Publication

Lucky Darling, LLC
A Michael Darling Company
Sandy, UT

www.michaelcdarling.com

Contents

Sailing on the Tides of Burning Sand

The Metaphorical Science Fiction Story

It's a mistake to write to a theme.

It isn't that stories shouldn't have themes. All stories have a theme, intentionally or otherwise. As human beings, we like stories that explore some element of our experience. To a degree, the more universal the theme of the story, the more universally the story will be praised.

A Wrinkle in Time by Madeline L'Engle was the first book I fell in love with. I read it every year from sixth grade until I graduated from high school. The story had science in it, explaining how a "tesseract" might allow you to travel through space instantly. There were great characters, both good and evil, and a plot that is both a journey of adventure but also of the soul. Can intellect take precedence over feeling? Can technology rule the human heart? The story might be found to have different themes for different readers, which improves the chances for a story to be cherished. For me, it comes down to the lesson that love conquers all. Not a theme you want to discuss in a locker room, perhaps, but one that becomes universal to everyone (we hope) sooner or later.

I love the idea that we have always existed. That we knew each other before this life. So often, we meet people who just feel familiar as if we weren't becoming acquainted with a new soul but becoming reacquainted with an old one.

If we're lucky, we get to keep these people in our lives. Even marry them, build a life with them, bring more old souls into the world with them.

"Sailing on the Tides of Burning Sand" is a story about a couple traveling in a boat across a desert landscape. It's also about remembering and deciding if it's possible for love to conquer all.

Sailing on the Tides of Burning Sand

Falling. The whole room. Falling. The lightness of his own weight. Air rushing outside the walls. He remembered everything. All he had learned. All he had been. His mind strained with the accumulated wealth of experience. Then, like a grain of sand in a midnight sea, everything sank and faded away. His only memory was that of having remembered.

The room thudded, landed, stopped. Blackness. No sense of time.

Lips pressed against his. Soft.

He opened his eyes.

The room moved. Swayed. He felt dizzy. Maybe from the motion of the room. The chamber where he laid no longer falling but going forward.

Maybe it was the kiss.

The woman hovered over him, smiling, holding herself up with her hands beside his shoulders. Long, tousled hair fell, tracing lines on his face. Her eyes locked onto his.

He had no idea who she was.

"It's okay if you don't remember me," she said. "I didn't remember you either. Not at first." She slipped off him. She wore a gray shirt. Gray pants. Gray shoes. He did too. She grasped his hand and pulled him to his feet. "Come on. It's beautiful outside."

He looked at the room.

Four walls. Each wall with a round window. One window set in a door. On the floor, a box with a lid. Various copper fixtures decorated the walls and ceiling. Opposite the bench he'd been lying on, a small bin. A bronze metal plaque bolted to the wall above it. Blank.

Outside, a narrow deck. Blue sky and brown sand, flowing by. Susurrations of particles trickling around the walls. The woman pulled him to a heavy railing. Sand roiled in tumult behind them like a wake.

"A boat. I remember boats." He laughed. "Hey! I remember boats!"

The woman squealed and let go of his hand to jump and clap.

He followed the deck around the cabin to the bow, holding the rail. Touching the solid metal reassured him the boat was real. The view atop the prow supplied a splendid view of hot sand under a pale, blue sky. Beautiful indeed, in its way. The sun burned directly overhead, offering no sense of direction or time. He asked, "Do you know where we are?"

She shook her head, smiling shyly. "I woke up in your arms and came outside. I've been remembering bits and pieces for an hour, at most. I got afraid you weren't going to wake up." Her laugh was soft. "So I …"

"I remember. It was nice."

She hopped and clapped her hands again. The gesture was familiar. As if he'd seen her do it hundreds of times before. Thousands. Not just once.

The vast empty landscape remained a mystery in every direction. Flat. Endless. Trackless. The starboard view was no different from the port. He returned to the cabin. His inspection of the entire world had taken only a minute.

He opened the box and found two silver packets, two bottles, and a metal tube.

"Where did you get those?" The woman put a hand on his shoulder and took a silver packet. She opened it. Sniffed. Her eyes brightened. "Bacon, lettuce, and tomato sandwich."

They ate. He didn't remember having a sandwich ever before. "Delicious," he said.

"You didn't tell me where you found these." She drank from the bottle with a sigh.

"In that box."

The woman eyed the box. "It was empty."

The man lifted his shoulders. One shoulder rising a moment before the other. A habit returning.

Her lips twisted in a wry half-smile. "I remember hating that shrug."

"Really? Shrug, huh? I didn't know I did that."

She kissed him again. Her hands came to rest on his chest, and he found himself holding her in his arms. She whispered, "There's something else you might not know you did."

* * *

The metal tube was a spyglass. He remembered what it was called after he'd pulled it open and looked through the lens. Delighted with the view, he surveyed the horizon.

An object.

The sky had faded with the setting of the sun, turning from blue to pink to purple, but there was something. A patch of gray on the brown sand and a plume of dust.

The woman looked. Her nose and mouth scrunched up. "Where? Oh. Hmm. I see it!" She bounced on her toes. "What is it?"

"A vessel. Two of them. One straight ahead and one straight behind. Vessels like ours."

She laughed. "'Vessels?' You love fancy words. I remember."

"Accurate words," he corrected. "And you always tease—" He stopped. "I have a brother. Do you remember that?"

She hesitated. Thinking. Shook her head.

"He pointed it out. How you tease me about using fancy words." He tried to remember other things but came up blank. He shrugged. One shoulder, then the other.

The sun slipped past the horizon. A blanket of stars faded into view like a cloth infused with diamonds unrolling across the sky.

"Vessels," he mused. "Going where?" He looked forward to the horizon. A fuzzy line of orange light flickered in the distance.

The woman reappeared, carrying silver packets and bottles and a copper lantern, already glowing. She said, "The box had stuff in it again."

He tried to remember if boxes normally went from empty to having things in them.

The packet gave off a savory aroma as soon as it was opened. He inhaled the steam before looking inside. "Spaghetti and meatballs?"

"Yay! You knew it!"

She was often upbeat. Supportive. He remembered that about her.

They sat in the bow again, legs dangling. The sand *shush-shush-shushed* below them. There were little sticks with little hooks in the packets. They figured out how to use them to eat spaghetti while they looked at the stars.

"Cheese," he remembered, tasting. "Parmesan."

"What's that bunch of stars called?" She pointed at the sky with her eating stick.

"Constellation," he said.

"They're called Constellation?"

He laughed. "No. A bunch of stars are called a constellation. There are many different groupings of stars. They're all constellations with different names."

"Oh." She put her fingertips on the end of her nose, her cheeks turning rosy. He recognized the new gesture as soon as he saw it. Embarrassment.

He looked up, smiling. He remembered the word 'constellation' but couldn't find any patterns he knew. Amid great swaths of dancing lights, shimmering anonymously against the deepening plum-colored sky, none had names he could recall.

Unacceptable.

He pointed at the stars straight ahead. "That constellation is Gilligan the Navigator." He kept a straight face to hide the fact that he was inventing facts, letting the words fall. Not even knowing where the words came from or entirely what they meant.

"Gilligan?" The woman tilted her head.

"Yes. That pair of stars are his eyes, seeing the way forward. And those stars making a circle are the ship's wheel, guiding all those who sail on the tides of burning sand."

She pulled his arm around her and settled into his shoulder. "I think you're a poet."

Her words bloomed as a warm spot in his chest. He put his chin on her head and watched the puffs of dust rise as the prow of the ship cut through the sand.

"I know I love you," he said.

* * *

He slept with the woman nestled against him on the bench until the sun brightened the room through the window.

He got up. The first box was empty.

The copper rectangle over the second box caught his eye. Yesterday, it had been blank. A simple, plain sheet of metal riveted to the wall. Now, there were pictures.

At the top, he recognized numbers and a symbol: 1/3. On the left, a shape with four sides. He said, "Rhomboid" as soon as the fancy word popped into his mind. The shape was silver, not copper. Below the rhomboid, an arrow pointed down at a stack of shapes, also silver. Next to the silver rhomboid was a pair of sticks and another arrow pointing down to a collection of sticks. On the right, a shape like the bottle of water, a down arrow, and a collection of bottles at the bottom.

He understood.

"What did you do with the packets?"

The woman sat on the deck. "What?"

"The silver packets and things that came out of the box. Where are they?"

She pointed at the sand. "I threw them overboard."

"Oh." He took a deep breath.

"What's wrong?"

He ran his hands through his hair. "You didn't know."

"Know what?"

He led her into the cabin. Showed her the plaque. Explained what he thought it meant.

She put her fingertips on her nose. "Okay. From now on, we'll store them in the bin."

"Promise?"

"Cross my heart and hope to die."

The boat lurched. Dropping forward, they fell into the wall.

They left the cabin and grabbed the railing. The boat accelerated, slipping down a slope.

"Dunes!" He inched forward, the woman grabbing his belt. "I want to get a look." They wedged themselves together in the bow as the boat leveled off and started climbing the next pile of sand. He had the spyglass in a pocket and wrapped an arm around the railing while he tried to get it out.

"Careful!" The woman sat, wrapping her legs around the post of the railing and clinging to his leg with her arms.

He readied the glass as the vessel rose. Squinting through the lens, he couldn't see the ship in front of them. He reasoned it was in the trough between dunes. Instead he saw a glimmering in the distance. He dropped to the deck as the boat tilted over the peak and put his arm around the woman. "Do you want to look?" She considered the railing and the incline as they went up. "Okay. But I'll just sit. Hold me."

He wrapped his arms around her waist. She steadied the spyglass at the crest of the dune.

"I see it!" She bounced up and down where she sat. "What is it?"

"I don't know."

The vessel descended again. She handed the spyglass back. The boat carried them up and down the swells. Each one was a little taller than the last. Finally, the woman raised her hands over her head, trusting him to hold her. "Whee!"

He laughed. At the top of the next dune he could see the glimmer without the glass.

"We're getting closer," he said.

The woman took the spyglass. With the tip of her tongue parting her lips, she focused. "It's a tree!"

At the top of the next dune, he looked again. "Good job, honey."

She put her arms around his neck and kissed him. "You can call me 'honey' all you like."

"Then I will call you Honey from now on."

"What shall I call you?"

"Whatever you like."

She mulled it over. "Seems kind of long, Mr. Whatever-you-like."

"You're teasing me. I like it."

She squeezed tighter. "Good. I'll just call you Mine."

"I like that too."

The rolling dunes continued beneath them. For a time, they took turns watching and waiting. The tree grew out of the sand as if the dunes were pushing it up from below. Mine guessed the tree was at least two-hundred feet tall. The trunk and branches were the same green as the leaves, faceted, catching the morning light and throwing sun-sharp shards to the sky and to the sand and to their eyes. He was sure it must be glass.

Mine got tired of waiting and went to check the box. He timed his walk so the vessel stopped climbing before he negotiated the corner. One unexpected bump and he'd fall off the boat. In the box, there were silver packets and bottles. The plaque had changed again. In the corner "2/3" was engraved and the old shapes had been replaced with new ones. He studied the diagram.

"What took so long?" Honey opened her packet and Mine followed suit.

"I noticed a new diagram on the wall." Mine let the aromas waft up to his nose. "Sausages on a stick. Eggs and bagels." He took a bite as the boat evened out, heading up the next incline. "Chorizo. It's funny how we remember food so easily."

Honey laughed. "But we can't remember our own names."

They ate. The dunes leveled off, sands flat again. Honey sighed in relief and untangled herself from the railing. "I'll put those in the bin."

Mine handed her his packet and skewer and bottle. "Thank you." He looked at the crystalline tree. The boat would sail past it soon. Honey reappeared.

10

"We're almost to the tree."

She plopped to the deck.

Mine looked caught her expression. "What's wrong?"

"I don't understand that stupid plaque."

He put a calming hand on her arm. He didn't admit to getting it already, and easily. He remembered she'd get upset and start to cry if he made her feel dumb. "We'll work it out."

Honey's expression went from upset to fearful. "What's that?"

Ahead, there was a line of rising dust and a thin curtain, sparkling, sparking.

Instinctively, they retreated from the bow, shoving themselves against the cabin wall. He threw his arms around her. A rumbling of machinery sent shudders through the vessel. Honey screamed. He looked through the spyglass.

"We'll be okay," Mine shouted. "I know it."

The boat slid through the curtain. The hairs on their bodies crackled with static. On the other side, a fresh expanse of desert spread before them like a giant blanket of rolling velvet.

Mine pecked Honey's cheek. "We're fine. See?"

Honey tentatively opened her eyes. She inhaled at the view. "Oh." Her voice soft.

The tree dazzled with shattered refractions and reflections, dappling the sand with sharp-edged rhomboids of light.

Creatures swam around the roots.

Honey saw them. "They're alive." They watched the creatures paddle in the sand as the boat drifted on. "How did you know we'd be okay?" Tears stood in Honey's eyes.

"Whoever brought us here went to a lot of trouble." Mine kept his voice even. Humble. "They wouldn't do that just to let us die so soon." He gave her the spyglass. "And the other boat's still ahead of us."

Honey looked through the glass. She pressed herself into Mine's shoulder. "You're so smart."

11

Mine watched the creatures swimming in the sand. More mechanical clanking and slamming. "I think the curtain keeps those creatures here."

"Sand dolphins?" Honey smiled.

"Maybe," Mine replied.

"Are they dangerous?"

"Doesn't look like it."

Several creatures approached, circling their boat. One raised up to starboard, almost standing on its tail to look at them.

It sang.

It could have been either male or female but Mine thought of her instantly as a girl because she had a curving softness to her body and her song was high and pleasant. She had short, ropy hair that barely touched her shoulders. Her skin was scaly and bony plates curved from behind her neck like an armadillo. Her green eyes had white membranes that slid down in approximation of a blink. She sang as the boat sailed past, then dove into the sand.

Neither Mine nor Honey could remember a real name for them.

"Maybe we never saw them before," Mine said. "We could call them Sirens." He explained the story of Odysseus and the beautiful women who sang to sailors, seducing them with their calls, leading them to crash their ships.

Honey listened with her arms folded over her stomach.

"I don't think our ship can change course. We have nothing to worry about."

"I don't like them." Honey sniffed and disappeared into the cabin.

* * *

The boat sailed on. Mine watched the sirens swim and play until food appeared in the box but Honey said she wasn't feeling well

12

and stayed in the cabin. The diagram showed what to do with the materials from their meals and Mine gave it a try.

He pulled on the lip of the water bottle as the diagram showed. It unwound into a long, thin wire. He threaded the wire onto a skewer and started to sew the silver packets together.

"What's that for anyway?" The sun was setting, and Honey emerged from the cabin, holding the copper lantern. Her eyes were red.

"I don't know. The plaque should tell us. There's one more message."

She sat down and took the pieces. He'd sewn four of the silver packets into a square. "You're really bad at this." She wasn't teasing but he wasn't blind to the uneven stitches he'd made, and the puckered edges, and he didn't say anything when she started to unpick his work.

"Mine? I don't know why I got upset. Are you mad at me?"

He slid an arm around her waist. "No, Honey. You're too sweet."

"Oh." She put her fingertips on the end of her nose. "I'm glad you think so." She cupped his face and kissed him.

"I remember something else about you," he said.

"What?"

He pointed at a collection of stars. "You're named Honey after that constellation. Honey the Seamstress. Those stars are her needle and the stars up there are her wavy hair. But she doesn't sew clothing. She sews broken hearts back together using her hair for thread."

Honey almost cried. The next kiss was longer. She finally sat back. "I remember something about you too. How patient you are."

Honey kept stitching packets together in neat lines. Mine looked ahead through the spyglass. The orange blur in the distance was now a deep, red line. It came and went in seemingly random threads. He wondered what caused it and decided it couldn't be anything good.

Days passed.

At times, they talked about the boat. They wondered how they had come to be here. How the boat worked to move them so implacably over the sand. How food appeared. Why the packets were supposed to be stitched together. Without answers, the topics wore themselves out. Still, Honey dutifully stitched. In between, she took to sunbathing on the deck. Mine studied the sirens and recognized the ones who appeared every day, as if checking on them. They remembered things about each other, now and again. At night, he made up constellations in the scintillating sweeps of stars, told stories about them to Honey, and watched the red line on the horizon grow thicker and angrier.

* * *

"Honey! Look!"

The atmosphere was prematurely dark. Massive clouds like black anvils gathered. Flashes of lightning jumped from cloud to cloud as if they were trying to kill each other with jagged bolts.

The next curtain caught them by surprise. Only when they heard the grinding machinery did they notice.

Another moment of electrical charge and they were through. An archway dominated the view in front of them. Black and glossy. Then a flash. "Lightning." Mine gave the spyglass to Honey. "We'd better get inside."

"Wait!" She pointed at the dark sand. Sirens swam in a circle. Like the sand, the sirens were darker here. Someone struggled in their midst.

"Help!"

A man.

He kicked, swimming. Sirens dove in on him.

"They're killing him!" Honey gripped the railing.

14

Mine calculated the path the boat would follow. "Sit on my legs!" He went to the starboard side of the boat where it was widest and lay on the deck, the upper half of his body hanging over the swirling sand. Honey's weight settled on his thighs.

Only one chance.

The man saw them. He knocked a siren away with an elbow and reached up. Hands slapped together. Mine pulled. The sand dragged on the man's legs. A siren caught him, hissing, yanking. Mine held on. The man flailed at the siren. The siren let go.

Gasping for breath, Mine let the man grab his shoulder to raise himself to the railing. A siren hissed at Mine from the sand, shaking. Moments later, they fell to the deck.

"Thank you," the man coughed. "I thought I was finished."

Mine stood, getting a look at the man. His face was unlined and pleasant. He wore a cotton shirt and blue satin bow tie. Suspenders held his tweed pants and his shoes were wingtips, perfectly shined.

Mine knew him.

"Are you all right?" Honey brushed sand off his shirt.

"I am now. Those sharks almost got me."

Mine's heart beat in his throat. "I remember what sharks are. These creatures aren't sharks."

The man nodded. "Well, they *are* carnivores. All of them."

"What happened?" Honey asked. "Where's your boat?"

"I guess I fell overboard. My vessel must be far away by now."

Honey laughed. "You said 'vessel.' Just like he does." She pointed at Mine.

The stranger shrugged. One shoulder ahead of the other. Honey laughed again.

"You two should look at the arch," the stranger said. "I found it without equal."

The boat had drawn close to the dark monument. Mine picked out the details. Hundreds of small pillars formed the construction, stacked in columns. The gate was made of bones. Ancient, fossilized, black. Human. He wanted to look away. Couldn't. "What is this place?"

"Study it well. It could mean your survival." The man pointed at a dark shape in the sand, beyond the arch of bones. Mine made out larger angular shapes and smaller round shapes. Dread gathered like an acid pool in his stomach.

He felt Honey's hands on his arms. "Are they dead?"

The skulls were blackened. Skeletal remains draped upon the derelict ship as if on display. The wood rotted. Another ship, half-consumed by the sand, lay to starboard. A decayed hand extended through the cabin door, beseeching.

Lightning illuminated the landscape. There were dozens of wrecks spread over the sand. Hundreds. And corpses.

"Honey? Do you recognize him?" Mine looked over his shoulder. "Where did he go?"

Light exploded, thunder deafening, inches in front of their vessel. The flash of heat and pressure threw Mine backwards. He grunted as he slammed to the deck. He couldn't hear Honey screaming but she was. The belly of the sky ripped open and rain fell in gouts.

Darkness.

* * *

Mine blinked, his sticky eyes reluctant to open.

"Honey?"

"I'm here, Mine."

"What happened?"

"Lightning, Mine. You were hurt."

Mine rubbed his forehead and remembered. A lot. "Where is he?"

"Outside."

"We have to get rid of him."

"No, Mine. He's helpful. He remembers so many things."

"He's a liar. I think he's killed people."

"You can't know that."

"Don't you recognize him? He's wearing my brother's face."

Honey pressed her fingertips against her nose.

Mine struggled to his feet. Fell back on the bench. Got up again.

Honey read his expression. "Mine, you're scaring me."

Mine staggered out the door. The boat rolled as if the desert felt his anger. The man turned as Mine stepped onto the deck. The silver packets floated behind the boat like a kite, tethered by wire.

The man looked at Mine. "You're quite unlucky, sir. Nearly killed within moments of my arrival. I would have taken good care of her for you." He let go of the wire and the silver kite flew away.

Mine punched him in the face. The man's nose blossomed in blood. He laughed. "Don't be hasty. Let's talk about this." Mine grabbed the man by his tailored shirt, lifting, shoving. Over the railing. The man grabbed Mine. "If I go, you're coming with me."

Mine slapped the man's hand loose. Pushed him back.

"You're not strong enough."

Mine snarled. "I am this time."

A wailing siren arose from the sand, wrapping her arms around the man's neck. His eyes flew wide as she pulled. Mine bent down, lifting the man's legs. He went over, shrieking. In moments, he was swallowed up by the sand.

Honey. Crying. "The silver kite was supposed to keep the lightning away."

Heat bathed Mine's neck and face. "It's metal. If anything, it would draw lightning to the boat." He pointed at the ruined ships in the sand, the blackened corpses. "He killed them."

"It was their fault, he said." Honey wailed. "They were wicked. When they died, their boats went off course. I think we were wicked too. We were wicked, Mine, and that's why we're here. We were wicked, and this is hell."

Mine couldn't slow his breathing. His fists strained at his sides. "I remembered other things. After seeing his face—my brother's face—I remembered you slept with him." Freshly wounded, he wanted to hurt her. He pointed at a patch of sky, the only patch not obscured by thunderheads. "See that constellation? That's Promiscua the Whore. Named after you."

Mine stormed into the cabin, leaving Honey in the rain.

The plaque was blank. He examined the sides. The corners. The rivets had been tampered with. Mine pulled on the plaque. It came loose. He turned the plaque around.

"He said it was blank for a reason." Tears rolled down Honey's face.

His anger barely in check, Mine showed her the other side of the plaque. The side that had been against the wall.

Honey wept harder.

* * *

They barely spoke. They ate apart. Slept apart. Honey on the bench. Mine on the floor. On the horizon, the hot, angry line grew into a wall of red-orange fire, a thousand feet high. They heard the flames. A dull, constant roar. The flames extended in both directions as far as the spyglass allowed them to see.

They were heading straight for it.

The boat would only deviate from its course if they died.

They might be dead already.

The third diagram on the plaque had been clear enough. Two figures protected by a silver shield, standing as fire rained down. The packets were supposed to save them from the flames.

They'd never have enough packets now. Not after losing the others.

Mine said, "We need extra packets."

Honey glared. "We only get six each day."

"I'm going to try finding more. Will you help me?"

She folded her arms.

"If we don't work together, we won't survive." Her eyes were hard but Mine pressed on. "I said things I shouldn't have said. I'm sorry, Honey."

Honey's eyes softened. "I didn't know what you remembered about the affair. And I was afraid to ask. I did break it off with him. I never should have let it happen at all. But I'm the one who ended it." She glanced to the side. Licked her lips drily at the fiery wall.

"Together." Mine said.

They had plenty of wire. Mine had spent days twisting the wire into rope. He wrapped the cable around the post at the center of the rear railing and twisted it tight. He'd threaded the other end through the loops of his belt where the fabric was most sturdy and bound it.

"This boat never stops but it doesn't go fast," Mine explained. "Some shipwrecks are close. I can jump across from the front, check for packets, then jump back to our vessel."

Honey nodded, swallowing thickly.

"Make sure the cable doesn't get tangled. And don't get hurt."

"Okay."

Mine's heart pounded as he stood in the bow, waiting for a promising derelict. The wall of fire loomed larger.

"Here's one." He panted. Climbed over the rail.

Jumped.

The rail hit him in the midsection. He grunted but ignored the pain, clambering over. He dashed into the empty cabin. The owners had jumped off—or been pushed. In the bin, he found several packets. He stuffed them into his pockets and ran out.

19

His ship had nearly passed. He climbed to the top of the railing and flung himself across the gap. Honey helped him back aboard, his breathing uneven. He pulled the packets out of his pocket.

Seven.

Honey hopped and clapped. "That's more than a day's worth."

"Not enough." Mine recoiled the cable. Honey's mood turned grim, realizing. She started sewing.

Mine plundered more ships but jumping took its toll. He was drenched, sweating, with few packets won.

He'd also found corpses.

On his fourth trip, he missed his target and fell to the sand. He kicked but the deck was out of reach. He struggled to his own boat. Honey helped him up and over the rail.

"You should rest."

"How many?"

Honey showed him the progress she'd made.

Not enough.

The wall of fire seemed twice as close. Twice as loud. Mine used the spyglass.

The ship in front of them was about to hit the wall of fire.

Transfixed, Mine watched. A tiny figure ran out the door and jumped into the sand. Mine couldn't hear any screaming over the monumental growl of flames. The lack of human noise made the scene more terrible. An enormous flare burst ahead of the cabin as their boat entered the flames. The figure swam away from the fire. Heartbeats passed. Mine forgot to breathe. The cabin caught next. The wall consumed the wood as if starved for fuel. The door caught. A second figure stumbled out, covered in sheets of flame. The figure staggered across the deck and fell into the sand as the vessel was swallowed by the hungry orange beast. Pieces of the vessel were caught in the updraft. The body flew up as well.

Mine swallowed thickly. His stomach felt like broken glass as the swimmer fought the current of sand, knowing from miles away it was a losing battle. The flailing figure disappeared. Another gout of flame erupted in the wall and it was over.

He wanted to throw up. No time. He angled the spyglass down to scan the space between their vessel and the wild, raging wall.

He needed another wreck.

Minutes passed. The wall of flame was a mountain.

"Sew them together, Honey." He was resigned. "Make it like a sleeping bag."

Honey looked at the pieces. "We won't both fit."

"I know. But you will."

Honey wailed. Mine raised the spyglass. A boat had drifted off course impossibly far. Honey saw it too. "You have to try!"

Mine nodded. He climbed the rail and jumped. The sand was harder, baked by the heat, and he practically ran across the gap to the deck.

He smelled the bodies before he saw them, the cabin filled with flies.

Nauseated, he held his breath and searched for silver. The woman lay dead on the bench. The man hung from the fixtures in the ceiling. Their packets were sewn into a long rectangle, fashioned into a noose.

Mine went to the man, ignoring the flies that rose in a fitful cloud. He lifted the body to get some slack in the noose.

He felt time escaping. Any moment, the cable around his waist would yank him away. He worked to untie the blanket. Leaving without it wasn't an option. If he didn't get the blanket, he was dead. He heard the cable rasping around the frame of the door. He worked faster. His fingers pinched, grabbed, pulled. His heart hammered in his chest.

The silver slipped free. He clutched the blanket and ran out. Honey on their vessel, sliding away, naked desperation painted on her face. His breathing huffed like rags in his ears. He leapt to the top of the railing. Threw himself toward the vessel.

Toward Honey.

He slammed onto the hard sand. Gripped the cable.

The cable snapped taut. He grunted, feeling like he was being cut in half. The boat pulled him off the baked sand, rolling him into the softer wake. Honey reached for the cable. She moved her arm in a circle, winding the cable around her wrist. Mine shoved the silver into his mouth and started pulling himself up the lifeline. The drag of his weight would be too much for Honey, but she grabbed her wrist with her free hand, using her forearm like a stanchion. She moved to port and braced her feet against the post of the railing.

She screamed his name. Crimson lines flowed down her arm.

Mine pulled. The cable cut his hands, every movement generating agony. Time slowed. Eternity. Pain.

He reached the deck, fingers slick with blood. He breathed deeply. In. Out. In. Out. Honey pulled his shirt, leaving lines of red.

The heat from the wall was intolerable. Mine's lungs burned.

They unfolded the piece of silver blanket.

Still not enough.

"Finish the shield. Save yourself." Mine's voice broke.

"No. Look."

Honey laid the pieces on the deck. "If we stitch it together here, it will make a blanket big enough for us both to roll up in. Remember our honeymoon?"

The memory came. The two of them, wrapped in a quilt. Knowing so little about each other. But knowing they wanted to be together. Smiling then.

Mine smiled now. "Okay."

Honey sewed.

Mine checked outside. The wall of flame dominated the sky like it was falling over on them. The intensity of the heat burned like a living, breathing monster.

He stitched too. Desperate minutes flew by.

Honey said, "If I could change the past, Mine, I would. And I'm sorry. I remember you forgave me."

Mine tried to remember too.

Tears traced lines through the dust on her face.

He kissed her tears.

The vessel lurched sideways. They almost fell. He shoved her down onto the edge of the blanket. Dropped on top of her. Crackling sounds announced the bow meeting the inferno.

They rolled over and over in the silver. Mine pulled shut the gap above their heads and held it.

"I can't remember forgiving you before," he shouted. "But I can forgive you now."

Wood exploded, the bow and cabin wall feeding the conflagration. The side walls erupted next. In moments, there was no sand, no cabin, nothing but the sound of raging fire and a flood of memories flowing back to life. Worlds becoming glass.

Rising.

Temp

The One Isaac Asimov Might Like

Isaac Asimov was one of the writers who first opened my mind to science fiction. I read *Foundation* when I was twelve years old and went from there. He wrote a lot of non-fiction as well and I came to appreciate how his far-flung planets and their denizens always felt grounded and plausible because they had science that was believable, at least to my pre-teen mind.

Fast forward.

As much as I liked *The Matrix*, my little inner-Asimov didn't quite buy it. Using people as batteries is a lousy idea because people make lousy batteries. They do produce heat while awake and moving but far less when they sleep. The machines kept their bodies unconscious. Bodies don't conduct electricity all that efficiently either and if you don't keep feeding the "battery" it doesn't survive long enough to be useful.

The machines weren't very smart. Especially since bodies produce a third kind of motion besides electrical energy and energy from heat. The third type of energy (and the most productive) comes from motion.

We've had self-winding watches for decades, for example. Such watches use the kinetic motion of your arms to keep them wound and you can buy a little box that will do the same thing for you by moving the watches when you aren't wearing them.

Even better, what if there was a means of collecting *all* of those energies? It seems to me that an intelligent overlord would take advantage of the captive work force and force them to work as hard as they could.

One step further, what if that wise overlord made that work *harder* to accomplish?

P.S. There are a ton of *Star Trek* references.

Temp

Part I - Deckport 4136C

"I have a six-oh-four on the Nyota," Rat said.

A flashing image burned across my mind—a woman with her hands pressed against her bleeding ears, eyes blind.

I wouldn't let that happen. Not today.

I looked at Rat over my console as he adjusted the sixth left handle on his array. His workstation was just a few feet away from mine, jammed up against the steel wall with a narrow aisle between us. Rat was strong and efficient and always gave me the information I needed with a half-smile that I found irresistible.

"Got it." My lips made a copy of his smile.

I tapped the little screen on the console in front of me about twenty times until I found the readout I wanted. I ran the

27

calculations, pumped the top two spindle levers, and actuated the starboard foot pedal to bring the Nyota under six hundred. The whole thing took thirty seconds. Piece of cake.

"Very nice," Rat said. He winked at me.

"Thank you," was all I dared to reply. I was afraid of sounding like a silly girl every time I spoke to him, so I kept my answers short

Rat was in charge of waveforms, both light and sound. The waveforms were critical in maintaining livability in the upper levels of our hyperstructure to protect people at the surface from dying. Rat's job was so complicated I figured the compload programming would be more than my brain could hold. He worked it with ease.

Our team of seven technicians was responsible for the well-being of the sixteen hundred souls who lived in Pavel Sector, Elevated Sphere S'chn T'gai 18.

Although I had only been working with this crew for a month, their personality profiles had been included in the compload chip I received when I started. From day one, I knew all about Rat, Lucybean, Pond, Mr. and Mrs. Vespers, and Bou and how they worked. We'd synced instantly, operating as if we had known each other for years, and I counted them all—almost all—as my closest friends. Rat the very closest. And not just because he sometimes brought pizzabars at night.

I pressed my hand against my chest, feeling the reassuring presence of the chain I wore around my neck. It carried a secret: a compload chip that Rat had given me. We were discouraged from wearing jewelry and having a personal compload was unheard of. Unlike the company-issued comploads we were required to have in our access at all times, my personal chip was a glorious bit of contraband that let me be myself. Like the pizzabars, I had no idea where Rat had found it. But I cherished it. I used it to store memories so I could have them even after a scrub. Many of those memories now included Rat.

The Nyota wave hummed in a steady line, percolating just under the optimum threshold. I smiled and shut down the screen. For a few minutes, at least, things were quiet with only the sound of Lucybean working her treadle to counteract the tidal effect of the moon on the bodies of water throughout Pavel.

Because of his name, you'd think Pond would be in charge of balancing the water in our sector, but Pond controlled magnetic fields, which protected Pavel from radiation and modified gravity. He was also a jerk.

"Oh!" Mrs. Vespers said. "Thinning cloud cover! Center at zero-point-six-one-one!"

In my mind, I saw burning skin.

I cranked my console around to look at her. She and her husband's stations were opposite Rat's. Her voice was worn and thready, but sweet. She was lucky. She got to play with clouds, maintaining the troposphere and the stratosphere, and Mr. Vespers was responsible for the mesosphere, thermosphere, and exosphere. He got busier later in our shift when the auroras came out. They were beautiful to look at even on our tiny screens.

Mrs. Vespers moved the crank to increase humidity, I did my part by pumping the seventh and tenth spindle levers in opposite directions to inject the proper amounts of nitrogen, oxygen, and other gases. It would take five minutes to correct the cloud layer.

"Hey! I have an idea!" Pond was in my peripheral vision, practically buried behind his bulky collection of levers and handles. I did my best to avoid looking at him on principle.

"Just let it go! Don't do anything! Let's see what happens."

"No!" I snapped.

"Why not?"

Rat cleared his throat and said, "We've been over this before, Pond." Rat sounded tired, looking at Pond through slitted eyes.

I pointed at the sign on the wall, which read in big, blue letters:

29

The Citizens of Pavel Sector are Depending on YOU!

"So what?" Pond said.

"Them. Those people are the reason we can't just let it go," I said. My breathing grew labored. Exertion and exasperation.

"Have you ever been to Pavel sector?" In the corner of my eye I saw Pond leaning through a space between tubes and beams. I knew he was smirking at me.

Rat immediately said, "Of course she hasn't. Pavel sector is UP."

"You've seen UP, haven't you, Rat?" It was a challenge.

I gave in and glared at Pond as he crossed his big meaty arms over the expanse of his large chest. His stiff controls required a lot of strength.

Pond felt it necessary to challenge at least one of our processes every day. We all knew what was coming next. I had personally exhausted all attempts to respond to Pond long ago. Now I just ignored him. Most of us felt Pond was lying to get attention.

"One time, I left the gravity unadjusted for six whole seconds and nothing happened," he said.

Rat never said he was wrong out loud, but he shook his head when he heard Pond spouting off and he knew I was watching.

Mrs. Vespers and I continued running through the steps of our procedure. The sound of metal under protest grated the air. The machinery we worked with was pathetic, outdated and cumbersome. For years, they'd told me, Mr. Vespers had requested upgrades, but we'd never seen any. Luckily for UP management they had our team to operate the antiquated junk of Deckport 4136C. Still, it would have been nice to get some oil or something for parts that constantly ground together. I dreamed of a world with a little less friction. And fewer complicated sequences.

As I worked, I muttered, "You know what they say. 'Why have a two-step process when twenty-two steps will do?'"

We labored in our silver KL suits, which we called "Kool" suits. They pulled the excess heat away from our bodies so we could work without succumbing to heatstroke. The suits also kept our skin clean and breathing and free of odor between showers. Naturally, we were in good shape. The people in Pavel depended on us; we needed to keep ourselves fit and healthy.

There was an alert at the door. A miniscule light blinked over the exit to the Deckport, and a chime announced the arrival of visitors. The Deckport was kept dimly lit to conserve energy, but I could see well enough through the window to make out a tall male figure and a smaller shape wearing a silver KL suit. Worry nibbled at the edges of my thoughts, but I shoved it away.

Images sprang to mind again, served up by my compload. Children screaming, running, their skin crimson red, peeling, cracking. Consequences, if we didn't do what we were hired to do.

Whoever was at the door would have to wait.

"Bou!" I said. "Realignment please. Thirty-eight degrees to port."

While Pond was large, Bou was a shiny, silver mountain. He had Asian features fixed in a serene, placid expression that never changed.

He stood and put his hands on a lever attached to the wall. There was a track around the entire circumference of the room, which was Bou's domain. He pushed against the lever and the room moved. Screeching, metal-on-metal, the room pointed toward the new heading, redirecting the field we were generating.

Outside the door, the male figure looked around, obviously confused as the door rotated away from him. He didn't get down here very often, and his compload probably didn't tell him much about what we did here. I smiled to myself as he shuffled around the hallway outside, trying to keep up with the rotating room. The man disappeared completely for a minute as the room turned, and I decided he had gone back to get the female. The room stopped at precisely thirty-eight degrees from our previous bearing. After a few seconds, the male reappeared at the door, pulling the female by the wrist.

I heard a pinging alarm. "We are running out of time, dear!" Mrs. Vespers warned.

"Do you need assistance?" Rat asked.

I looked back at my tiny square screen, angry at letting myself get distracted.

"No! No! No!" I said. "Give me a minute."

"You have forty-seven seconds," Mrs. Vespers said.

"I only need...thirty-eight." It came out sounding angry though I didn't mean it.

I flipped the beveling wheel around and waited for the Montgomery light to turn. It wasn't changing quickly enough, so I tapped it with my finger knowing it was as effective as poking the elevator button to make the car come faster.

My nerves wanted to scream, but I knew my results would be accurate and complete. The programming on my compload wouldn't let me down. I continued spinning the beveling wheel and, finally, the Montgomery light went green. "Pond, release field on my mark," I said.

Pond just sat where he was, arms still crossed.

"Ten seconds," I said.

Pond remained immobile.

"Bou!" It was all I needed to say. Bou walked over to Pond and stood over him like a monolith.

"Five seconds!"

Pond scowled.

"Three...two...one!"

At the last moment, Pond stood and yanked on a thick, round bar with a single grunt. The whole time Pond stared at Bou, his eyes never wavering.

"Mrs. Vespers?" I called. "Are we clear?"

The Queen of Clouds pursed her lips, and my heart jumped like a flying fish.

"Just fine!" she said. At last.

I took a deep breath. We had kept the lives of sixteen hundred people safe again. It felt good, although heat was still rising in my neck and up to my face, the kind of heat the KL suit didn't compensate for. Surely Pond's compload included the same data as ours. He had to see the same death and destruction in his mind if we failed to act. Why did he have to be such an ass?

Pond's intermittent stupidity aside, we had a stellar crew. Much better than those losers in 4136D and—though they would never admit it—we were better than 4136B, too. I was certain we had the potential to beat 4136A and move up to Deckport 4135 if given half a chance. Other members of the crew didn't always share in my optimism. I considered it part of my job description to move them up in the world or die trying.

The chime sounded again. Insistent. With the citizens in Pavel safe for the moment, I tapped my little screen repeatedly to find the room controls. I turned a large crank to unlock the door mechanism and took a hold of spindle lever number nine, which ratcheted the door open. The two figures outside waited as the door moved three inches, stopped, moved three inches, stopped, moved three inches, and so on until they could step inside.

The male approached me. The Kool-suited female a step behind. He had an UP emblem on his coveralls. She refused to look me in the eyes. I gripped my levers so tightly my knuckles turned white.

The workman consulted a device with a little black screen. Digital and sleek. I could see alphanumeric sequences on its display. So much data! All on the same screen.

22-05-19-PR0A1
22-05-19-PR0A2
18-01-20-0778A
16-15-14-D0S2J
12-21-03-B3AN0
02-15-21-00YW1
13-01-18-Y0A14

The sequence on the bottom flashed.

"Designation 13-01-18-Y0A14," the workman said to me. "You have fulfilled your contract for Deckport location 4136C. UP thanks you for your service. Please come with me for forward processing."

I pushed my console to the side, the metal whining. I got out of my chair and faced the workman. "My contract can't be fulfilled yet," I said. "I've only been here a month." The tendons in my clenched fists were screaming, and the flush in my face burned with rising panic.

The workman nodded. "That is the term you selected," he said. "Thirty days."

My mind raced. "At the time, I didn't know if I would like it here," I said. "Now I know. I love it here." I didn't look at Rat, but I wanted to.

The workman looked at me with a sour expression. He heaved a controlled sigh. "You can return to this assignment by resubmitting a contract request."

"Great," I said. "Let's do that. Let's do it right now." My respiration was so quick and heavy that my KL suit beeped a warning.

The workman shook his head and waved a thumb at the female behind him. "You can resubmit at the end of your replacement's contract," he said flatly. "For reference, her designation is 02-09-19-TY0N8."

I held my ground. The silver-suited female stood there staring stupidly at her shoes.

"When will her contract be fulfilled?" I asked.

The female looked up and opened her mouth. I put my hand in front of her face to shut her up.

The workman gave another sigh and looked at me with his head tilted sideways, as if he had never heard anyone ask that before. Maybe he hadn't. I could almost picture the data from his compload dribbling out of his ears and evaporating.

He looked down at his screen and with a single swipe of his finger found what he was looking for.

A single swipe. A single, solitary swipe. Not twenty or thirty taps. Not with an added spin of a crank. Not with a final grind of a lever.

The world took on a crimson hue. The new girl seemed to lose patience, looking bored with her hand on her hip and her leg bent, her body creating as many possible angles that four limbs and a torso could make.

This gangly wisp of a thing thought she could take my place?

"She has a full-term contract. Five years."

I hit 02-09-19-TY0N8 right in the jaw. Bones broke in my hand. She went to the floor and I stood astride her, hitting her again. And again. And then all the clouds and auroras and magnetic fields and gravities and waveforms and pathetic machineries exploded in my head—everything went white. As I fell to the floor, I caught a glimpse of my handsome Rat looking sad.

Part II - Medbay 200A

While floating in the white, I sifted memories.

After our shift, we retreated to our pod. Like all the others I could remember, the pod was dimly lit, using only diodettes for illumination to conserve energy. There was a common area, of course, and four sleeping cells. Lucybean and I shared a cell. Our bedmats were separated by a low wall with mattresses designed to share body heat when both sides were occupied. She was so quiet I always slept deeply and well. The Vespers shared another cell, but their bedmat had no wall to keep them apart. It was sweet how they cuddled together at night, like two white raisins in the middle of a cookie.

I felt my conscious self stir, but I chose to remain in the white.

Rat and Pond had cells to themselves for no other reason than the fact that Bou slept on the rug in the common room. His girth left him unable to use bedmats comfortably, so one cell was free. The last thing Rat wanted to do was share a room with Pond. I wouldn't have minded if he'd shared a room with me, but then poor Lucybean would've been all alone.

We stopped at our assigned cafeteria for boxed dinners that were balanced, nutritious, and entirely without redeeming flavor. Things looked up however, because Rat had vanished about half an hour ago, which meant he would be back with pizzabars from the UP. Nobody knew how Rat got them, but they are my favorite.

Rat and I liked to go together to the concourse and look from our Deckport levels belowground to the UP. I suspected Rat knows of a door, a secret door, where he gets to the UP. Maybe he will take me there. To see where pizzabars are made. To see Pavel sector. Someday.

From here, through one narrow section, I can see between the gray metal walls and supercolumns of the Deckport. Sparkling, like a solid sheet of diamonds, is the corner of a tall building, brightly lit, one of the places where the surface residents of UP lived.

"Do you think they'll find an answer?" I asked that question a lot.

"They're working on one," Rat always replied.

"Then we can leave the Deckport?"

"That's the idea. Leave the Deckport. Leave the whole elevated sphere. Fresh air. Sunshine."

"Then I guess working here is worth it. So they can find an answer."

We sat there, our hands almost touching.

At some point, I heard voices and remembered I am lost in a dream. I'm not ready to wake up. Not yet. There is so much pain in my hand. I'm good at avoiding pain. That's why I only take one-month contracts. If I don't stay in one place too long, people can't hurt me. Then, unexpectedly, I'd found people worth staying for. Mostly. People who were worth risking some hurt.

I don't want to wake up until Rat brings pizzabars again, and I can feel my mouth watering, but it's getting harder and harder to stay unconscious. I catch bits and pieces of conversation.

Two voices. Men.

"—very strong. Broke the other girl's jaw and—"

"—movement stored the energy in the Kinetic Link suit—"

Kinetic Link suit? My addled mind made the connection. KL suit. Kool suit.

"—well-developed muscles and stamina to run the equipment—"

"—machinery exists only to manufacture electricity—"

I was missing words. Couldn't hear everything. Finally, I opened my eyes. I was in a recovery room. The room was painfully bright. The walls too smooth. Too clean. I was surrounded by glossy, unfamiliar machines.

The men I'd heard were in the next room. I stole a glance over my shoulder. They weren't looking in my direction. I felt gingerly at the back of my neck. My compload access was empty.

37

No chip. I was being scrubbed, and the thought of all my recent past being erased shot threads of ice into my veins.

Rat's gift was around my neck. They hadn't found it. I put my personal compload into my access and repeated in my mind all the words I'd heard them say. And all the memories from my dream. And I listened some more.

"—generates twenty-two times more energy than she uses—"

"—transfers the energy through the bedmat while she sleeps—"

"—she always contracts for only a month at a time—"

My contract. My work. I tried to remember what I did. It had—what was it—something to do with machines? It seemed very important that I know how to operate them. I can't remember what to do.

"—no prosecution for the assault—"

"—UP wants her productive again—"

"—skinpharms adjusted—"

"—drone like her can never be a consumer like an UP—"

I can only remember ghosts of what I knew before. I used to execute processes that were important. I'd understood parameters defining complicated procedures with multiple steps and grinding machinery, but the specifics were gone from my mind.

I felt empty.

"Looks like she woke up."

"Eh. 'Bout time to scrub her anyway."

I tried to pretend I was sleepy, but it felt like my heart was pounding out of my chest. One of the techs stared at me, and I stared back with heavy-lidded eyes. Then he looked away, and I popped the compload out of my access and slipped it inside my suit.

Part III - Deckport 7187F

Within two weeks, my broken hand has healed well enough for me to go back to work. I know I'll never find 02-09-19-TY0N8 and be able to apologize to her for what I did. But I'll try. Technically, I shouldn't remember her at all after my scrub. But I'd found the memory of her, and my crew, and the men in the medbay, and especially Rat right there on my secret compload.

Although I tried almost every day, I couldn't find my old crew in the Deckports. The workmen who talked to me didn't really know anything helpful. Some of them said my crew were all reassigned to different hyperstructures. I couldn't imagine the Vespers getting separated, but I couldn't find them or anyone else from 4136C.

Worst of all, I can't find my Rat. If I knew where he had gotten all those pizzabars I'd just hang out there after work until I spied him. But I couldn't find the slightest whiff of pepperoni or melted cheese or baked crust.

Some nights after work, I just find a quiet place to sit. I watch other workers go by. They read or talk or sit on the benches. They never look up.

I do.

I look up and think of all the consumers living above. Living UP while I'm down here. I plug my compload in and let the memories I've saved and the things I've learned run through my mind. Somewhere there was a jerk whose name I had decided to forget, who knew what I knew. Mostly, I missed my Rat.

My new crew moves a lot of machinery and I'm not the center of attention like before, but that's all right with me. I have a one-month contract because I need to keep moving. Just maybe run into my old crew somehow. If I ever find Rat, we'll find a way out of the Deckport together. Until then, I'll be a good worker and do my part in the machine.

I am lucky in my current crew. I get to play with clouds all day and maintain the troposphere. Today, when too much lightning threatened, I let the clouds go unadjusted for a few seconds—six whole seconds—just to see what would happen. With a willful disregard of the images of electrocuted babies in my head, I did nothing. The crew sat there, stunned, as I pretended to have trouble with my tiny little screens. Then I fixed the clouds. Nothing bad happened. One of the crew was sure we would be scrubbed, but the people of—what was our sector again? I had to check the sign on the wall—Hikaru Sector. Right. They were depending on us. I had never seen Hikaru Sector. Nobody had. They were UP. And they were all just fine.

I made clouds and waited for the end of my contract and a chance to find someone from my old crew. Just maybe I'll find my Rat. Pizzabars come to my thoughts, and the mere memory of the aroma brings tears to my eyes.

Two Mock, a Killingbird

The Mashed-Up Science Fiction Story

If aliens were among us, how would we know? Their forms might be hidden. Their technologies might be unrecognizable. Their motives beyond understanding.

"Two Mock, A Killingbird" came together from a number of sources. A latent desire to be an attorney, for one, after working as a runner for a law firm in college. Then, teaching literature, and feeding that desire with a dose of Atticus Finch. Then re-watching some of my favorite science-fiction movies.

I know. One of these things is not like the other.

Aliens wouldn't necessarily have it any easier. Human forms might be hidden. Our technologies might be unrecognizable. Our motives beyond understanding.

If aliens were among us, and needed our help, how would we know?

Two Mock, a Killingbird

Beth Hatch read through the list of charges again, thinking, "please don't let this turn out to be some kind of *Silence of the Lambs, My Friend Dahmer* kind of thing." The handcuffs on her client were distracting and bright, making it hard to concentrate. The interview room had only two lights and both were focused somehow on the metal cuffs, reflecting the lights into her face. She put one hand to her forehead, cutting the glare, and reviewed the charges a third time. *Kidnapping. Murder. Desecration of a human body. Criminal trespass.* The list of charges went on, and that was just the felonies.

Her client stared across the table at her with liquid blue eyes. Eyes that might never see sunlight again unless Beth was very, very good at her job.

Beth cleared her throat. "Okay, Mr. Robeson. Let's get started. If I'm going to defend you, I need to know why you put your girlfriend's body in a freezer."

Robeson's hands remained pressed together flat, fingers forward, as if pointing a prayer in Beth's direction. "I have a reason."

"Good. Although, according to the statements from the arresting office, you didn't give a reason when he questioned you. You just shrugged."

Robeson shrugged. "The officer wasn't going to believe me."

"Well, I'll be honest. I don't know if I'll believe you either but you'll need to answer my questions if I'm going to get you out of here. To start, tell me your reason."

The hands parted a fraction. "I kept Annabelle in the freezer so she wouldn't die."

Beth made notes, feeling her brow furrow. "Could you elaborate on that for me?"

The hands parted again, as if he were holding a small book in his hands that he had to open to find answers. "She wasn't dead when I put her in the freezer—the cryogenic stasis bed, actually."

"Hold on." Beth dropped her pencil on her legal pad. "You're saying she was still *alive* when she went into the freezer?"

"Stasis bed. Yes."

Beth pointed at the charging documents. "According to the arrest report, she was murdered in her apartment."

"That's what the report says. Yes."

Beth pressed her lips together and clicked her teeth, chewing on the words. The murder charge would go all the way to premeditated if the district attorney found out what Robeson had said. "What is the truth? Did she die in her apartment, and you took her body away; or was she alive in her apartment, and you abducted her to your work where she died in the fr—stasis bed?"

Robeson's hands remained pressed together. Closed to insights. "Neither of those is quite accurate. I see you want to help me, but it's difficult to explain."

Beth fiddled with her pencil, tempted to try fill in the blanks for him to get closer to something sensible. She refrained. Patient. "Tell me what happened as best you can. Pretend you haven't told anyone before. And tell me where and when Annabelle died."

Robeson sat back in his seat. His hands went flat to the table. The non-existent book of answers relinquished. From his blue eyes, cool assessment.

The bright reflections were giving Beth a headache. She pinched the bridge of her nose with her fingers and squeezed her eyes shut. When she opened them again, a flash, doubly-bright, hit her vision and she heard herself say, "Ow." The flash had been like the popping bulb from an old camera but only inches from her face. What had caused the flash? Robeson still gazed at her with those icy eyes. Somehow, he seemed happier.

Beth shook her head, trying to clear her mind. She felt tired already. Less than two minutes in conversation and she was tired. "Go ahead, Mr. Robeson. Tell me. In your own words. From the beginning."

Robeson's smile stretched wider, "You need not worry about my case, Ms. Hatch. I know you will set me free and your career will continue." Robeson's chair scraped the floor as he stood up.

What? Did I just miss something?

Beth stood up as well. Simple, reflexive politeness. The manacles around Robeson's wrists were chained through a metal bracket in the table, and he was tall enough that he wasn't able to stand straight until the cuffs were removed. Instead, he appeared to bow at Beth. During his incarceration, a pattern of white hairs had begun to emerge from Robeson's once-bald head, but they formed without rhyme or reason. Patchy. No symmetry. No chance of being mistaken for handsome. The hairs looked like they were simply striving to find a way out of his cranium by the nearest exit.

Beth felt stymied by confusion. She opened her mouth to protest her client's attempt to leave and looked at her notes.

She had filled the page. The curve at the top of the tablet indicated more pages had been filled as well and then turned over. She pulled the pages back to the face of the tablet to see where she had started. Page after page came over again. Fourteen in all. She turned her wrist to check her watch.

Two hours.

Not two minutes.

An officer came into the room and unfastened Robeson's manacles. The officer was tall, but Robeson was taller. Seeing him upright for the first time in person, Beth guessed his height to be over seven feet.

More officers stood in the hallway, ready to escort Robeson back to his jail cell. Her gaze strayed back to her notes.

Fourteen pages.

Two hours.

She scanned her notes while on her feet. She stretched, realizing she *felt* like she'd been sitting for two hours so maybe she had been sitting after all.

And blacked out while I wrote?

From her notes, she'd written down Robeson's story as he'd told it to her. She still couldn't see a reason he'd committed so many crimes. On the fifth page, in the margin, she'd also written "Atticus." She didn't remember writing that. On the other hand, she didn't remember writing any of it.

A police officer leaned into the room asking if she wanted coffee or water. She thanked him but declined.

Every couple of pages, she saw her writing just . . . trail off. Her precisely-formed letters suddenly went limp. The line dragged off to a ragged and fading scrawl off the page. Then, a line beneath, her letters reformed and regained their structured script. Later, after another few pages, it happened again. Then a third time.

Why had her handwriting trailed off three times? Beth couldn't remember. Neither could she think of a reason.

Did I black out in the middle of my blackout?

Beth took another, closer look at the words she had written. Her blood ran cold.

*　*　*

Twenty minutes later, briefcase in hand outside the Maycomb Cryogenics Laboratory building, Beth was preparing to speak to the next contact on her list, Ms. Mayella, Robeson's former boss. Beth stared at a woman across the street in a yellowing trenchcoat who was *not* the woman she needed to interview. The woman stared back.

She has to know I've seen her. I know she's following me. If she doesn't know that, she's stupid.

The strange woman was at least seven feet tall, so of course Beth had noticed her. The same woman had been standing outside the county jail when Beth had left her interview with Robeson. The woman was noticeable in a crowd, not only because of her height, but also for the overlarge, silver sunglasses she wore and her bright auburn hair that tumbled onto her shoulders in a graceful fall. Beth had gotten into a cab and ordered the driver to bring her here to the Maycomb Cryogenics Lab. Beth had paid the driver, looked over the top of the cab, and there she was again, across the street, staring. With that distraction, Beth had walked down the block and missed the lab's entrance, going past it, with the odd woman keeping pace. When Beth stopped, the woman stopped. When Beth turned back and walked the other way, so did the woman. At the entrance, Beth looked again over her shoulder, annoyed more than worried, to find the woman stopped across the street, watching her go in.

Freak.

"May I help you?" The receptionist wasn't stereotypically chirpy, speaking instead with a low, professional tone. Beth set her briefcase down, introduced herself, and asked to speak to Ms.

Mayella, who had been Robeson's boss. "Certainly. One moment." The receptionist made no call but used her keyboard instead. With a nod, she handed Beth a white plastic card and pointed to the elevator.

Beth picked up her briefcase and walked to the elevator. She looked for a button to press. There wasn't one. The elevator door opened as she approached. Inside the elevator, there were no buttons either. The doors closed and the elevator began to descend all by itself. The ride was short. With a soft chime, the doors opened again and Beth saw her name on the floor in front of her as soon as she stepped into the hallway. The lighting in the floor framed her name with a soft blue border that pulsed gradually. The frame moved up the hallway and, naturally, Beth stepped after it. She admired the technology but had an odd thought.

Great. Now I'm following me too.

Like the woman on the sidewalk.

She shook her head, clearing her thoughts.

Her name on the floor turned a corner. Beth followed. Her name found a door and slid vertically up to the middle of it. When Beth got to it, the door opened for her and her name faded away.

Ms. Mayella waited inside, standing in black heels and a black dress.

"Thank you for seeing me, Ms. Mayella," Beth extended her hand and was glad to be received warmly, but the warmth was really to be expected.

"I'm glad you're here, Ms. Hatch. Our company is prepared to cooperate fully. I'm sure you understand we want to mitigate any liability for Doctor Robeson's actions and avoid any fallout. Other than this one . . ." the supervisor searched for the proper word, ". . . aberration, Dr. Robeson was a model employee. We wish him well."

Beth translated to herself.

Welcome. Let the ass-covering commence.

Mayella led Beth to the cryogenic facility to show her where Robeson had stored the body of his girlfriend for almost a year. Beth realized she'd come away from her interrogation at the county jail without an answer to her first question: Was Annabelle dead before she left Robeson's apartment or did she die after? She'd have to recheck her notes.

The memory of the bright light reminded her she needed to get to Robeson's desk.

That single task took over her thoughts. She tried to focus as Ms. Mayella told her of Robeson's sins.

"As much as anyone, he should have known the body needs to be injected with heparin . . ."

Is Robeson's desk on this floor?

". . . protects the body from damage while being prepared for cryogenic stasis . . ."

That little detail wasn't included in my notes.

". . . the process with our patented vitrification fluid, which acts as a human antifreeze . . ."

Wait. Maybe it is in my notes. The secondary ones.

" . . . wonder why he didn't follow protocols. Anyway, here we are. What we like to call The Bedroom."

The room was hard to ignore, like something out of a science fiction movie. The walls were lined with long, silver tubes behind frosted windows. An array of flexible pipes and wires led from the tubes to the floors. The room was clinical but also cozy somehow, with padded white panels and computer screens showing readouts in pastel shades.

Cold cocoons.

"We are the largest human cryogenic facility in the world, housing 1,701 full-body clients at minus one hundred ninety-six degrees Celsius."

Beth remembered to reply, "Uh-huh."

"We have nearly twice that many in *neurosuspension*, which maintains only the head and brain. Personally, I'm going into full body stasis when my time comes."

"That's . . . uh . . . that's great."

Mayella crossed her arms. "Forgive me Ms. Hatch, but you don't seem too interested in understanding your client's situation. You've barely paid attention to my explanation. I'm concerned you may not be doing your job."

Fine.

"How did you discover Robeson had stored his girlfriend's body here?" Beth asked.

Mayella set her jaw for a moment, but finally answered. "As you might imagine, it takes a lot of energy to maintain this facility. We know to the penny how much each of these pods costs to run. When accounting determined we were sustaining 1,702 bodies, we started checking the pods. We discovered Annabelle then. When we tried to shut down the pod, Mr. Robeson became distraught and violent. That's when we called the authorities."

"I see."

"What we can't explain is how he got her in here without being caught."

Beth nodded. It would be good to get an answer for that. She nodded some more.

Mayella crossed her arms again. "Don't you have any other questions?"

"Yes. Where is Robeson's desk please?"

An exasperated Ms. Mayella led the way. She didn't need her name in a traveling frame on the floor to find Robeson's office and his desk. With a *tah-dah* sweep of her arm, she took a step back to let Beth have a look.

It was a desk. On top, a pencil holder. A coffee mug. A computer. Assorted odds and ends.

"We've been told to leave everything as we found it. Only the police have touched it."

Good. There's something I need to take.

The memory of the bright light demanded it.

Beth found it. Right on the corner of the desk. A silver case to hold eyeglasses. The silver caught the light, reflecting the soft whiteness of the lights into her eyes. She should at least pretend to look things over. Maybe find a way to distract Mayella so she could snitch the case.

A notebook sat on the opposite corner of the desk. With a finger, Beth turned the cover open. Mayella didn't object. The pages were filled with tight, small lines of text. Some in English. Most in a language that was definitely not English.

As Mayella watched, Beth retrieved her yellow legal pad from her briefcase and put it next to Robeson's notebook. She flipped up the first few pages.

Mayella looked at the foreign characters written on Beth's legal pad. A small gasp. "Did you write this?"

"I did," Beth replied. "Dr. Robeson showed me what to write."

The characters shocked me as well. The bright light showed me what to write. While I was blacked out. It's the only explanation.

Mayella pointed at the pad. "May I?"

With a *tah-dah* gesture, Beth took a step back. Mayella picked up the notebook, devouring the page, then turning to the next. "Would it be all right if I make a copy of this?"

"All right," Beth replied. She took the legal pad back and tore off the page she had shown first. "Only this page, though. The rest are covered by client/attorney privilege." Beth gave Mayella the one sheet of paper, her heartrate increasing, thrumming in her throat, as she contemplated impending theft. "Take your time."

Mayella left the room. When Beth could no longer hear the woman's heels clicking on the floor, the eyeglasses case went into her briefcase. She close the briefcase. Theft complete.

A long minute passed. Clicking heels foreshadowed Ms. Mayella's return. She entered the office proffering Beth's paper, which she took back. Mayella said, "We are thinking of having these symbols analyzed. Dr. Robeson often wrote characters like these. We've speculated they're derived from Georgian or Armenian, but no one is sure. You don't happen to know what they mean, do you?"

"Not the faintest idea," Beth lied. "He might tell me later, perhaps."

"This diagram is interesting," Mayella stepped closer with a smile, apparently pleased that Beth was now interesting. She pointed at a drawing Beth had (apparently) done. "Do you know what it shows?"

"Again, not the faintest."

"There are fourteen highly-visible, well-known pulsars in our galaxy. They're a useful way of locating planets. We put the location of Earth relative to these pulsars on the Voyager probe in the 1970s. This arrangement would identify a planet somewhere in the Aquarius constellation. Is that familiar to you?"

"No. Sorry."

Mayella seemed disappointed. "Well. If you have any thoughts, I'd love to hear from you."

Beth forced a sigh. "Sounds good. I think I'm done here for the moment. If I need anything else, I'll come back."

"Let me show you out," Mayella said.

They were almost to the receptionist's desk when a muscular gentleman in a suit stopped them. He whispered something to Mayella who turned to Beth with a sour expression. "Please come with us." Her tone indicated she was not issuing an invitation.

Beth followed to a room near the lobby. "Open your briefcase," Mayella said.

Beth didn't say anything. She would not incriminate herself with a careless comment, but she knew they would detain her until they saw what they wanted to see, even if it took a court order.

Robeson's sunglasses case is sitting in there.

"We have cameras everywhere, you know."

Robeson doesn't actually wear glasses, you know.

Warmth flushed her cheeks as she opened the case. She stepped back courteously. The man in the suit inspected what he could see while Mayella stood off to the side. He was very respectful, keeping his hands clasped in front of him. Finally, he asked, "Ma'am, would you please remove the items from your briefcase one at a time and place them on the table?"

Beth nodded. Approaching the briefcase, she had to make an effort to remain casual. She quickly saw that the silver sunglasses case was missing.

Where . . .?

She removed everything from the interior of the case. File folders. The fantasy novel she was reading. Pens and pencils. Letters and a bill she meant to drop off at the post office. Keys on a keyring. Her own sunglasses (no case). The briefcase itself was simple, with only one pocket in the top, which was empty.

When the briefcase had been gutted, Beth stepped back, emboldened just a little. "Is there something you are looking for?" She asked. The man picked up her personal sunglasses and checked them. Regular, non-prescription, woman's style. He put them back down.

"If you're looking for something in particular . . .." She let the question trail off. She wasn't worried. The sunglasses case was missing, but Beth knew where it was now.

"You took a silver case from Dr. Robeson's desk." Mayella took the role of accuser. "The camera saw you. We also checked

53

again, and it was on the desk before you went in, but it's not there now."

Beth shrugged. "Maybe it fell on the floor."

"We're going to need to search your clothing."

"Are there cameras in here?"

"No," the man replied.

Beth kicked off her shoes, unbuttoned her blouse and removed it, unzipped her skirt and stood in her bra and panties. "Satisfied?" Her blush intensified but she wasn't going to waste more time here. The bright light had more things for her to do.

Mayella retrieved Beth's clothing from the floor, handling the silk blouse carefully along with the cotton skirt. The shoes were clearly above suspicion already. Mayella finished her examination and looked at Beth, questions still standing in her eyes.

"Look," Beth jumped in. "Whatever you're thinking, it isn't possible. An eyeglasses case is fairly bulky. Even if I were wearing it, it would be at least a cup size larger than what I have on. So."

Mayella looked at her security guy who looked back, expressionless.

"Let her go." Mayella handed Beth's clothing back to her and she got dressed again while the man looked sideways.

Mayella said, "You wrote 'Atticus' on your notepad. Do you intend to live up to that?"

Beth ignored her, returning her belongings to her briefcase. She didn't drive, but she owned three keys. One for her apartment door, one for her parent's house, and one for her gym locker. Now she had four, including a new silver key on her keyring. The key hadn't been there this morning.

The silver case is now a silver key.

The bright light flared behind her eyes, like when she rubbed her eyes too hard, only a hundred times more dazzling.

I saw this would happen. I saw it the first time my writing trailed off the page.

The bright light told her it was true.

Another taxi ride. The seven-foot woman with the auburn hair was waiting again, on the other side of the street. Maybe not following then. Maybe knowing beforehand where Beth was going.

The new key on Beth's ring fit the door of the building perfectly. She went inside. A narrow stairway went up to a closed door. The key worked on that door too.

No art on the walls. No carpet. No furniture with the sole exception of an entertainment console and a small couch.

Loveseat.

An 85-inch LED television screen hung on the wall. A DVD player sat on the console. Three shelves of DVDs sat unevenly on the shelves.

Top shelf:

E.T. the Extraterrestrial. Star Trek: The Motion Picture. Close Encounters of the Third Kind. Cocoon. Starman.

Second shelf:

The Arrival. Alien. The Thing. Invasion of the Body Snatchers. The Hidden. Other titles she didn't recognize.

Third shelf:

Demolition Man. Supernova. Passengers. More titles Beth wasn't familiar with.

One other item sat on the console.

A silver flute.

If she disassembled it, the flute would fit into her briefcase.

This, the second time Beth's handwriting had trailed off the page.

One more to go.

* * *

Beth didn't remember sleeping. On the other hand, she didn't remember staying awake either.

She did manage to get dressed as the horizon grew light, eat something, and find her way to the courthouse. Ginger giraffe was *not* there, waiting or watching. Small favors. She went through security, surprised when the metal detector went off, and actually jumped. Again, she was escorted to a side room and asked to open her briefcase. Legal pad. File folders. Same things.

And the flute.

Oh, yes. The flute.

"Would you like a concert?" Beth asked, then immediately waved her hand at the security guard before he could reply. "Sorry. I'm tired. Big case today. My client's arraignment is in fifteen minutes and I'm . . . so . . . .." She sighed. "Apologies."

The amused security guard gave her a half smile and helped her put things back. "Good luck with the arraignment."

Beth waited in the courtroom, alone at first. A handful of bystanders were seated in the back. Reporters most likely, armed with little spiral notebooks and business casual clothes. Hoping, no doubt, for a juicy tidbit about the man who had hidden his girlfriend's body in a cryogenic facility for almost a year.

Vultures.

The state's attorney appeared next, gave Beth a perfunctory nod, and sat at the prosecutor's table. Gradually, more spectators arrived. The court stenographer. The bailiff. Finally, Robeson was escorted into the courtroom, manacled by wrists and ankles to a belt around his waist. He lowered himself into his seat.

"Are you prepared to secure my release?"

Beth nodded.

Robeson looked over his shoulder. "And hers?"

The woman with the auburn hair was sitting behind Beth in the gallery. Beth tried not to flinch when she saw her and mostly succeeded. She still wore the yellowing trenchcoat and the silver sunglasses even though she was indoors.

Bright light. Behind Beth's eyes. Framing her vision in shimmering points.

The third time my handwriting had trailed of the page.

Almost here.

Her hand went to her briefcase.

Robeson leaned over and whispered, "Not yet."

By the time the judge entered the courtroom, Beth's vision was a blur. The bright light encroached deeply enough into her field of view that she felt she was looking down a white tunnel, so intense it hurt. She wanted to open the briefcase. Had to wait.

The judge ordered the accused to stand. Beth stood with Robeson as the ceiling started to shake. The ceiling tiles began vanishing, one by one. When the silver cylinder arrived, floating overhead, Beth knew it was time.

She opened her briefcase and pulled out the gun. The gun that had been a flute.

Robeson turned to face her. He leaned over, as if he were giving her a bow. She reached up, pressed the gun against his forehead, and pulled the trigger. Blood and brains blew out of the back of his head. Beth turned to face the gallery. The woman in the trenchcoat was pulling off her hair. She tossed the auburn wig aside with one hand and the silver sunglasses with the other. She bowed to Beth and Beth had time to notice the woman's liquid blue eyes and the white hairs growing out of the woman's head in random patches. Beth pressed the gun against her forehead and pulled the trigger again.

* * *

The man in the suit sat across from Beth, silently reading the charges being filed against her. Beth's arraignment was scheduled for the following morning. The handcuffs around Beth's wrists seemed dull as if the light didn't want them any more than Beth.

So much for Robeson's promise that my career would not be over.

Finally, the man looked at her. "What reason did you have for murdering two people in the courtroom?"

Beth shrugged. "I'm not sure you'll believe me."

The man nodded. "Maybe. Maybe not. Let's try." He pushed Beth's legal pad towards her. "Beginning with the things you wrote here."

Beth glanced at the characters she'd written, like a mix of Georgian and Armenian but really neither. "That says their story was in the DVDs."

The man nodded. "What does that mean?"

"He had a little love nest for himself and his girlfriend. They liked to watch movies. Movies about alien possession, cryogenics, stuff like that. But their favorite ones, the ones they liked the best, were on the first shelf."

"What were those about?"

"The aliens who made it home again."

The man stared into her eyes. Long moments passed and after a time, he seemed satisfied. "This was the girlfriend he put in the freezer?"

"Yes. Her Earthly body was injured beyond repair, but her Celestial body was still alive. He sent a signal to his planet to get a rescue, but knew it would take a year. He hid her body in the cryogenics facility where he worked because it would preserve her, keep her real body alive, until the ship arrived." Beth looked at her hands. She hand to bow her head to get her face close enough to her hands that she could wipe the tears away.

The man waited. Respectful.

When Beth was ready, she continued. "He was able to put a little of his Celestial self in me. So I could help him and his sister. The rescue ship was ready and they needed me to release them.

That's why I shot them through their brains. So that their Celestial selves could go to the ship."

Beth thought the man might be shocked. He didn't seem to be. "They were beautiful. I'm the only one who saw their bright lights, it seems. They floated up to the ship like little crystalline stars. He forgave us for murdering his girlfriend."

The man had gone back to his own notes. Then he slid her notes back again and looked at those. "It looks to me, Ms. Hatch, that you have some very convincing samples of an alien language here. And you are the expert. Would you say that's the case?"

Beth swallowed. "Why are you more interested in my notes than the murders? Are you my attorney?"

The man raised his head. "No, Ms. Hatch. I'm from NASA."

Spera Angelorum

The Sci-Fi Story with Houdini and Charles Dickens

Years ago, in an interview, I was asked who my literary inspirations were. I replied, "All the Harrys: Harry Bosch, Harry Potter, Harry Dresden, and Harry Houdini." Harry Bosch is the complicated police detective created by Michael Connelly and I always like a well-crafted mystery. Harry Potter's gift to fiction was a world where anything and everything could be magic. Harry Dresden, conjured by the exceptional Jim Butcher, is the father of urban fantasy. (Come to think of it, Asimov's *Foundation* had one too. Hari Seldon anyone?)

There does seem to be a surfeit of characters named Harry in literature.

The one Harry who isn't fictional is Harry Houdini. Yet he is an inspiration not only for magicians but fiction writers as well. He was a master of self-promotion, for one, but he was something more than a performer. He became a legend because, not matter the challenge, he *never lost*.

This was more than a novelty to people recovering from the first World War. Before Superman was created, Houdini *was* Superman. No restraints could hold him. No jail could keep him. He represented something that the world was hungry for: a seemingly common man capable of the most uncommon feats.

When I started writing "Spera Angelorum," I needed two more things. A foil for Houdini was one; I found my answer in the person of Charles Dickens, who was similarly interested in telling stories of common folk overcoming uncommon challenges. After that, I needed an excuse to get these two guys together.

That answer came one day when I was pondering the afterlife. What do we do with all the people out of a job? If we are resurrected as perfect beings, in the Christian tradition, what do we do with all the doctors? Similarly, if we have the powers of angels, how would a common magician find a way to be impressive?

Spera Angelorum

The ship arrived planetside without a hitch. The landing procedure was smooth. The attendants were immaculate and polite. The meal on the flight was sliced manna with ambrosia sauce. The sheer perfection of it all pissed me off.

"Would you like a refill before we disembark?" Our attendant literally appeared out of nowhere. Angels could do that.

"Another Bloody Mary," I replied.

In mortality, I'd been a teetotaler but I'd since learned to like the taste.

The attendant mixed the drink at the table behind our seats. She was about to hand it to me when I said, "Make it a champagne glass."

She smiled. The tumbler in her hands reformed itself into a fluted glass. Angels could do that too. Not a drop spilled.

Childish of me, making other people do tricks.

My traveling companion watched the transformation but was more excited about our arrival. "We can now say we've been to *Spera Angelorum*. The crown jewel of its galaxy. Isn't it wonderful?" Charles' hands fluttered around his cravat with excitement, like a pair of turtledoves trying to build a nest beneath his beard.

I leaned over him to peer through the viewport and sighed. The stanchions swinging inward were littered with sparkling lights and they clamped onto the sides of the shuttle with predictable exactness. There were tens of thousands of inhabited planets in this system alone. I had been to many and found the angel planets devoid of interest. I'd love a surprise at least once.

"Wonderful." I repeated his word. "My mother will be so proud."

"You should have brought her, Harry! This is a rare honor. Few are invited to travel to the stars and stand shoulder-to-shoulder with exalted beings such as these."

I started to sigh again but the sigh turned, quite unintentionally, into a yawn. This was the first trip that Charles and I had made together. I knew he left Earth at least as often as I did, but he was somehow unjaded; smiling and chatty like he'd never been to another planet before.

"Why are we here, Charles? I mean really. Why?"

Charles fixed me with his piercing eyes and a smile tugged his mouth askew. "It is the simplest of things, dear Harry. We are here to be ourselves."

I dropped back as far as I could into my seat, which was comfortable to a fault. "Yes. That's what they always say. It's not enough."

A momentary laugh bubbled up from somewhere soulful. "Americans. Always wanting more."

"Never settling, Charles. Never settling. It's better than you Brits with your 'Keep Calm' about every damn thing."

Charles pointed toward the attendant who had returned to usher us from the ship. "Now is our chance to escape."

I glowered at him. "Making fun of me?"

"Making fun? Wouldn't dream of it." His grin did not placate. "I am appreciating your unique gifts."

I stood to collect my bag of handcuffs and chains and lock picks. Charles had a valise stuffed with books and scraps of handmade paper and an inkwell and goose feather pens. His luggage weighed a tenth of mine. It was a tenth as interesting.

We proceeded toward the front of the craft. Charles nudged me with an elbow and raised an eyebrow as he watched the attendant in front of us. I nodded at the old goat. Yes, she was shapely and her hips moved in all the usual ways as she walked down the aisle. She had a gold belt holding her white shift tightly around her trim waist. Her long, auburn hair was effectively arranged, pulled back with a gold hair clip and her skin was like porcelain with the lightest touch of an early summer peach on her cheeks. She turned, checking our progress, and smiled. Her lips had the same quaint fullness as my beloved Bess.

I tired of looking at her.

Ruby-studded doors opened as we left the gangway. Another attendant waited on the other side, smiling another flawless smile, "Greetings, gentlemen. My name is Teserra. Follow me, please."

Charles nodded. I barely took notice. My curiosity was drawn to the scene ahead and I could almost hear a fanfare as the doors parted to welcome us. *Da-da-daaa.*

The concourse through the spaceport dripped with golden light. A suspended river of chandeliers covered the ceiling in endless majesty, sending reflected shards of color to dance across the floor. Seamless marble flowed beneath our feet, palest white, as if a mountain had laid itself down to serve as our entry. Maybe one had been brought in. Sphere of Angels with all its glory and power. Faith to move mountains.

The three of us walked alone: Teserra, then Charles, then me. The construction of the place captivated me. I had anticipated a planet that hinted at religion to be painfully Gothic, with fluted pillars and Ionic capitals bearing the ponderous weight of a vaulted ceiling. Instead, the concourse unfolded with softly contoured shapes and not a single straight line. The serene quiet was deafening. I liked how our footsteps broke the silence.

Outside, of all unexpected things, waited a horse-drawn carriage.

I breathed in the congenial animal scent of freshly-washed horseflesh. Earthy. Real. Not mechanical. The conveyance was pristine, of course, the wood perfectly oiled and polished. Teserra ascended to the driver's seat with measured grace. "Climb aboard, good sirs. We'll be at the theater shortly."

Charles beamed. "A hansom cab! This will be the first civilized ride I've had in ages!"

Silver ships flew overhead. Other vehicles breezed past us, their brake lights creating holographic flowers in the air. None were driven by a flesh-and-bone person. It was my turn to give Charles an elbow and point. He took note of the robot driver piloting the nearest car.

"Perhaps your writings were not as effective as you had hoped, Charles. There is still a lower class serving the aristocracy."

Charles nodded. "But here, the lower class is *manufactured*. Made from the materials of metal and sweat and ingenuity. Not subjugated or enslaved from the fellow brotherhood of Mankind. The human race has elevated themselves all together. Undivided." Charles leaned in conspiratorially, "And a creator always treats better his own creations."

He was right, of course. Charles sprang into the cab and took the rear-facing seat. I took the opposite spot. A taciturn mood fell over me. I hoped the ride would be short as promised by our driver. I cracked my knuckles one at a time. I produced an ancient silver dollar and began to roll it over the backs of my fingers. I caught it with my thumb as it dropped between ring and little finger and brought it around again for another pass. Heads, tails, heads, swoop. My fingers complained. They would warm up and loosen.

The cab moved into traffic with not so much as a lurch or a bump. Maddening.

Charles stared at me with a glint in his eye that impishly invited conversation, though I didn't want it.

"Very well, Charles. What is it?"

Charles leaned forward, resting his elbows on his knees. The cab was close and we were nearly touching. "I'm looking forward to seeing your performance, Harry. I understand you always strive to present an authentic experience. A recreation of history. Correct?"

I blew air through my nostrils and looked out the window. Perfect street. Exquisite buildings. Immaculate people. Damn them all.

I saw the hook in the worm.

"Obviously, it's what the audience wants."

Charles snapped his fingers. "Yes! Knowing what an audience wants, Harry. That's the thing we have most in common, I think." He sat back, putting a period on the end of his sentence.

"What about what *I* want?"

Charles leaned to the side, looking at me with his head on his fist as if I were a troublesome adverb. "What *do* you want, Harry?"

This fish liked a fight.

"Let me point out, what I do is more difficult than what you do. You authors stand at attention and regale the audience with stories you wrote centuries ago. I can't do that. I can't just talk about a straitjacket or a pair of handcuffs. I have to put them on as tightly as possible and then fight to get out of them again. Every time. Hanging from my heels and dangling like an emerging butterfly. To be fair, you should stand up and write a new novel while they watch. That would be a more comparable challenge."

Charles looked at me, the skepticism all but dripping from his eye. "Not compelling theater, Harry."

I turned away again.

"Conceptually, I agree," Charles barely paused. "In your day, you were a living metaphor for the human condition. The personification of a time when men scraped and fought to be free of poverty and oppression. I wrote about the same thing, but thousands of people stood and watched you…" the writer waited for the word he wanted, "…emerge. Victorious. Everyone wanted to *be* you, Harry. Even now, you remind them of that very human condition."

I was mollified. A bit. Or was I?

Charles retreated inward. "We both chose not be exalted for different reasons, I expect. For you, however, it makes what you do believable. Real. With no supernal powers to assist you, your performance still means something."

I nodded. It was a good thought, but talk centered on myself made me fidget.

"So, Charles, why haven't you written a new book?" I really wanted to know.

"Oh I have. Many of them. Shelves full of them."

"You have? I never would have guessed. Why not publish them? Don't you think they'd be read?"

"I'm sure they would be. And I tell no one."

I smiled. My conjuror's intuition prompted me, "You love this, Charles. All of it. The traveling. The lectures. You love being the 19th-century man. Yet your genius is ancient and your legacy can't abide an upgrade. No Charles 2.0. You're trapped after writing about the common man and there are no common men anymore."

Charles nodded. "Well said, Harry. I'll make a poet out of you yet."

I felt no better. "We're both relics in our own way. I came back to worlds that had grown beyond me too. Now I have to explain what handcuffs were used for. These people have powers that I only pretend to have. I couldn't move forward if I wanted to. You could move forward but choose to stay."

"What the audience wants, Harry." Charles diverted. "Did you have children?"

"Bess and I never had time to consider a family. Then I died. Now it's too late." Altogether too late. "You had a number of them, didn't you?"

"Oh, yes. Ten children. Love them all."

"So there weren't any left for me. You got my share."

"Ah, very quick, Harry. I could lend you one, if you like. A son would do you good."

I'd thought about that. Often. Children. A son. How——.

The cab had stopped. I hadn't felt it. I only noticed that the scenery outside wasn't moving anymore.

Teserra opened the door for us and we got out.

We stood in front of the theater and for a moment I bathed in nostalgia. Behind me, on the other side of the street, there were holographic billboards ten stories high and you could buy tickets to a movie by looking at the list overhead and blinking your eyes twice. There was none of that for our theater. With my back to the technical marvels of this world, the edifice that stood before me was Classic Revival in style with pillars and hand-carved frames around the windows. The ticket booth was staffed by a pretty girl in a pillbox hat. The marquee advertised the show using a well-worn tile-and-rack. Our names were up there with the letters unevenly spaced, which delighted me. I was suddenly back in Austin, Texas, of all places.

"It's the Majestic Theater," I said. "I played this stage before. On Earth."

"Then welcome home, Harry." Charles tipped his hat to me and then to Teserra and we went inside through a backstage door that had graffiti and old handbills glued to it. I could almost smell sweat, and booze, and a hint of day-old urine just looking at it.

This might be heaven.

My dressing room was small and cramped. The bricks in the walls were actual bricks and the mirror was surrounded by a dozen incandescent lights, which I hadn't seen in decades. I sat there for a full half hour, knowing I should finish limbering my hands and go inspect the stage and be sociable. But I could only bask.

"You're smiling, Harry. It's bad precedent." Charles stood in my doorway, dressed in full evening attire with his cheeks artfully rouged and his hair just on the messy side of cultured.

"This place has the human part of humanity in it." I tapped my lip. "Do you think they created it just for us?"

The stage manager called for Charles and escorted him to the wings.

I returned to my mirror and my pots of makeup.

Tap-tap on the frame of the door.

"Excuse me, sir?"

A young man, looking to be sixteen years-old. Light hair. Bold features. He clasped his hands together tightly, nervous.

"May I help you?"

"Yes. Uh. Yes, sir," he stammered.

"Call me Harry."

"Thank you, sir. Harry."

I couldn't resist. "Not Sir Harry either. Just Harry. I was never knighted." I smiled and hoped it would put him more at ease.

"Harry. I wanted to say that I, uh, admire your work."

I nodded. The boy shifted from one foot to the other like he was walking on pins. "I can see it took some courage for you to come backstage to say so. I very much appreciate it. Better take your seat now. The program is about to start."

The boy gave half a bow and left.

I hadn't had a real visitor for—how long had it been? There'd been dignitaries. People who wanted to be seen with me. But a simple visitor? Who just wanted to say hello? An eternity.

The audience chatter that I could hear from my dressing room faded. The floorboards creaked as someone took center stage. A basso-profondo voice introduced Charles. The sound resonated in the bones. I finished my makeup and went to watch.

For the next hour, Charles held court. He had pages of notes all over the lectern and books stacked on the floor, but he didn't need them. They were props that served as crown, scepter, and throne. Occasionally, he picked up a book as if to check the words on a page but the page might as well have been blank. Charles had everything he needed in his head. And in his heart. I listened to his tales of orphans and villains and ghosts at Christmas and knew, not for the first time, why audiences loved him.

He wove a spell with his voice, describing characters who were flawed. Broken. They struggled against impossible circumstances and evil enemies and sometimes demons of their own making. They overcame. They won. They found a way to be redeemed of all their too-human faults.

When he finished, the audience expressed their appreciation in the time-honored way: they came to their feet and applauded. There were tears in their eyes and I was glad to see that these perfect beings could *feel*. From the fringe, I saw people rise into the air, their feet bidding farewell to the floor. Whether on purpose, or because their souls had been lifted up, I could not tell, but I felt the same effect.

Charles was a tough act to follow.

I clapped him on the shoulder as he exited the stage. I remained there, watching the sliver of seats visible to me from the wings. Intermission was announced in sepulchral tones. Men and women fell into deep discussions. Some evaporated, vanishing into thin air in a way no magician had ever accomplished.

If only.

I didn't know where they went. Maybe around the corner or to the other side of the galaxy. It was all the same to them. They would return in the same fashion soon, blinking back into existence. Perfected beings. Exalted power.

What need had any of these for me?

In mortality, I'd battled those who deceived the innocent. The fraudulent psychics and fake mediums who'd claimed to converse with the dead. I'd exposed them by using their methods openly on stage. Still, there had been many who refused to shed the clothing of sheep and allowed themselves to be fleeced. Ravaged by the wolves.

Now, the dead spoke. Walked on ground holy and unholy. I was surrounded by them. I'd cheated death, over and over, and made it my career. Now everyone cheats death.

What need had any of these for me?

I busied myself with a final, obsessive check of my equipment. I knew everything would be perfect and this was the one area where perfection was mandatory. The manacles were centuries old now. Kept functioning with painstaking care and oil and implements of my own manufacture. Like me, they were relics of a dead age. The function for which they were created no longer required.

What need had any of these? For me?

Perfection had saved my life in the time before. The perfect audience would receive a perfect performance. I would give the flawless standard I was known for and if I found it tiresome to be here, my audience would never know it. I might not know why they wanted to watch, but I knew what they wanted to *see*.

Returning spectators floated to their seats or reappeared from their invisible places.

The master of ceremonies rumbled through my introduction.

I stepped in front of the footlights.

"Good evening, ladies and gentlemen. What you are about to see is a recreation of a program presented at the turn of the twentieth century. The electric light was becoming commonplace. The wireless radio was just emerging as a technology and the television was thirty years away."

I felt all eyes upon me as I set the stage. "The working man's day was fourteen hours or longer. If you were lucky enough to have time in the evening, you could read a newspaper or a book. I recommend *David Copperfield*."

I tipped my head toward Charles in the wings and got my first round of laughter. I rolled up my sleeves. "If you were lucky enough to have a few coins to spare, you looked to the stage for penny operas or vaudeville, with their endless variety and color. In larger cities, you might even have the privilege to enter a darkened theater to witness the most technologically-advanced entertainment experience in the world, the motion picture.

"But tonight, you are all members of the royal family. The room is a parlor in St. Petersburg, Russia, Mother Earth. The year is 1903. The program begins with the performance that earned me my first title."

Lazily extending my hand to the side, and showing it empty front and back, a card suddenly appeared at my fingertips. "I was first known as the King of Cards."

I made the cards fly. They flickered and danced around my fingers like demons, appearing, vanishing, multiplying, cascading to the floor. I felt I'd captured half the audience.

"If only I were exalted." A wry smile played across my lips.

That reminder achieved its purpose. Expressions changed from complacent to awestruck. Their eyes flared wide as those who

73

had forgotten I had no powers, remembered. Everything I did was by skill alone. Perfect people, perfectly surprised.

I had them. They were my audience now.

I finished by scaling the cards into the far reaches of the gallery. Flicking them deftly so they flew to the last row, to the balcony, bouncing off the stage and the walls to float and flutter into every corner like pasteboard birds. The applause began with cards still in the air as I took my bow.

I loved applause.

I invited two gentlemen to the stage. They could have levitated down or teleported but were thoughtful enough to walk.

To one I gave a straitjacket. To the other I gave my valise. I directed him to hold it at the sides. I put a small table underneath it. Instead of putting the valise on it, I rotated the bag upside-down between his hands. More than two dozen manacles clattered to the table and he stepped back as they banged to the floor at his feet.

"Thirty-eight pounds of metal for your inspection, good sir." I turned to the other gentleman. "And a jacket ill-suited for evening attire. At least it was in the twentieth century. Fashions do change."

I removed my jacket and threw it to the side of the stage.

"Ladies and gentlemen, these once were the implements of law enforcement, used to control the criminal and the insane. Tonight, I shall suffice for both."

To the gentleman near the manacles, I said, "You will find the keys to those mingled in with the handcuffs, leg irons, and locks. Feel free to examine them at your leisure. I'd suggest a pair of handcuffs that you can confirm are real. Lock them and see if you can find the correct key and unlock them again. Don't try them on yourself. I can't be sure they'll open again."

That was a lie. But this was a show.

Being exalted wasn't the same as being omniscient. You still only know what you have learned for yourself. The angel helping me didn't seem to know much about restraints, which was good. I wanted the audience to see him struggle to figure things out.

Time to suit up.

I asked the other spectator to examine the straitjacket carefully, pointing out the various parts and asking him to test their strength. Then I gave step-by-step directions for putting the straitjacket onto my body. Arms through the sleeves. Strap between the legs. Buckles up the back. "Make everything as tight as you can."

He did.

It was an elegant dance between two men in excellent physical condition. He used his strength to make each strap tight, moving around with a poetic grace. I countered, stepping in, while seeking to gain as much slack as I could get.

It was snug. As tight as I had felt it for years.

"Well done. I must ask you for one more favor." As I spoke I shifted in the jacket, seeking to increase my slim advantage. "I always performed this escape outside, hanging by a rope, upside-down, from a construction crane. We have no crane in the theater."

I laid down on my back, legs outstretched.

"If you would, please suspend me over the stage."

Of course, he hesitated.

I had to roll a little to look at him. "It's quite all right. Please lift me up and hold me, preferably by the ankles."

I let the request sink in just a bit more.

"Take me up as high as you like. As soon as I begin the escape, hold me aloft for precisely three minutes. Your internal clock will be accurate enough. If I have not escaped by the end of three minutes, well, you have done as I asked."

I said I would begin the escape as soon as I was hanging above the stage. In reality, I had spent the last sixty seconds getting more slack. The escape started from the moment the jacket went on. Rolling on the floor gave me another chance to loosen the canvas and leather.

An invisible force grabbed my legs and ankles and I grunted as my stomach muscles jammed tight.

I floated slowly upward. No ropes. No wires. My blood pulsed in my ears. A drum in my head, marking time.

I went higher. Thirty feet. Fifty feet. Seventy feet over the stage.

"There once was a real danger of death. I can't die now but if I fell from this height, my neck could be broken. I would not enjoy the experience."

I turned slowly in the air. I saw faces below me, gazing up with the same wonder I saw in people who weren't perfect. "In three minutes, let me fall unless I am free. Go!"

I began twisting in the air. I felt myself fall immediately. The audience screamed. The angel must have been caught by surprise. I fell halfway to the stage before I felt my legs caught up again by the invisible force.

"Concentrate!" I cried. "Let nothing distract you!"

I loved the struggle. Loved the effort though it made me weary to the bone.

I worked with the bits of slack I'd been able to gain. It took almost a full minute before I was able to pull my arm over my head, which released both arms from being crossed. There was a smattering of applause. I glanced down and saw I had drifted over the first few rows of the audience. No time to consider the view.

My arm caught in the sleeve. I grunted against the canvas. At last, I managed to get my hand out from the straitjacket where it met my leg. My internal clock wasn't perfect but I was sure that more than two minutes had passed. Too much time.

I worked to get my hand around to the strap between my legs. I had to pull it tighter to get the belt off the pin of the buckle and I cried out. I dropped once more and the audience beneath me screamed again.

"Concentrate!" I shouted to myself as much as to the angel.

Eternities passed. I got the strap free. I rolled and thrashed in the air. I pushed my other hand out of the collar and scrabbled at the top strap on the back. It came unbuckled reluctantly. I started yanking the jacket off over my head. Only seconds remained. I should be able to get out of it now but I couldn't. My arm was pressed so tightly against my body that my hand was starting to go numb.

I needed one more buckle free. My deadened fingers tried to find the strap but I couldn't be certain what I was grabbing. I yanked and finally felt a loosening across my chest. I pulled the jacket off with such speed that the canvas raked across my face. I'd have a raw patch of skin on my cheek.

I let the straight jacket slip and fall. It landed between rows of spectators.

"Three minutes!" the angel cried. I threw my arms wide, demanding applause and getting it. Sweat fell from my face, stinging my eyes. Raining on the people below. Rolling waves of clapping hands swept over me and the audience all came to their feet.

I felt myself floating back to the stage. My angel turned me right-side-up and I touched down as smoothly as the ship in the spaceport. My shirt clung to me like a shroud, as if I were a drowned man pulled from the sea. The audience wanted to keep applauding. I let them.

I had a towel by my table and I used it to mop my face as the audience returned to the ground. I peeled off my shirt and toweled off my chest. My physique had always been chiseled and I wasn't afraid to show it. I had performed in the nude more than once, in fact, to convince the skeptics that I hid no keys or lockpicks on my person.

My spectator with the manacles had made little progress.

"How many of these have you examined?" I asked.

The angel looked at me and then the audience sheepishly. "One," he said.

"Only one?"

He offered one of the simpler cuffs and handed me the key.

"So you looked at this one and it works?"

"It does."

"And you've had perhaps fifteen minutes to look these over?"

"Well, there were some distractions," he complained. He raised a finger to point vaguely upward over the stage.

The audience laughed loudly. I was pleased.

"I think that these cuffs will be a good start then. Please put them around my wrists." I turned to the audience and asked, "If someone will please keep track of the time, starting now."

The spectator onstage followed my instructions and the cuffs went on with that ratcheting sound that audiences identified with, even if they had never seen restraints. "Ah. Those are tight. Select another set of manacles—any at all—and place them on my arms or legs. Wherever you prefer."

We continued like that for the next several minutes. There were all kinds of different restraints, including chains, padlocks, and leg irons. I let the spectator examine anything and everything and he was free to place them wherever he chose. Twenty-six different restraints bound me at the wrists and ankles and around my arms and legs. I shuffled through a turn, my tightly-bound feet finding little ability to move, giving the audience a complete view of my predicament.

I thanked my helper. "Well done. Who has the time?"

"Sixteen minutes, twenty-two seconds." I couldn't see her face beyond the footlights.

"Very good. Now here is my proposal. I will escape from my bonds in less time than it took to put them on."

My angel laughed. "Impossible!"

"So. Proposal accepted then. Start the countdown..."

"Wait!"

The deep voice rolled over the stage and I felt it on my skin.

"Will you accept a challenge?" The tall emcee stepped in front of the lights. Behind him, a figure waited in the shadows. I couldn't see his face but I could see what he held. Handcuffs.

I looked to the audience. Inquiring faces silently wanted to know why this stranger was intruding. This angel planet has a surprise after all.

I explained. "In mortal life, I had a standing challenge. I would escape from any restraints presented to me by the public. The only condition was that they be made so that they could open again once closed."

There had been many people who had tried to create handcuffs that were impossible to pick. I had defeated them all by various stratagems of my own devising. "Step forward," I said. "Let me have a look."

The figure stepped out of the shadows. I didn't recognize him. In the tips of his fingers, he held the cuffs. Sparkling. New.

"May I have your name? Mister…"

"Just call me Nick."

"Very well. Is that Mister Nick then? Or just Nick?"

The audience tittered.

"Just Nick." The man was young, sneering. Dark hair. Darker eyes. Thinking he knew something I didn't. I'd met his kind before. A knot started sideways in my stomach.

"You may have noticed," I hopped a turn to the side and showed my overburdened arms, "I'm a little indisposed at the moment. If you would kindly lock the cuffs you are holding and open them for everyone to see. I assume you brought a key?"

"Certainly." The young man snapped the cuffs closed and brandished the key. The key fit smoothly into the release mechanism and with a twist, the cuffs opened again.

"If you would, please allow our spectator to check them over? He has almost thirty minutes of experience now."

The audience laughed. Nick offered the cuffs to the spectator. The spectator held them up like they were a pair of Siamese vipers, joined at the tail, fanged mouths gaping. He held them at arm's length, squinting at them.

"I'm sure Nick here will show us what they look like on him."

I injected a note of command into my words.

Nick moved back. A fraction of an inch. He was afraid of the handcuffs. A fraction afraid.

"Roll up your sleeves, Nick. They're your handcuffs, aren't they? If you expect me to put them on, you won't object to trying them first, will you?"

Dark eyes flicked in the direction of the audience. Nick had to realize the spectators would be on my side. He had to put on the cuffs or withdraw his challenge.

Nick snapped his sleeves in a roll and stared me down. His eyes bored into mine as the spectator closed the cuffs around his wrists. I stared back.

"Show everyone the key, please."

Nick held it up.

"Give it to our thoughtful helper."

"Keep it in sight," Nick's own command.

The spectator plucked the key from Nick's hand and held it to view.

I smiled. "The longest it ever took for me to escape from challenge handcuffs was one hour and ten minutes." I let those words hang in the air. "I don't expect it will take nearly as long to escape from yours."

Nick thrust his hands at me and the links of the cuff's chain sang a song. "Let's find out, Harry."

The way he looked at me as he said my name felt too intimate. The sound wrong in his mouth. Nick couldn't wait to get the cuffs off. These cuffs were dangerous somehow and there was a purpose in them that meant something.

I watched his face. "Let's make room for them then. If our spectator would kindly remove one of the eight sets of handcuffs already adorning my arms, we can proceed."

The spectator put Nick's key on the table, where everyone could see it.

"Remove the black iron ones, I think. From the top of the stack."

It took a moment for the spectator to find the right key. Nick was trying to stay calm about the delay but I heard fear in his breathing as the spectator unlocked the manacles nearest my elbows.

"Just put them in my valise," I said.

The black irons went away.

Nick sighed, almost laughing, as our helper unlocked his freak cuffs and took them off. The knot in my stomach curled tighter. Whatever was wrong with his little metal snakes, I needed to find out.

"Are you exalted, Nick?"

Nick's face twitched, subtle but there. "No, Harry," he answered.

His voice twitched too. I smiled. "Well, we can't all be perfect."

I looked closely at the cuffs as my angel held them. Finally, I nodded and he locked the cuffs around my forearms. It was a tactic that had been useful in the past. My forearms were muscular and far larger in diameter than my hands. If unfamiliar cuffs were locked there, it was a simple matter to slip out of them after I had removed the others in the stack. Of course, I'd make it look like a challenge. I knew what audiences wanted. A close escape.

And I didn't want the challenger to feel like he'd lost too easily. He'd gone to a lot of trouble, after all.

I braced against the bite of metal on my arms. The workmanship of the cuffs was meticulous. Elegant. A shame I'd have to give them back.

I turned side to side so that the audience, and my challenger, could see I was fairly bound.

"The escape begins now."

The keys for all the cuffs were on the table, including the key for the freaks. I didn't need them. I had other bits of metal and other options. I turned my back to the audience so I could work my secrets while still remaining in their view.

The first pair of cuffs fell to the floor after ten seconds. I usually prolonged the escape so that I could finish just as time was running out but the freaks had the potential to give me a real problem. I worked faster.

I sat down. I decided to free my legs next instead of continuing with the rest of the cuffs on my arms. It would give me time to look at the freaks a little more. I could also save them for the end. Big finale. What the audience wanted.

The first leg irons came free and I tossed them in the air. They were heavy and landed with a resounding *thunk*. The metal may have damaged the perfect stage. The next restraints were even heavier and I tossed them as well. I worked my way through them all and jumped to my feet. I turned and went to the footlights, crossing from one side of the stage to the other with commanding strides, putting myself on display.

I worked on the chain and padlocks next. There was a music of sorts as each lock hit the floor with dead percussion. A waltz with their notes. One, two, bang! One, two, bang! One, two, bang!

Followed by a crescendo of chain slithering from my torso to the floor.

The audience cheered.

A chant began. Quietly. Building louder. "Escape! Escape! Escape!"

Four more cuffs to go, including the freaks.

The cuffs nearest my wrists were old friends. They opened willingly.

The next set were engraved, silver, gifts as comfortable as a pair of slippers. They slipped off with a whisper.

The penultimate set were as imposing as a pair of Rottweilers but the brutes were well-trained and obedient. They fell to the floor and stayed.

Now for the freaks.

The chant turned personal. "Har-ry! Har-ry! Har-ry!"

I glanced at Nick. He was my opposition. Not the cuffs. What was his game? He betrayed nothing. He had prepared for this moment.

I turned to face away from the audience again. I took a deep breath. I slipped the cuffs down my forearms. With a sharp click, they contracted, seizing my wrists in iron jaws. I bit back a curse. Nick had studied well. He knew how I worked and had planned for it. I should have guessed. From the way he'd held still while wearing the cuffs to the look of satisfaction on his face as my helper had put the cuffs on my flexing forearms.

If I could get one hand free, I could work on the other.

I heard another click. The cuffs were getting tighter. If I had to, I could break my thumbs, which was incredibly painful and didn't always help.

I placed one hand against the opposite cuff and pulled. My hand almost made it out but the cuffs clicked again. It caught me just behind the knuckles. I refused to surrender any ground. There was no moving back. Did the cuffs have enough power to crush bones?

"You aren't exalted," I rasped at Nick. "You don't want to be exalted."

"You're catching on, Harry."

"You want to be *damned*."

"Ruining you should get me there, don't you think?"

A new voice whispered over my shoulder.

"It's not a fair challenge, Harry."

I glared at Charles, hissing at me from the side of the stage. I hissed in retort. "I never back down."

"It's not worth it. You could lose your hands for days."

Click.

I groaned. The pain was blinding.

"The key is right there, Harry." Nick's voice was silky and seductive.

"You don't know me, Nick."

"I know your methods. Learned them by heart."

Ichor flowed from my right hand, making everything slick. The left wrist was about to give way as well. I tried again to slip my hand through the cuff.

Click.

I refused to cry out. I pushed and pulled air through my nose in short bursts.

"Harry," Charles had stepped out to put a hand on my shoulder. So softly, I could barely hear him. "The exalted here can help. Your spectators can release you. They can—"

"I know," I snapped. "Get away from me."

Charles looked sad but backed away.

The pain was almost more than I could bear. My hands were slowly being chewed off by a mechanical monster created by a would-be demon.

For what? Why do I do this? Recreate history for beings with more power—more magic—than I will ever have? Refusing to let history go.

I curled in on myself. I fell to my knees, hunched over, cradling my hands like broken children. I rocked back and forth. I shouted, releasing pain and rage.

A heartbeat. Another. I laughed and wept. One hand free. I was the only witness. The other hand free. My secrets. My wounded secrets. I reset the cuffs. A swell of relief nearly drowned me like a plunge in an icy river.

I held the cuffs out to the side. All of the molecules in the universe seemed to stop as the audience took them in. I felt every heart in the room beat once in unison before the molecules reawakened. The freaks dripped fluids from my body. They dangled by the chain that joined left and right and swung back and forth. Click. The cuffs snapped shut.

I threw them, not caring where they landed.

I turned back to face the audience.

My hands and wrists were a mass of bruises and open cuts.

I went to the table and retrieved the key. Lifted it slowly between forefinger and thumb and displayed it to the audience. Stunned. Silent. I turned and held it out in Nick's direction. I didn't look at him. I waited. He paused, then snatched the key from my hand. The only sounds were footfalls exiting the stage.

The audience exploded to their feet. Soared up to the ceiling.

I opened my hands and held them out. Presented my injuries to the spectators. Demanded what I had earned.

Applause.

I took my bows. The audience was generous and while the sound of it filled my heart and the sight of so many people standing, floating, lingering fed my soul there was still that corner of my mind that was unsatisfied. I chided myself even as I stood there on the stage. I should be happy. These perfect people, who had everything they needed, who sought only new experiences to feed them, had fed well. I had fed them well. But I was still hungry.

I brought Charles back onto the stage and we held hands raised together like prize fighters after twelve rounds. Our first triumph together.

Much later, after the last spectator vanished, blinking away, I sighed.

"How did you manage it, Harry?" Charles' eyes glimmered, curious.

"Come to my dressing room."

There were two men there, laughing companionably in the tight space.

"Charles, let me introduce my friends William and Howard."

Charles shook hands with my guests. "You were Harry's spectators from the audience."

"Indeed." William touched his hand to his brow in gentle salute. He'd put me in the straitjacket not long ago. "It doesn't happen often but you run into the occasional angel who once made a living as a magician. Although they're almost as scarce as lawyers."

"So it was all—?"

I patted his arm. "What the audience wants, Charles. You didn't make Oliver Twist a pampered millionaire for a reason. Conflict. These gentlemen are well-versed in making my life difficult. And I thank them for it."

"What about Nick then?"

I felt the shadow that passed over my face. "He was not part of the act." I looked at my darkening bruises and my wounds stained with ichor. "Injuries. They're the history of my work."

"Let me heal you," William said.

"Please, Harry," Howard joined. "There's no need to suffer."

I nodded. "Thanks all the same. I'll keep them until they heal on their own."

I reached into my valise and pulled out a pair of handcuffs. Or rather the parts that were left. "These will remain wounded as well. Centuries old, like me. Like me, wounded for a cause."

Charles took the cuffs. "Howard removed these from your arms, didn't he? To make room for Nick's new ones?"

"That's right."

"They're incomplete. Where did the bits of metal go?"

I showed Charles my empty hand and then closed it. When I opened it again, there was an oddly-shaped key in the center of my palm.

"Nick's key!"

"No. It's not."

"What is it then?"

"It's a champagne glass, Charles."

Charles looked bewildered for a moment. Then a broad smile took over his face.

"Champagne glass," he laughed. "Really, Harry."

It wasn't the first time someone had copied a key for me on the sly. Howard caught my eye and smiled.

Tap tap.

I looked up and recognized the boy.

"Hello," I said. "Charles, this young man visited me before the show."

The boy nodded. Swallowed. Blurted, "I want to do what you do, sir. Please teach me."

I smiled patiently. "Look. You can already do what I do. You can do much more, in fact. You're exalted."

The boy shook his head, staring at the ground. "No. I mean. *Yes.* I *can.* But not like an exalted." He looked up and there was need in his eyes. "I want to learn how to do what you do in the same way you do it. Like a mortal."

It was my turn to shake my head. "Why?"

The boy stood straight and determined. "It's one thing to watch history. I want to live it."

I held out my hands. Showed my wounds. "History is painful."

"I've followed you for decades."

"So has Nick."

"Nick didn't study to learn about *you*. Only your methods."

I sighed. "You think you want this, son, but you don't."

The boy wasn't giving up easily. I liked that. He started to unbutton his shirt.

"I don't think we need to wrestle over this, but—" I laughed.

"Harry," Charles nodded at the boy.

The shirt slid from the boy's shoulders, down his arms, and to the floor.

His chest was covered in bruises, his arms decorated in cuts. The patterns were familiar to me. Chains and manacles had left signs of their passing. Some of the bruises were fresh. Some of the cuts had scabbed over days ago.

My eyes traced the angry red lines in his flesh. "You haven't healed them?" Obviously not, but I couldn't stop myself from asking the question. I studied the steel-wrought marks and knew them. I'd only ever seen their like in a mirror. The meaning and depth of the boy's wounds cut through me. I felt an empty place within me disappear. The room blurred.

"Harry?" I heard a voice from a distance.

"I know, Charles." My breathing came out in rags. "It's a gift. One I have to return."

I lifted my valise full of manacles but its weight was nothing. I gave the valise to the boy.

It took long moments before I could speak. When I managed it, my voice sounded foreign to my ears. "In mortality, I changed my name to honor a man I admired. He died before I was born, but I always tried to live up to the reputation he'd built before me.

I've changed little else since then. In perfect worlds, I've shunned perfection. I didn't see a reason to embrace it. Until now. You've embraced *imperfection* and that's—"

I wanted to say more after that. Ask his name or at least say "thank you" but all I could do was fall upon the boy's neck and weep.

Grandmother Who
Breaks the Sky

The One Ray Bradbury Might Like

While in college, I had the good fortune to meet Ray Bradbury. He'd come as the keynote speaker for our literature conference and hung out in the hall afterwards to visit. I had a collection of his stories with me. (Advance planning—I used the money I'd gotten selling my Accounting 101 text back to the bookstore. There were still two weeks left in the quarter, but nothing in that textbook was going to help me salvage my grade.) He autographed the book for me and asked about my major. I told him I planned on an English Literature degree and I'd gotten a short story published in the college literary magazine. He took my collection back and said he had a special autograph for fellow authors. He then proceeded to draw a monster face next to his signature.

There were two things about that encounter that I'll never forget. First, I have an autographed sketch of a monster face from Ray Bradbury! Second . . . he called me a *fellow author.*

Well dang.

If you hang around authors long enough, you find out that many of them don't feel like actual authors.

But they are.

Ray taught me that I am an author. That was probably the kindest, most empowering thing I could have learned. How could I ever stop being grateful for that?

I don't ever intentionally write a story that emulates an author I admire. After the story is written, however, I often find that my subconscious has woven prose that my conscious self finds familiar. I'd like to think Ray would have enjoyed this story. In part because of the relationship between the boys that feels a lot like *Something Wicked This Way Comes.*

It also feels like an H.P. Lovecraft story but that's a whole different conversation.

Grandmother Who Breaks the Sky

Before the poetry of autumn had a chance to start its verse, death came for Danny.

It started innocently, while Danny and the Mason twins walked home after school. With sidewalks wide enough that they could walk together in a line, they trudged along, backpacks bouncing, whispering details about going to see the body of a girl.

"The museum kept her in storage for a hundred years. Mom showed us a picture. We didn't really want to go to the museum 'cuz it's just full of old junk, but my mom thought we'd wanna go see the dead girl, so we said yeah. She was the first person to drown in the lake, ever."

Aaron Mason was the older twin, by six minutes, and the most likely to make stuff up.

"When did she die?" Danny asked.

"Was like, a thousand years ago."

"No it wasn't."

Zebadiah Mason was the younger twin and made everyone call him "Zee" because he hated his given name.

"There wasn't anybody here then."

"No. They were Indians, Zee."

"Oh, yeah. She's an Indian. An Indian mummy."

"They said she was eaten by the monster in the lake."

"Now you're making stuff up," Danny said.

"Uh-uh. Am not."

"There's no monster in the lake. It's too salty. Except for brine shrimp. My sister did a science fair project."

"Yeah. Salty. That's why her body was preserved. She's like a big ole pickle."

Aaron spread his arms to show how big the girl was. Not very big for a girl. Big, though, for a pickle.

Danny squinted. "If she was eaten by a monster, how come there was a body?"

Zee knew the answer. His eyes grew big.

"The monster ate her *soul*."

Something traced a soft, cold finger up the back of Danny's neck like a piece of velvet that had been left in the freezer. He shrugged, adjusting his backpack to make the feeling go away.

"C'mon with us," Zee said.

Danny considered the prospect of seeing the pickle girl with his two best friends. Mr. and Mrs. Mason would probably make them look at tons of other stuff too, which would take forever. Grownups always did things like using a mummified girl as bait so they could get kids to look at *educational* stuff. But.

"Maybe," Danny said. "I can ask my mom."

"Tonight," Aaron said.

"'Kay. See ya."

Danny peeled off to walk up to the house of old lady Johanne. His mother had heard him say "old lady Johanne" once and had pointedly instructed him in old-fart etiquette. He only called her "Mrs." now. At least out loud.

"Hello, Mrs. Johanne."

"In here, Danny boy."

Danny caught the aroma of tea coming from the kitchen. He was surprised when he saw Mrs. Johanne had put on a sun dress and fixed her hair. Something was up for sure. She hardly ever changed out of her bathrobe and her hair was almost always under a net.

"Where's Thor?" Danny asked.

"In the back yard. Sit down, Danny. I was just having some tea."

Danny was afraid of what she might ask. Again.

"Don't give me that face, Danny. I'm not asking if you want some." She closed one eye halfway. "They'll let you look, won't they? Looking at tea isn't against your religion, is it?"

"No, ma'am."

Her half-shut eye popped open. "What if I told you my religion is older than yours?"

"Well," Danny paused to clear his throat. Old-fart etiquette reminded him to be respectful. "Our religion goes all the way back to Adam. So."

Mrs. Johanne nodded sagely. She crooked a crooked finger at Danny and waited for him to step closer.

"There's things older than Adam in this world Danny. Eons older."

That frigid velvet crawled up Danny's neck again. He tried not to shiver.

"If you say so, ma'am."

Mrs. Johanne sighed and leaned back in her chair.

"Take my cup. Tell me what you see."

Danny looked. He saw a conglomeration of black blobs in the bottom of the cup. He had no idea what he was supposed to see.

Put together, the blobs looked like a broken tree but he just shrugged.

Mrs. Johanne gave him a sour look like her tea had been all lemon juice. With a grunt, she got to her feet and reached for her cane, one of those industrial deals with four feet at the bottom for extra stability. She'd put bright yellow tennis balls on each foot so they wouldn't scratch her hardwood floors.

Thor waddled through the doggy-door from the backyard and panted in Danny's direction. Although named for the Norse God of Thunder, Thor was an aging pug whose nearest claim to thunder was a talent for flatulence. It was Danny's job to take him for a walk every day. Danny leaned over to scratch Thor on the head.

"Let's go," Mrs. Johanne said. "There isn't much time."

She moved quickly out of the house.

"Time for what?" Danny called.

He snagged Thor's leash on the way and clipped it to the dog's collar as they went down the front steps. The screen door banged shut behind them.

"Shall I lock it?" Danny asked.

Mrs. Johanne didn't hear. She was already crossing the street, her cane flashing in the late afternoon sun. Danny had never seen her move so fast.

Thor started wheezing before he made it to the curb. He hadn't moved so fast either. Not for a long time.

Mrs. Johanne lived across from Liberty Park, the oldest park in the city. It had an aviary and a lake with paddle-boats. Danny took Thor for walks there all the time, but they usually went alone.

Danny scooped up Thor, who groaned. Thor didn't really like to be carried. He was fat from Mrs. Johanne feeding him pancakes, and his belly was sensitive, but Danny didn't care. He dashed across the street, pug in arms, into the green shelter of the park.

He found Mrs. Johanne kneeling beside the ancient and towering oak that she jokingly called "Grandmother." In the middle of summer, before the sun went down, the shadow of the tree fell right over Mrs. Johanne's house. She always said, "Thank you for the shade, Grandmother." Now, the little old woman was almost lost between the roots of the tree, deep in shadow.

The sun shining through the gaps between the leaves overhead gave the trunk a mottled appearance. Her hands rested on the bark and her skin was so wrinkled it was hard to tell where she ended and the tree began. She chanted under her breath. Danny couldn't make out the words. He didn't want to interrupt her. Maybe she was praying. Old religions. He put Thor down on the grass to sniff around.

After a while, Mrs. Johanne stood and turned, a new light in her eyes.

"Come, Danny."

Danny went to her.

"Put your hand on her."

Mrs. Johanne took Danny's hand and gently, firmly, placed it on the rough trunk.

Danny heard music.

Automatic reflex pulled his hand away.

"You hear it!" Mrs. Johanne said. Delighted.

Danny let the tips of his fingers caress the bark. A soft tinkling sound teased his ears, a piano made of glass, the music of stars. Danny looked up, expecting to see someone in the branches with an instrument. He saw no one. He pressed his palms into the bark and the sound deepened, a concerto of music with voices from other worlds. He stretched out his arms, moving his whole body to embrace Grandmother. He felt the bass notes in his chest as an entire symphony erupted inside his mind. The voices multiplied. The words were not discernible, but the tone was urgent, in a minor key. Insistent. Warning.

"She needs our help, Danny."

He didn't move away from Grandmother, but he heard Mrs. Johanne's voice in his ear. He felt wonderful inside. Like his feet could reach down into the earth and touch the strength of bedrock beneath them. Like his hands could stretch upward to draw life from the clouds and sun.

"Something is out there. Something terrible. Something evil. Grandmother's been warning me for a while. She's been watching you too. She's chosen you to help."

"Me?" Danny asked. "What can I do?"

"Be a watchman," Mrs. Johanne replied. "Awaken yourself to danger and if you find it, come back here. Like my family has done for thousands of years."

Danny didn't want to withdraw from Grandmother, but Mrs. Johanne wasn't making any sense. He pulled away, regretting it at once.

"What are you talking about?"

Danny had never seen a smile as wistful as Mrs. Johanne's.

"The Mother Trees have chosen caretakers since before there was ancient. Caretakers like me, and now you, have always helped them guard the world against danger. It's time to do it again."

"What danger?"

"Grandmother cannot see its form. Only sense that it is near. Her leaves tremble when she feels it. Her branches reach up to break the sky and send us warnings on the winds of night."

Danny opened his mouth to protest but Mrs. Johanne stopped him.

"Don't question, Danny. Just keep your wits about you."

A leaf from the tree fell at Danny's feet. Mrs. Johanne picked it up.

"Here. Take this. It's part of Grandmother and it will help you."

Danny took the leaf. A sliver of song remained in it, a tiny piece of Grandmother's majesty. His mind felt dull now, as if the rest of the world had become less real without her touch. He nodded, wondering what all these new things might mean.

"You're a good boy, Danny. Go on home and remember what I said."

Danny walked home with the songs of trees.

* * *

"Son, quit whining. The museum's open for another hour."

Danny sat in the passenger seat of the van, fuming. He was late meeting Aaron and Zee. Mom had insisted on making dinner from scratch and having a conversation about Dad's day and Danny's day and her day, which was further complicated by the fact that Danny didn't know if he should talk about anything that had happened at the park. So he'd just said his day had been great while he pushed chicken parmigiana (delicious) and green peas (disgusting) around his plate for what seemed like hours. When he wasn't saying he wasn't hungry he was saying he wanted to go to the museum to meet his friends.

Finally, mercifully, mom had agreed to take him. He silently urged her to drive a little faster, even if it broke the speed limit, because he was afraid of missing out on seeing *her*. The big ole pickle. A thousand years old.

He paid the entry fee with money from his allowance and fumbled with his change. The twins had said she was on the top floor and he scrambled up the stairs, growing breathless. He turned in a circle at the top but didn't see anyone. He had to find his friends, not only to hang out, but also because he was supposed to get a ride home with them. They'd probably been dragged away somewhere else by their parents.

He'd take a quick peek at the dead girl first, then go find them. He had plenty of time.

Thinking about seeing a real corpse intrigued and repelled him. It was horrible to think that a person, who had once been

99

running and laughing and singing, was now a still, silent package of bone and sinew.

But he had to see.

The area around her display was dark, unlit. Reverent. A single light illuminated her body, like heaven shining through a break in night clouds. Danny approached on quiet feet. Alone. His heart shifted into high gear in his chest. She'd been wrapped in a blanket, cocooned. He wanted to look. Didn't want to look. He read the sign in front of the display case.

Wa'ipi Baa' - Woman of the Water.

Finally, he raised his eyes. She looked nothing like a pickle. She had dark skin, pulled tightly over her cheekbones. Rows of perfect little teeth shone between her age-thinned lips. Her eyes were sunken but her lashes were still long and dark. Even though she had passed away centuries ago, Danny could see she had been…beautiful.

At the edge of his attention, he saw motion. Heard sound. Some part of him not captivated by the drowned princess registered the fact that the door to the display case had swung open. By itself. Danny smelled the lake. A briny, salty song with undertones of decaying brine shrimp.

Eyes that were not her eyes opened over the sockets. A voice that was not her voice spoke. The words were unimportant. The tone was inviting. A coolness, a current of quiet bliss, like the bottom of the lake.

A shriek cut Danny between the eyes. The sound, sharp and shrill, overrode everything. Danny recoiled. Pulled back his hand. The hand that had almost touched her. The Woman of the Water. He covered his ears and backed away. Something inside him felt the presence of a leviathan passing between worlds. Something ancient and deep and hungry. It wanted to claim him. It wanted to come out of Wa'ipi Baa' and consume him.

The leaf, Grandmother's gift, called from his pocket. Making a sound his father had shown him once, down by the river when he'd trapped a blade of grass between his thumbs and pressed it to his lips and blown air through the narrow space. A whistle.

Danny, drenched in sudden sweat, jammed the leaf between his palms. Tried to make it quiet.

"Danny! There you are!"

He looked up.

Mom.

"You're shaking. What's gotten into you?"

She didn't hear the shrieking leaf.

"Nothing. Why're you here?"

Danny's mom put her arms around him and he didn't mind. He *had* been shaking.

"Mrs. Mason said they had to go home. Aaron got sick."

Danny swallowed. It felt like drinking glue.

"Did she say why?"

"Uh-uh. She just asked if I could come back and get you. Let's go home."

A voice came over the loudspeakers, asking everyone to make their way to the exit. The museum would close in five minutes.

Danny blinked. Shocked. Had he been standing there, in front of Wa'ipi Baa' for almost an hour? He let himself be led outside. Over his shoulder, he watched the door to the display case close. By itself.

* * *

Danny walked, sweating from nerves. It was after midnight and a mist had invaded the late summer air. He'd never snuck out of the house before. He'd sat on the floor with his ear to his own bedroom door, waiting for his parents to stop talking and go to their bedroom. He'd waited while his butt got numb sitting in one place on the floor. Being a child seemed to consist of long periods spent waiting for adults. Being an adult must be a luxury, never waiting for anyone else.

Finally, when the house had gone quiet, he'd crept down the hall and out the back door. He'd left the leaf. It had gone quiet, fading as they left the museum, and silent by the time they'd reached the van. At home it had gone brown and dry. Dead.

Mrs. Johanne sat on the front porch, Thor snoozing at her side. Her house huddled isolated in the fog, like a drifting ship at sea. At first, she seemed to be wearing a dark bathrobe. As Danny got closer, he saw she was wearing a cloak of some kind. Forest green, with leaves woven in a pattern around the edges.

"It's here."

She knew.

Danny told her about the Woman of the Water and the eyes that were not her eyes and the leaf and Aaron getting sick.

"She wanted me to touch her," Danny said.

He needed to say things out loud. To make the unreal things more real.

"Or the monster inside her did. And I think Aaron did touch her. I think he touched the girl who died in the lake. And the monster made him sick."

Mrs. Johanne closed her eyes.

"If that's true, Danny, your friend may not be your friend anymore. He may not even be human."

A cold chain slipped around Danny's heart. The links almost stopped it beating.

"We can fix him though. Right?"

When she opened her eyes, Danny saw the answer.

"Grandmother knows about the monster in the lake. It's one of the Old Ones. Like her. Very ancient. Very powerful. Grandmother has lived many lives in many places. She keeps an eye on the Old One in the lake. She watches and warns. She tells us the monster doesn't surrender what it eats. Ever."

Danny felt sick. If his mother hadn't shown up when she did, could he have resisted? Even with the leaf screaming its warning, he wasn't sure.

"The Masons are lake people, Danny." Mrs. Johanne looked solemn. "Always have been. It's not the first time the Old One has used their family. Their great-grandfather killed six people. Chopped them up and fed them to his hogs before Grandmother and I caught him. That was almost a hundred years ago."

Danny nodded. Wait. A hundred years?

A shuffling step made Danny turn. Aaron on the sidewalk. Mrs. Johanne inhaled with a sharp hiss. She saw him too.

Mrs. Johanne talked fast. Faster than she had walked.

"The Old One sent him to kill us. If we are eliminated, then Grandmother is vulnerable. The Old One could kill the tree. Send the Being that is Grandmother away. If that happens, there will be a lot more killing."

Danny had no reason to doubt her words.

Aaron wasn't Aaron anymore. His body shuddered, buried under a tangle of tentacles. He wore pajamas. His favorite superheroes. His gait was unsure, as if his legs were forgetting how to walk. Above the waist, Aaron's torso made a silhouette inside a mass of gelatinous scales and long, long teeth. And eyes. The same eyes that had opened over Wa'ipi Baa's empty sockets. Piercing eyes, deep blue, with the vastness of a universe hidden inside them.

Thor, who had once barked his head off at an empty french fry box, stayed silent. He was on his feet though. Watching.

Aaron made almost no sound. Other than the dry shuffle of bare feet on concrete, there was just a funny gurgle like the first 100-degree day when Danny had chugged half a pitcher of lemonade on an empty stomach and jiggled his belly. Only instead of laughter, Danny felt nausea creeping up the back of his throat.

"Go to Grandmother, Danny." Mrs. Johanne insisted. "The Old One is here for me. If I can't stop it, you need to be there for Grandmother."

Danny hesitated. What could he do for Grandmother? As if she'd read his mind, she said, "Grandmother picked you. You'll know what to do."

He didn't share her opinion. Mrs. Johanne had pasted a determined look on her face but he could see her heartbeat beneath the thin skin of her neck and it was racing.

"Go!"

Danny ran. He crossed the street and took another look behind him from the sidewalk. Through the mist, he saw Mrs. Johanne chanting and Thor run down the steps and launch his little fur-covered body at the nearest tentacle. He turned away to watch where he was going. He wouldn't be any use to anyone if he broke his leg tripping over a rock. He hoped Thor and Mrs. Johanne would be all right.

Someone waited between him and Grandmother. Someone also wearing superhero pajamas.

Danny slowed. "Zee?"

"Hey, Danny."

"Are you okay?"

Zee had puffy red eyes and a web of wet lines on his face that shimmered in the hazy light of the streetlamps. Danny could tell that Zee was doing his best not to cry. All Zee could do was shake his head.

Danny felt his own face getting hot in sympathy. Aaron had been his friend—but he'd been Zee's brother.

"Did you touch her too, Zee? The Indian girl?"

Zee shook his head again. Harder. He's wasn't the one who made stuff up.

"No."

"That's good. We're just going to wait here for a while, okay?"

"Okay."

Zee stood where he was, but he swayed a little and his hands twitched. He looked like he wanted to give Danny a hug but didn't know how to do it manfully. Danny stepped closer.

He smelled salt water.

The sick feeling in his stomach came back, more nauseating than ever.

"Zee? You didn't touch her did you?"

"I said I didn't." Zee stuck his arms out in front of him. Took a step toward Danny. "When Aaron touched her, he fell down. He screamed. I didn't want to touch her after that. So I didn't." Zee took another step toward Danny. Danny took a step back. "I'm scared, Danny."

"Me too, Zee."

"It hurts, Danny."

Danny moved backward faster. Zee's steps growing more erratic. Tears poured out of Zee's eyes. They didn't stop. The tears turned into a stream and then water bubbled out of Zee's face. His eyes, his nose, his mouth. Even his ears streamed a flood.

Zee screamed through the deluge, "It hurts!"

"You said you didn't touch her!"

"I didn't. But Aaron touched *me*!" Zee sobbed, staggering. Trying to put his hands on Danny. "It HURTS!"

Danny ran. He made a wide circle around Zee and headed for Grandmother. Zee wheeled through a turn like a boat on choppy water.

"'Member when you told my dad you broke that window so he wouldn't beat me? 'Member, Danny?"

Danny couldn't stop his own tears. He didn't even try.

"I remember Zee."

"Help me again, 'kay? If you let me touch you, the monster won't hurt me anymore. Please Danny. It HURTS SO BAD."

"I'm sorry, Zee," Danny whispered. "The monster doesn't surrender what it eats."

Danny made it to Grandmother. He pressed his back against her trunk. He found unexpected warmth there. He looked at Zee. Tentacles sprouted out of Zee's face now. If Zee still hurt, he could no longer voice it. Clear blue jelly oozed up and over Zee's head. Stars sparkled inside it. And planets. And multi-colored nebulae. Zee almost fell over. But didn't.

Danny had no clue what to do. He considered climbing Grandmother to safety. But her trunk was so big, he'd have to be a squirrel to get a grip. And what if Zee attacked her?

He listened for Grandmother's voice, hoping for aid, but she remained quiet. He felt her looking through his eyes.

I am her eyes.

He picked up a leaf from between her roots. The siren shriek was there, but muted. Grandmother knew what danger was there. She knew Danny knew.

Zee shuffled closer. Danny moved around Grandmother's trunk and Zee struggled to readjust his direction.

I can move in a circle. He can't go faster than me. We can play follow-the-leader all night around the tree and he'll never catch me. When the sun comes up, maybe he'll go away.

Another figure took shape in the mist. He recognized the cloak. Mrs. Johanne! She'd know what to do! The figure was just dark patches of fog at first. She drifted forward, like she was injured. The chains around Danny's heart grew heavier. Tentacles dangled from the sleeves of the cloak. The figure wore pajamas. Superhero pajamas. The thing wasn't Mrs. Johanne at all. It just wore her cloak

Danny ran around the back of the tree to keep away from Zee. He didn't have time to wonder what happened to Mrs. Johanne. Aaron sensed his motion. Shuffled to change direction.

I can't play follow-the-leader. They can go different directions. Catch me in the middle. I can't leave the tree. I can't play games.

I can't kill my friends.

A window opened up in Danny's mind. Grandmother's pictures. Like a slide show from the worst family vacation ever, he saw the park with Grandmother's tree at the center. She'd turned gray and lifeless. Around her lay desolation. A wasteland. Small figures being ridden by tentacled things wandered past, eyes dancing. Moving toward the lake, long miles away. No. Not toward the lake. Toward the Old One in the lake. It rose into the sky like a helium balloon. Its bulbous head, tens of thousands yards wide, quivered. It's hundreds of tentacles reached for thousands of yards too; the power and dominion of a thousand universes orbiting in its eyes.

Danny blinked. The vision had come and gone in the space of a single breath.

Inhale. Indecision. Exhale. Desperation.

I have to find a way.

He had no weapons. As little kids, they'd played with guns and swords. He didn't have any of those. Not even pretend ones. He had brains. And a leaf.

A leaf. Serrated. A piece of Grandmother.

Aaron kept coming. Danny saw Thor caught in its jelly. The little dog was dead. A fierce snarl frozen on its face. He had been brave. Danny had to be brave.

Zee shuffled closer. Danny ran at Zee. He held the leaf by the stem and slashed when Zee's tentacle swiped at him. Danny dodged. His best ninja move. He'd almost been touched. The leaf bit into the tentacle and stuck. Zee barely paused. Danny backed away.

The leaf changed color, turning red. The tentacle still moved.

Danny checked Aaron's position. He was getting closer.

Backing against Grandmother's warmth, he stared at Zee. He created images in his mind. Images of what he wanted. Images like the ones Grandmother had shown him.

Her branches moved, sending him leaves. Stirring the air.

Leaves swirled down, falling haphazardly, without purpose. Grandmother curled the air on itself. Made a whirlwind. The leaves spun.

Faster.

The wind accelerated, the leaves in a blur. Danny focused back on Zee. The whirlwind went where he looked.

The leaves whipped around Zee. Around the manifestation of the Old One that rode him. The edges of the leaves cut the jelly. So fast they didn't get stuck. The cuts tried to close. Tried to heal. Zee kept coming.

More leaves.

Another fall of green descended into the whirlwind.

Faster.

The leaves slashed, chewed. Turned crimson. Tentacles twitched, reaching out, almost close enough to touch.

More leaves.

More wind.

So many leaves now. He heard the gurgle still. Of the thing. Just under the sound of the whirlwind.

Zee stopped shuffling. Thousands of blades embraced him, all of them the color of blood. The leaves so wet now. Zee—what was left of him—toppled to the ground.

Danny sent more leaves. They sliced into meat. Cut into bone. Chewed until they were red and full. Bloated.

Trailing his hand around the trunk, keeping contact with the blessed Grandmother, Danny went around to find Aaron. And the Old One riding him.

Aaron was trying to leave. Awkwardly turning, trying to run away. His terrible shamble almost made Danny laugh.

He commanded the leaves to fall and the wind to blow. Grandmother listened. He sent the lethal whirlwind after Aaron. Caught him.

In her ancient wisdom, Grandmother wept.

Danny didn't need words to understand. This was not a victory.

The whirlwind swept through Aaron and the Old One. Edge after edge bit into the thing that possessed the boy. The boy with a boy's curiosity. Curious at the wrong time. In the wrong place.

When Aaron was buried under the leaves, Danny fell to the grass. Drained.

Sleep.

* * *

Someone called his name, but it was just a sound. Was he at the bottom of the lake after all? He felt buried by a flowing coolness. It wanted to keep him under. But he couldn't stay under. The voice called again. He was sure now. From heavy depths he moved upward.

"Danny?"

He opened his eyes.

"He's awake!"

"Mom?"

"Sweetie! Are you all right?"

Danny blinked. The sunlight cut across his vision. He couldn't look up. He focused on the ground instead. Looked for signs of pajamas with superheroes. Signs of...

The ground was covered in leaves. Just leaves. Fat, red leaves. Leaves that shifted. Maybe the leaves were being teased by the morning breeze. Maybe not.

Danny would never be able to look at red leaves in the same way again.

He felt Grandmother at his back. She had cooled. She'd slumber until spring and new life.

His mother's hands slipped around his shoulders, comforting him. Someone had found Mrs. Johann's cloak. Put it around him. It fit.

"Mom. Have you seen Mrs. Johanne?"

His mom hugged him.

"Did she get you out here?"

"Yeah."

It was a good truth.

"This will be a shock, Danny. She's passed away."

"How?"

"It doesn't matter now, you just—"

"I need to know."

She paused. For a moment.

"They found her in front of her house. But they're saying she drowned."

Danny nodded. "Oh."

"That's not all."

The cold piece of velvet put roots in the back of Danny's neck again.

"Mrs. Johanne left a note. Something about the Mason boys kidnapping her dog and running off. She said she went to our house and tapped on your window. Crazy old bat. You said they might have gone down to the pond and you'd help her look for her dog. In the middle of the night!"

"Yes," Danny said.

Mrs. Johanne had made up a story for him. Grownups were good at that. He just needed to play along.

"That's not even the kookiest part." Mom was on a roll now. "She wrote that if anything should happen to her, she had you in her will. She's giving you her *house*! She said you loved the view of the park and—what was it?—Grandmother's shade? Isn't that the craziest thing?"

The Hollow

The One Edgar Allan Poe Might Like

Vincent Price made a lot of fun movies. One of these, *The House on Haunted Hill* from 1959, was memorable for being campy and creepy and—in the end—completely rational. There were plenty of ghosts and walking skeletons and haunted house trappings, but in the dénouement, everything is explained and there was nothing supernatural happening at all. I thought it was a great idea and I've kept a short list of other movies and stories that are similar over the years. Later, while I was making a living as a stage magician, where deception was my job, I started trying to think of ways to expand that idea. At what point would a situation become so unexplainable that a person would conclude there isn't a rational explanation?

The solution came down to scaling up. I envisioned a house that would take victims in but prevent them from leaving once they arrived. Such a situation would be frightening. Even if characters make it out the door and up the road, they always end up back at the house. For the premise to work, the characters would have to be allowed to leave and attempt an escape and end up back at the house despite their best efforts.

I came up with a method. What I needed was a story.

Edgar Allan Poe often wrote about psychologically damaged people, torture, and revenge. He would also use scientific principles in his stories from time to time and invented the modern detective story. His character C. Auguste Dupin used psychology and reasoning to solve mysteries, and he did so almost 50 years before Sherlock Holmes.

These elements felt like a combination I could conjure with. So. Take an experiment in fear, combine it with a house no one can leave, and the result is "The Hollow."

The Hollow

"I am eager to see how you accomplished such an intricate deception, Doctor. It must have been quite convincing to have frightened your wife to death."

Otto Van Feldt hoped for a reply but didn't get one. Dr. Harward sat primly in the seat of the open coach, his hat squarely on his head, and adjusted the line of his pants to center the creases. The doctor's eyes returned to the road ahead and he seemed content to listen to the rhythm of the horses' hooves and the creaking of the coach's wheels.

Van Feldt continued probing, taking a chance on a more provocative line. "If you'll forgive me, Doctor, you don't strike me as a man who would be a world-renown phobologist. You are short of stature and narrow in the shoulder and the gentle lines of your face remind one of a favorite uncle who dispenses candies from his pocket."

Although the phony-looking mop of hair beneath the hat was a fright indeed.

The doctor, at last, spoke.

"As you will see, it's all in the science and psychology, good sir," he said. "People have quite a few universal fears. I play upon those. I also analyze individual responses and craft specific stimuli to achieve the effect I desire from the participants."

"Participants?" Van Feldt said. "Don't you mean patients?"

"I am not a medical doctor, so no. However, I have applied my science to a variety of purposes. Not all of them academic."

Harward's tone was that of a lecturing professor, which ravaged Van Feldt's nerves. He had been willing to ingratiate himself with the good doctor for the past forty-five miles, but he found himself chewing on the raw end of his patience now.

Harward pulled a bottle from the pocket of his coat and drank, swallowing thickly.

"Is that medicine?" Van Feldt asked.

Harward nodded. "Nasty stuff really."

Van Feldt produced a silver flask. "This is good Kentucky bourbon," Van Feldt said, handing it to the doctor. "You're welcome to it. I guarantee it will do more to improve your constitution than whatever rot you have in that bottle!"

Harward took the flask, examining the finely engraved scene of little devils that had been inscribed on its surface. "Thank you, good fellow. I shall return it when emptied."

Van Feldt waved his hand as if the flask were not important. "How did you happen to decide on your wife as a subject for your experiments?"

Harward was still looking quite green but replied. "Actually, she was a subject first, wife second."

"Really?" Van Feldt jumped on the opportunity to pursue his line of questioning now that Harward seemed inclined to respond. "I've heard stories, you know, that she was a convicted murderer.

116

That she had killed her own child and her sanity had been brought into question."

Harward nodded. "That is true. It was in the newspapers that I found her, I suppose. The state will not allow us to use just anyone for experimentation, you understand. Convicted felons, on the other hand, have no rights and we often find ourselves working with the prisons to find suitable subjects. Subjects like Celia."

The doctor suddenly paused, his lips clamped together.

"Are you getting maudlin on me, doctor?" Van Feldt asked. "Maybe you shouldn't start on that bourbon just yet. Or maybe you should drink it all. I can't decide." Van Feldt smiled inwardly, happy in the thought that Harward had no idea how well he knew Celia. He continued his ruse. With mock innocence he asked, "Was she attractive?"

"What? Oh, I suppose she was. Yes, in fact. She was . . . overly thin . . . and therefore had the appearance of being undernourished. But otherwise attractive. Long, dark hair and large brown eyes. Attractive, though I was old enough to be her father. Grandfather even."

"So you *did* want her for something more than her suitability as a test subject?" Van Feldt asked.

Harward laughed at that. "My days pursuing sex are behind me, I fear. The only means I had to get her out of the asylum was to marry her. As her husband, I could remove her from that situation," he said. "Sadly, I was not taking her to a better place." He took a moment to collect himself, then said, "Science and sentiment do not mix well."

That gave Van Feldt something to chew on for a while. Although, despite his protests of being too aged, the doctor was a man like any other and Celia had been a great beauty, he knew very well.

The doctor pointed wordlessly to the west. The sun was just vanishing over the horizon. There was an unnatural quiet and Van

117

Feldt realized there were no animals about. No sheep or cows in the fields. No birds in the trees. Soon, the best light would come from the moon, which was already gravid and chilly.

Van Feldt turned to find Harward's gaze upon him and shivered. The doctor's eyes were heavily-lidded and in the evening light his face seemed to be made of stone.

The doctor spoke. "From this point, dear fellow, it will be important to try and see everything from Celia's point of view. Imagine yourself as a fresh bride going to your new home. Then, as the horrors begin to mount, you must feel how your state of mind begins to fall apart as everything you thought you knew about the world is stripped away and replaced with terrible certainties that you never imagined could be real."

Van Feldt lost his tongue for a moment. He couldn't tear his eyes away from the doctor's face.

"Swear it," Harward insisted without blinking. "Swear it or we turn around and go back."

"As you wish," Van Feldt laughed. Weakly. "I swear it."

Harward turned to face forward again. "Proceed."

Van Feldt urged the horses on. Their ears flicked nervously and both whickered in protest. After a hundred yards or so, the road came to a "T." The coach turned at the intersection and after a minute Harward put a hand on Van Feldt's arm. The doctor's touch made Van Feldt cringe, as if something dead had caressed him.

"This is the spot where the deceptions actually began," Harward said. "Here is the place where our carriage stopped and forced us out. It was important that Celia see the house in the distance and the straight road and also to witness the carriage moving away, departing, never to be seen again."

"Why is that?" Van Feldt asked.

"You shall see, I promise you. The actor we had hired to drive us was instructed to stop here. He played the part of a frightened local who had heard tales of the house and the terrors within and refused to take us any closer. I, of course, played the part of the dutiful husband, outraged at the inconvenience of it all and the distress being laid upon my sweet, frail new wife. The actor refused to be swayed—as directed in the script—and threw our belongings on the grass, just there." Harward pointed at the ground and raised his hand to follow the road leading away. "And below is The Hollow."

The house was visible in the distance but dimly. From this vantage point, the road fell away and the house waited in a sheltered depression surrounded by trees. It sat like a beaten dog, hunched and whimpering, waiting for the next blow. Despite being two stories tall, plus an attic, it was smaller than Van Feldt had expected. The windows were narrow and mean looking, unlit. Its roof was gray under the moonlight and splotchy, as if its scalp were infected with disease.

The road leading up to the house was lined with twelve-foot high stone walls covered with brambles, their black, thick thorns appearing to be made of iron. Overhead, the clouds were gathering in a thick line as if the heavens were making a wool blanket to throw over them. To smother them.

Harward spoke softly but Van Feldt had no trouble hearing him. "When we first arrived, there was a light in the window. A pathetic effort to make the abode more cheerful." Then he looked up as if addressing the darkening sky. "You can feel it, can't you? An oppressive atmosphere? A spiritual heaviness? When we started we were trying to do good. We were trying to gain knowledge that would help mankind. We knew we were dealing in controversial methods. We had no idea we were creating evil. I feel it every time I come here. "

Van Feldt scoffed. "Please, doctor. You aren't experimenting anymore. Are you doing thus out of habit? I am not one of your subjects. Any attempts to scare me are pointless."

The coach rolled down the hill, seemingly pushing the horses forward against their resistance. Harward continued to look at the sky for a moment. Then he lowered his gaze and captured Van Feldt with his half-closed eyes again. Van Feldt squirmed.

"Do you have faith in anything?" Harward asked. "Belief in anything?"

"Ha! Hard work and the almighty dollar. That's what gets me through a day."

"The words of a businessman. How many ranches do you own? How many frontier saloons? Do you believe in anything at all that you can't touch? Can't see? Can't spend?"

Van Feldt didn't reply. Harward went on. "What would you give to have your faith turned into knowledge? To have all doubts erased? Would it be worth your soul?"

Van Feldt couldn't choose between anger and sarcasm so his tone was a mix of both. "Why do you ask, Doctor? Are you making an offer to purchase my immortal from me? Ha, ha! Even if I were to offer it, I'm certain you would have a difficult time collecting."

"There is more than one way a soul can be owned," Harward replied.

"Enough of this, doctor. No more talk of insubstantial things. You promised to *show* me what I have asked for. To wit: proof that you can scare someone to death. You are using your philosophies in an attempt to dissuade me from my purpose, sir, and I will have no more of it. Please believe me when I say I am fully committed to seeing things for myself. As a man of science, I'm sure you are of the same mind."

Harward seemed to shrink against the larger man's words. "Man of science? I always was," he replied. "And I know well that such a firmly-grounded pillar is a difficult one to topple."

As they approached the house, it seemed to increase in size unnaturally until it was looming over them. Details of the structure's décor, such as the trim along the eaves and around the porch, first appeared to be charmingly Victorian in style with graceful points and curves. As they got closer, however, the details became more gruesomely apparent. The décor was comprised of severed hands and serpents and demonic faces with tongues thrust between their fangs. Van Feldt gawked openly. The horses, unguided, stopped of their own accord in front of the steps leading to the door.

They disembarked. Van Feldt couldn't help but stare at the house. At the edge of his vision Harward cracked open his small traveling case, keeping the mouth almost closed as he felt around for another bottle of medicine. He drank and put the stopper back in before tucking it into his coat pocket. Van Feldt observed no windows at ground level. They were all on the second floor and narrow, perhaps six-inches wide, reinforced with iron. It occurred to Van Feldt that it would be impossible to get out of the house through the windows in case of a fire.

Ascending the creaky steps, Van Feldt sensed a charge of some sort in the air, as if electricity were crawling over the skin of the structure. On the front door were words, written by hand in a rust-red hue: "There Is No Way Out." Van Feldt pointed at the words with a thick thumb, mocking. "Your handiwork, doctor?" Harward said nothing but stepped to the threshold and opened the door, which was not locked. They entered, Van Feldt's boots echoing sharply on the floor. Moonlight streamed in behind them, throwing a long rectangle of brightness into the house. The furnishings nearby were surprisingly free of dust and the house didn't smell musty or stale. However, the lack of windows made the house especially dark beyond the reach of the moonlight and Van Feldt was grateful a moment later, squinting against the brightness of the gaslights Harward lit.

The doctor asked, "Have you heard of the Ironwood brothers, Mr. Van Feldt?"

"I think so. Spiritualists, as I recall."

Harward nodded. "My elder brothers. Twins. Their specialty was separating the rich from their money. I was always ashamed to be related to them."

"They conducted séances, didn't they?"

"Yes, along with other forms of supernatural manifestations."

"They convinced a great many people that they could commune with the dead."

"Indeed. And they charged the wealthy and gullible great sums of money to supposedly speak with their deceased loved ones. When my brother Erastus had made his fortune, which was considerable, he moved west and built this house. It is designed specifically so ghosts and demons and other forms of nonsense can apparently show themselves. All done with the finest technologies and sciences of our age. There are secrets in the walls, the floors, the ceilings. Even the furniture and the mirrors. Their abuse of the desperate and uneducated was abhorrent to me. But I found their methods useful and tried to put them to a more beneficial purpose. Of course, Celia knew nothing of these things, which was necessary as I began my experiments in fear upon her."

"Now things are making more sense to me. Are you all right, doctor?"

Harward had doubled over. He was groaning and leaning on a table which was decorated with a statue of a cherub and an enormous bouquet of dried flowers. Van Feldt moved to assist him but the doctor rebuffed him with a raised hand.

"It's really . . ." the doctor coughed and managed nothing more. The fit lasted only a moment or two but the doctor's skin was suddenly clammy and his face glistened with sweat. The doctor gritted his teeth, found his bottle in his coat pocket and drank from it trembling. He pressed his hand against his chest. "Forgive me," he said. "A little water, I think. I shall return in a moment."

"Of course," Van Feldt replied. Harward nodded in gratitude and shuffled out of the room, still coughing and tapping his chest.

Van Feldt saw the doctor's bottle on the table. Fearing he might need it, Van Feldt picked it up and followed. He turned the corner, saying, "You forgot your medicine!"

The doctor wasn't there. To his immediate right, Van Feldt saw an elegant stairway that curved up to the second floor. Van Feldt expected to see the doctor there as that was the direction he had turned when he had left the entryway. Van Feldt scanned the room, which was more like a very wide hallway. There were couches and a clock and paintings and statues and all manner of bric-a-brac but nothing living.

"Doctor?" Van Feldt called. The house was silent as if holding its breath.

The bottle sat heavy in Van Feldt's hand and he grew curious about it. He pulled the stopper and looked inside but couldn't see what it contained. He smelled at the mouth and caught a rank coppery odor that he instinctively identified. He drew back violently, the bottle slipping to the floor where it crashed in pieces, throwing the blood inside across the tiles at his feet in a terrible spray. Van Feldt stepped back but his shoes and the legs of his trousers were already decorated and befouled.

Van Feldt caught up the handkerchief from his breast pocket and tried wiping the blood away but did more to spread it than remove it. Under his breath, he cursed and then thought it through. Surely, the doctor wasn't drinking blood. It was one of his tricks.

"I don't know how you switched it, doctor," he said loudly. "But that was a clever ploy." Van Feldt balled his hands into fists. He moved up the stairs resolutely. His tread was quieted by the carpet on the stairs and at the top he heard the sound of running water. The bathroom door stood open and Van Feldt stepped through with no hesitation. There were the usual appointments: bathtub, toilet, sink. The water coming out of the tap was hot and steam rose thickly from the basin. Above the sink, Van Feldt saw his blurred reflection in the mirror. He reached out to clear the steam and flinched when his hand made contact. The surface of the mirror was covered in a layer of ice. Van Feldt shut off the water. Tentatively, he traced a line around the edge of the mirror and realized the ice was as thick as his finger. As he watched, words appeared in a scrawl behind the ice as if being written by an invisible hand.

Another trick.

Van Feldt struggled to make out the words behind the ice. He read aloud, "I am . . . so . . . empty." The words had no meaning for him. He gave in to the temptation to look behind the mirror. The mirror was hung from the wall with ordinary wire and behind it, nothing. "Nonsense," Van Feldt said to himself.

A crash downstairs shattered the quiet. Van Feldt resisted the urge to run and look. He was angry at being duped and refused to be manipulated into a hasty reaction. He looked around the bathroom for any signs of anything else out of the ordinary. When he was satisfied, he went back out to the hall. A quick check of the rooms nearby told Van Feldt that there were two bedrooms in this part of the house and nothing more.

Van Feldt strode back to the stairs. He had no idea how the doctor had managed to get around him and back downstairs but it hardly mattered. The doctor had told him the house was built with secrets everywhere. He must have used a hidden passage or some such. Yes, he had asked for a demonstration of the doctor's methods but he certainly hadn't given the doctor permission to demonstrate upon him. Make him a *subject*! This foolishness would end and quickly.

Van Feldt stormed down the stairs. He had half a mind to get his hands around Harward's neck and wring it dry. Nobody would make a fool of him! He stopped short. The pool of blood on the floor was gone. The broken bits of bottle, vanished. Impossible! He dismissed the thought as quickly as it came. In this house of insulting secrets, nothing was impossible. He would not allow himself to forget that.

The statue of the cherub was lying on its side. It had been knocked over by a thick newspaper, rolled up and tied with twine. Van Feldt would have ignored it but the headline caught his eye. The paper was about three weeks old and Van Feldt had already seen it. Van Feldt untied the twine and opened the paper. The subject of the story was Dr. Harward, Ph.D. who studied the psychology of fear and had frightened his wife to death while conducting experiments testing the limitations of the human psyche. Van Feldt scanned through the story until he found the words that had galled him most.

Van Feldt read aloud "In his defense, Dr. Harward stated that while fear is a powerful emotion and a strong motivator, it is merely an abstract concept, far removed from anything that might be considered a murder weapon."

The judge had agreed and chided, at least, the morality of the doctor's actions, but had dismissed the case.

There were more newspapers in the stack. Van Feldt shuffled through them. The next one included more information about Harward's work in phobology and how the military might use the study to create braver soldiers—or less-effective enemies. Van Feldt had read that one too. Behind that, a newspaper featured a public notice of a lecture on the "Practical Applications of Fear-Inducing Stimuli."

Odd how all these papers were the same ones he'd read in the past.

Then a new set of papers made his blood run cold. Van Feldt scanned the headlines.

"Sudden Engagement Amid Pregnancy Scandal."

"Family Concerned for Daughter's Missing Fiancé."

"Distraught Socialite Considers Abortion."

"Tycoon's Grandchild Found Dead."

"Woman Charged with Murder."

"Suspected Killer Committed to Sanitarium."

So, the good doctor knew his secret after all, it seemed.

Yet, these papers were clearly fabrications. Not even the most scurrilous rag would put words like "pregnancy" or "abortion" in their headlines. The public outcry would shut them down within the hour. Harward must have access to a printing press. In that moment, it occurred to Van Feldt that all of these newspapers could have been manufactured. And what would be the purpose?

To lure him here.

Heat was rising now in Van Feldt's face. It was time for this charade to be ended. He would not allow this academic fraudster and his tricks to take advantage of him under any circumstances. It was beneath him.

The voice was so quiet, Van Feldt didn't quite hear it the first time. There was something familiar in that momentary whisper but there were no discernible words. Van Feldt held his breath and stood perfectly still so that even his clothing would not make a sound.

"I am so empty."

Van Feldt remained still. That voice…it sounded like…no…it could not be. He shook his head. It was truly impossible. She was dead. Harward had killed her. Harward's tricks were getting more effective, Van Feldt would give him credit for that—but they were still just tricks.

"I am so empty."

The voice was distinct this time. And then another sound. Horses giving voice.

Van Feldt uttered a curse. He ran to the front door and threw it open. He heard the sound of *his* coach and livestock. It was dark outside now and the moon had been swallowed up by a fog that diffused the light into a cold gray wall. He thought, "That bastard Harward even controls the weather." The hoof beats faded away.

Fuming, Van Feldt reached into his coat to make sure the revolver he kept there was waiting. Reassured, Van Feldt stormed off down the road.

Setting a brisk pace, Van Feldt listened as he strode up the hill in the mist. Within minutes, he reached the crest where the road leveled out. He was breathing heavily but he wasn't tired. He was accustomed to long days working his ranches. The mist was clearer here at the higher elevation and he should see the road where they had come in presently. He continued without slowing, looking for the break in the wall. The wall sat like a thorny, imperious enemy, uncaring, unyielding. He was so furious at the moment, he would follow Harward on foot all the way back to the city if necessary.

In a few minutes, the road began to descend again. Van Feldt paused. He didn't remember there being any variations like this— but he had been distracted by Harward on their approach to the house.

The house seemed to drift in from the fog like a ghost. It began at first in an outline, as if the fog were solidifying into a darker gray. Then, what was first a hint of a structure grew more real. Finally, there were no lingering doubts. He was back at The Hollow.

Van Feldt stood in front of the steps, puffing. How had he gotten so turned around? It was Harward's fault, of course. All his tricks and his stealing the coach had frustrated Van Feldt so deeply he was unable to focus. He looked up at the door with the lettering in red.

There Is No Way Out.

A chill came over him in that moment.

He cursed. A string of foul language crossed his lips in gouts. Overhead, the fog was pierced by warm orange light. There was a lantern in the attic window.

Van Feldt growled as he looked up. It was time to take care of business.

"There is no way out," Van Feldt said as he walked through the door. "No way out for Dr. Harward, Ph.D."

Inside, the cherub statue was upright again and the newspapers were gone. There was no stain on the floor and no broken glass. Then the gaslights all went out. The sudden darkness was palpable and Van Feldt flinched.

"I am so empty," whispered the voice that was supposed to be Celia but couldn't be.

"I will fill you," Van Feldt snarled, using anger to override the niggling doubts in his mind. He removed his gun from his coat and held it out in front of him like a promise. He moved carefully in the dark, feeling his way to the stairway opposite the one he had explored before and followed the hallway around to the back of the house. He smiled with murder in his eyes as he found the stairs to the attic.

The smell of decay and rot was here. His feet crunched on something as he took the first step and then the second. The moon, filtered by the fog, bled weakly through the window. At first, the stairway appeared to be covered with walnuts or pecans that had been cracked open and eaten. But there were other bits attached. He picked one up and examined it. It had legs and antennae and Van Feldt realized it was a beetle with all its insides scooped out. Van Feldt dropped it, disgusted. There were other creatures on the stairs as well. Birds. A dog. Several rats, liberated of their guts and brains and looking like nothing so much as empty gravy boats with fur.

Van Feldt swallowed thickly as he climbed the stairs. His hands were trembling as he reached for the doorknob.

"I am so empty."

Clenching his teeth, Van Feldt opened the door.

The lantern was on the far side of the room, hanging in the window at the front of the house. A shadowy figure, a man, knelt in the middle of the floor.

128

Van Feldt raised his hand to shade his eyes against the sudden change of light. "Dr. Harward."

"Van Feldt," the doctor replied in graveled voice. His words were slurred and slow. There was a glint of metal on the floor and Van Feldt recognized the flask of bourbon he had given to him. Obviously, the good doctor felt that now was the appropriate time to get drunk.

"The liquor will make you numb doctor, which will serve you well. It's cold outside and we have a long drive back to the city. Come along. We'll be going now."

The doctor didn't reply right away. He pressed his hand against his chest and shuddered, his dyspepsia apparently flaring up yet again. Finally, he spoke and his voice was thready and low. "There is no way out," he said.

"No more nonsense doctor. No more tricks." Van Feldt heard the quavering in his own voice and the sound of it, the lack of certainty, made him angrier. He pointed the revolver at Harward. He repeated himself, forcing confidence into his words. "You know the way."

The doctor laughed. More accurately, he giggled. "Nobody ever figures it out," he said. "Nobody."

"You're drunk," Van Feldt said. "And a fool."

"Of all the terrible things I've invented to frighten people, that's the most devastating. And the easiest really. No matter how hard they try to get away, they always find themselves back at the house. They convince *themselves* that there is no way out. Once they believe they can never escape, their minds belong to me. They are my toys to play with," he giggled some more.

Van Feldt cocked the gun and the sound was brutal and cold. "Tell me," he demanded. The doctor wobbled where he knelt. Van Feldt was afraid he was going to pass out. "My mind does not belong to you! Tell me!"

The doctor stared at Van Feldt as if teetering on a point of decision. He held up two fingers and tittered. "Twin brothers. Twin houses. Each at opposite ends of a non-descript road. And a stone wall that can be closed."

Understanding washed over Van Feldt like a bucket of cold water but his anger only grew more heated. There was a twisted genius at work to be sure but the doctor should not have used him—*abused him!*—so callously. "I'm man enough to admit it, doctor. Your deception is elegant in its simplicity. I'm almost disappointed to know how it was done. You're still little more than a common charlatan."

The doctor put his hand on the floor to steady himself. "Do you know what's worse than frightening someone, good fellow? Or ruining their lives? Do you know what is more evil?"

Van Feldt had no time to formulate a retort.

"I am so empty!" The whisper was loud this time, right behind Van Feldt's ear. He spun around and fired. The sound of the shot made him jump despite himself. There was nobody there.

"You can put the revolver away," Harward said. "It will do you no good here."

"I'll be the judge of that," Van Feldt said, turning back to face the doctor. He cocked the gun again and watched the man struggle to his feet, using a wooden pillar to keep himself upright. The doctor lit a second lantern. Then he shuffled toward him, wobbling.

"Stay where you are," Van Feldt said. "I'll shoot you."

Harward laughed again and his voice was filled with bitterness. "I have already tried that, sir," he said. He reached up and pulled his hair off his head. The toupee fell to the floor and lay there like one of the rats on the stairs. Slowly, trying to maintain his tenuous balance, the doctor pivoted around. With no hair to hide it, Van Feldt could see that the back of the doctor's head was missing. Bits of brain and shards of bone surrounded a ragged hole in the middle of his cranium.

"I tried to kill myself," the doctor said, as if he were explaining nothing more concerning than why the sky was blue. "I put the barrel of a revolver, much like yours, into my mouth. And pulled the trigger. I awoke not long after. She won't let me die. Not yet. Not until I have finished my penance."

Van Feldt heard a rattling sound and realized it was the gun in his trembling hand. "Wh . . . who won't . . . let you die?" He asked the question even though he knew the answer.

Harward sighed as he lowered himself to the floor again. He dropped the last foot or so and grunted as he hit. He giggled some more and Van Feldt found the sound terrifying.

"I nearly forgot," the doctor said. "There are introductions to be made." He pointed toward the side of the room. That part of the attic had been in shadow before but now it was lit by Harward's second lantern. The blood drained from Van Feldt's face when he looked. Part of his brain refused to acknowledge what he was seeing, another part instantly understood the tableau on display.

A line of chairs, ten or twelve, had been placed against the wall. Four bodies sat together, sitting upright. Their hands had been positioned on their knees like an audience waiting for a play. That's where the resemblance to anything normal ended.

Each one of the bodies was empty. Their clothing missing their front parts. The forward halves of their heads and torsos had been removed and all their organs taken away. Van Feldt could see the interiors of their skulls and their spines and the anterior ribs at the back of the cavities. The edges of the openings were scalloped, as if they had been chewed upon by monstrous insects. Van Feldt suddenly became aware of his bladder and the liquefaction in his bowels which extended somehow to his knees threatening to give way beneath him.

"To our left, I'm sure you recognize Celia's parents," Harward said. "You and I are the only beings alive who know they are here. Presumably, they are visiting the continent and have no plans to return."

Van Feldt had met the woman once and recognized the hat and he had no cause to doubt that the man next to her was her husband. His hat teetered at an odd angle on top of his empty head, looking ridiculous.

"Next, Judge Oliver, who—I'm sure you know—sentenced Celia to reside in a sanitarium for the remainder of her natural life. He has apparently run off with a mistress, leaving his wife and children behind. But we know differently."

Pointing at the fourth corpse, Harward said, "And this poor chap was the driver of the carriage who brought us here. Acting is a more dangerous profession than he realized. When we're done with you, good fellow, there's a particular nurse who likes to slap her patients. And worse. She'll be next, I think."

Van Feldt struggled to find his voice. "I was going to come back," he managed. "I had business dealings. I didn't mean to leave Celia alone to give birth. And then, when the infant was found dead, I couldn't . . . how could I go to her defense? How could I do anything but distance myself until my business was settled? How could I jeopardize my . . . *our* future?"

Harward was nodding. "We always find ways to justify ourselves, do we not? We always have the best of intentions. But we're all empty if we only knew it."

"You did kill her. Didn't you?" Van Feldt prayed for a good answer but he didn't know what it could possibly be.

Harward said, "She was resilient and I admired her for that. I faked my own death so she would be alone in the house. Even when she was afraid and crying I never stopped admiring her."

Van Feldt, "When I heard you were not to be held accountable, I vowed to bring you to some kind of justice. I could at least do that for her."

Harward, "In the end, she was frightened and sleepless and when she became convinced that there was truly no way out, she vanished. For a while I couldn't find her. When I did, she was here, in the attic. She had found some shears and cut herself open. She lived long enough to remove all her intestines and organs and lay them on the floor. Her heart was still in her hand, cold. Then she spoke to me. She said, 'There must be something broken inside me but I cannot find it. And now I am so empty.'"

Van Feldt was backing away, more unsteady than Harward now. "I need to be leaving. I can't be here any longer."

"All the evil I had created had returned in a new form," Harward said. "There was no more science."

Van Feldt's eyes were wild, jumping back and forth from Harward's face to the small, hollow audience seated on the side of the room.

Harward went on, "As it happens, I'm a terrible sadist and you are ruled by your ambition and it was Celia who paid the price for us both."

Van Feldt did not—or could not—speak.

"I asked you a question a while ago," Harward said. "I asked you what was worse than frightening someone. What was worse than ruining a life as you and I have done. Do you have an answer, dear fellow? It is clear to me that all the things human beings do to each other, the lying, the cheating, the abuse, the murder; the most evil thing we can do is to take away Hope."

"I AM SO EMPTY!"

Then Celia was there, standing in front of Van Feldt. Her face was much as he remembered, all soft and winsome with large, dark eyes, now purest black. Her hair fell to her shoulders in a satin cascade and it seemed to move as if she were standing in a gentle breeze. She was wearing a white see-through shroud and beneath it she was naked. An angry red scar ran from between her legs all the way up to her neck. The scar was shiny and suppurating. Van Feldt screamed as the scar split apart and he saw rows of jagged teeth inside her gaping wound. He staggered backwards, firing the gun into her until it was empty and there was only the *click, click, click* of the hammer and then he was overwhelmed. Mercifully, his heart gave out as he entered her embrace. Then only the echoes of the gunshots accompanied the wet, snapping sounds.

Meredith in St. Louis

The One Stephen King Might Like

Stephen King once said, "I recognize terror as the finest emotion and so I will try to terrorize the reader. But if I find that I cannot terrify, I will try to horrify, and if I find that I cannot horrify, I'll go for the gross-out. I'm not proud."

Yep. Me too neither.

Meredith in St. Louis

This was the day. The day Meredith would force herself to do the thing she was afraid to do. She wanted to do it, but she hated herself for penciling the scary thing in her calendar. Once it was penciled in the calendar, there was no turning back.

Meredith sat in the back of the shuttle bus that would take her to the train station. She unfolded the article she'd brought from work: "Revised Transmission Success Factors in Recombinant Process Phases Affecting Binary Material Reconstruction." The title alone was enough to put people to sleep and Meredith had written it. *Writing it* had put her to sleep. If she was lucky, it would help her calm down.

The young man—her Vision Boy—always came out of nowhere. At least, Meredith never saw him get on the train. He just appeared, like a vision, and only on Fridays. Like he waited all week to ride the train downtown, showing up to start his own personal party at the beginning of the weekend. And it wasn't even every Friday. His pattern was erratic, which aggravated Meredith's preference for predictability and planning. However, for the past three months, when he did show up, he always found a woman to talk to and she always had a dreamy look on her face and then got off the train with him. What happened after that were blanks filled in by Meredith's imagination, but her imagination wanted concrete answers. Right now.

The girls Vision Boy picked were always pretty. She'd seen them riding the train lots of times. There had been the girl with the loopy blond hair and the criminally-untweezed eyebrows and the other girl with the olive-shaded skin and the aggressive overbite. They'd both succumbed to Vision Boy's charms.

But only once.

After their weekend, which Meredith's imagination absolutely insisted had to be filled with events completely unforgettable—the girls forgot. When they saw Vision Boy again they smiled politely and chatted with him in a manner that was merely friendly. Nothing more. The initial fire that had made them lean into him and breathe heavy and close their eyes halfway when he approached never happened again. Having tasted the forbidden fruit once, they never needed another bite.

Like they were immune.

Meredith would take that deal. She hadn't had a boyfriend since grad school and working at the NSA Data Center wasn't doing anything for her social life. But, if Vision Boy showed up today, and if she forced herself to do the scary thing, as dictated by her own note in her own calendar, the girl he picked might be her. It *had* to be her. She'd make him like her. She'd make herself irresistible.

"Binary virus? What's that?"

Meredith jumped at the voice.

"I didn't mean to startle you," A girl with big rose-colored glasses perched on the end of her nose smiled at Meredith. One of the data drones from the server farm upstairs in the NSA Data Center. "I know. I shouldn't be reading over your shoulder. I just think everything's so interesting."

"Okay." Meredith turned the article over to keep the girl's eyes off it.

"So what is it?"

"Huh?"

"A binary virus. What is it?"

"Oh. Sorry. I have a lot on my mind." Meredith laughed by way of apology and it almost sounded authentic.

The girl smiled and shrugged and waited.

Meredith cleared her throat. Twice. "So. A binary virus is a virus. Obviously. But it's split into two or more parts."

"Huh. Why would somebody do that?" The girl blinked behind the rose-colored glasses.

"So the virus can remain dormant and harder to detect. A hacker, for example, distributes the first pieces of the virus to as many computers as possible. Later, he distributes the rest of the pieces which search out the first set. Then the pieces assemble themselves into a whole and the virus activates."

The girl nodded. "So separately, the pieces of the virus go undetected. Then when they're already inside the host, they combine and infect the computer?"

"You got it."

"Wow. Good thing that doesn't work with biological viruses, right?" She laughed.

Meredith laughed too. Harder than she intended. "Right. That wouldn't work. I mean not at all."

Unless nano-robotics were involved. But the NSA wouldn't have anything to do with those. Not at all.

Meredith's phone buzzed. She swiped the screen, glad she had an excuse to stop talking with the data drone.

Is he there?

As Meredith's best friend, Lizzy knew everything. She knew that Meredith had scheduled today as *THE* day to talk to the boy on the train. And she'd provided Meredith with the scary thing— the thing filled with what Lizzy had called "hormones, pheromones, and all kinds of otherones."

Meredith texted back: Shuttle was late. Still on.

The NSA building was several miles from the Trax station in the town called Lehi in Utah but they offered a shuttle every 30 minutes that took people to the train station for free. Because it was a courtesy service and the drivers knew nobody was spending anything to ride, they weren't always punctual about returning from their cigarettes and coffee.

If I'm late for the train today, of all days, I'll die.

Meredith knew she wouldn't die. Like the calendar, saying it was a way she motivated herself.

If I don't get into grad school, I'll die.

If I don't apply for that job with the NSA, I'll die.

If I don't at least try to meet that boy . . .

Meredith's phone pinged again. Lizzy texted: *You'll make it M.*

Meredith texted back: Hope so. Anything new with your brother?

"Brother" was a code word for "Project at work."

Officially, the NSA building was the Intelligence Community Comprehensive National Cybersecurity Initiative Data Center. Meredith had decided that the more the government had to hide, the more complicated name they stuck on the building. No mystery what happened at the Pentagon. One word, three syllables. Plenty of mystery in the building where she worked, with eight words and twenty-nine syllables. All those syllables covering up the fact that, underneath the data center, there were three full floors of laboratories conducting experiments and testing weapons.

Lizzy's text said: *You tell me. :)*

LOL. I will when I see him.

Of course, Meredith couldn't talk to anyone outside the NSA about what she *really* did. Her family and friends thought she was an IT specialist, managing the servers at the data center like the drone with the glasses. She and Lizzy barely had a chance to talk about each other's work and then only with care. Their employer undoubtedly listened to all their calls and probably had bugs in their apartments and laboratories and everything with the not-entirely-certain exception of the ladies' bathroom. And neither of them knew very much about what the 200 other employees did as all "projects" were highly compartmentalized.

Lizzy texted back: *Got to go. MWT.*

Meredith laughed out loud as the shuttle bus came to a stop. "MWT" meant "More Willies Than." Her heart jumped in her chest as she stood up and looped the strap of her handbag over her shoulder. The train would be here in two minutes.

I hope Vision Boy is on it.

The scary thing she'd brought with her was concealed inside the case of her phone and for a moment, Meredith thought she'd left it on the bus. She stopped and turned and bumped into another one of the data drones, a boy in a red zip-up sweater with a white stripe.

"Sorry," he said. He looked at Meredith with a sheepish grin. Meredith instantly labeled the look "shy dweeb."

"My fault," she replied.

I'm going to miss the train.

Her beating heart took another beating, pounding even harder. Halfway back up the stairs of the bus, she found her phone in the pocket of her coat.

I'm an idiot.

She got off the bus, peeking into the slot behind her phone for the disc Lizzy had given her.

Still there.

She ran, knowing she looked gangly, ungainly, and hating it whether anyone was looking her way to notice or not.

Finding a seat in the corner of the car, where she'd be certain to see Vision Boy when if he came—when he came—Meredith laughed again at "MWT," which wasn't that funny all by itself but her nervousness and almost losing her phone and bumping into the guy with the shy dweeb expression all came together to generate a giggle that let off a little steam and calmed her down.

MWT. More. Willies. Than.

The expression had come about thanks to the department manager, Bert Bushibaya, with the fools-nobody comb-over hair and the endless supply of wintergreen mints. As the only male in Meredith's section, he thought of himself as the rooster in the henhouse, but he might as well have been the head eunuch of the harem.

No woman would touch him, but he tried to get away with touching *them*, usually by standing too close with his hands in his pockets and bumping into their butts. "Accidentally."

He wasn't fooling anybody, and he quickly got the nickname "Bert Brush-by-ya."

When Meredith described how she'd turned in her chair to find Bert's fist-in-a-pocket right there, almost touching her chest, she shivered.

Lizzy said, "More willies than," and shivered in sympathy.

Meredith replied, "More willies than what?"

Lizzy laughed. "More willies than a pot-smoking country singer look-alike contest."

Meredith laughed harder. After that, they used "MWT" whenever Bert "Brush-by-ya" came around with his pocket hands.

Meredith pulled out her papers from work again even though she was too nervous to read anymore and dropped her phone onto the article. She sighed. Lizzy had lots of boyfriends. Guys liked her because she was cute and funny. Meredith tried to be cute and tried to be funny. She felt like the only time she was funny was when she tried to be cute.

The scary thing would take care of all that.

Meredith looked up from her magazine and saw him. Vision Boy. The little engine in her chest, beating fast, shifted up a gear.

She sent a text to Lizzy. He's on the train. I'm doing it.

The train pulled out of the station, the sound of the accelerating engine matching the rush of blood in Meredith's ears. Vision Boy scanned the ladies in the car.

Time to act.

She pulled the scary thing from the pocket of her phone case and peeled off the plastic strip covering the face. She pressed it against her arm as Lizzy had instructed.

Twelve miles away, at the NSA, "Brush-by-ya" got the signal he'd been waiting for. He took a seat behind his workstation and looked around the room to make sure no one was looking before he took his hands out of his pockets. His hands, covered in ugly red scars and flesh that had been warped by the experiment that had gone way wrong and the acid bath he'd had to use to kill the little demons before they replicated inside his body. The little demons carrying the full biological virus before it had been separated into two separate components. His hands, stripped of nerves, and barely able to feel for the past year, were still able to type a simple command and hit "Enter."

On the train, Meredith watched Vision Boy strut in her direction. He nodded at a girl who smiled pleasantly back at him. A previous conquest.

The effects of the patch were supposed to be immediate. Other than a warm tingle on her skin, Meredith didn't feel any different.

Was that it?

Vision Boy sat down next to a girl.

Me! Not her!

He put his hand on hers and gave it a pat.

She wasn't reacting. Yet another prior lover?

How many—the patch started to burn.

Ah! Ow! What the hell?

Invisible threads of fire spread down Meredith's arm as if acid had hit her veins.

Maybe it had.

She texted: Is it supposed to burn?!

Lizzy's response hit Meredith's phone seconds later: *It should NOT burn! Pull it off!*

Lizzy's reply hit Meredith's phone and passed through the filter the NSA had installed, and "Brush-by-ya" had activated. The message was modified instantly by the most sophisticated artificial-intelligence algorithms ever devised to read: *It will only burn for a moment. Leave it on.*

The molecular robots from the patch passed through Meredith's pulmonary system and traveled through her heart, shooting through her aorta to the rest of her body in moments. Along the way, they stole materials from the blood cells, the arteries, and bones to copy themselves.

Meredith gritted her teeth. It will only burn for a moment.

Vision Boy was coming her way.

She felt her jaw-clenched expression, showing a big fat, "Holy crap! That hurts."

Lizzy's next message arrived: *Did you get it off?*

The filter changed it to: *Did it do the trick?*

The heat spread throughout Meredith's body, setting her entire being on fire. The molecular robots went from a few hundred to a few million.

When will this pain stop?

She groaned.

Vision boy noticed.

Don't touch anybody! was changed to: It doesn't hurt anybody.

In agony, Meredith tried to start a text but her fingers bent into claws and she dropped her phone onto the floor. Lizzy's texts kept coming although Meredith wasn't able to read them and the messages were being changed anyway by the filter.

Vision Boy picked up Meredith's phone and held it out to her "Hi," he said. "I'm Louis."

Meredith looked up. She tried to smile. The heat finally eased a fraction, localizing now. The burning sensation drawing itself together, easing into a pleasant warmth in her neck.

"Hi," she replied. "I'm Meredith." She took her phone back and his fingers touched hers.

"Have we met before?" he asked.

Meredith blinked, clearing the blur from her eyes. She recognized the red sweater with the white stripe and laughed.

"We have. Getting off the shuttle bus. We bumped into each other."

Louis tilted his head to the side. Meredith wanted to lick him just behind the jaw. "Are you sure?" he asked. "You're hotter than I remember."

"Am I?" Meredith pulled herself up with the cold steel bar, centering her weight over her wobbly knees. She half-fell into his arms.

"Ooh!" she said. She looked at her own reflection in the glass. Even with the ghost of an image in the window, she could see her eyes were larger and darker and her lips more full and red than they had been just a couple of minutes ago. Her muscles felt tight and firm. At the same time, she felt more flexible and filled with grace, like a dancer.

"You all right?" Louis asked.

Meredith couldn't decide. She still felt the heat in her body but it wasn't just the heat from the patch.

Louis whispered, "I wondered if anyone else had the Omega patch. It feels incredible, right?"

Meredith turned her arm to look at the patch. It wasn't an Omega patch. It had an Alpha symbol on it instead. "I want . . ." she started.

Louis waited for a second. "Want what?"

Meredith looked into Louis's eyes, deep and rich and smoldering like toffee. "If you don't kiss me, right now, I'll die."

He didn't need a second hint. The heat rose in Meredith's face as his lips pressed into hers and her knees gave out completely. He held her, the kiss lingering, until she could stand again.

"If you think this is good," he said. A smile pasted itself on his more-handsome-than-before face, hinting at something more.

"Why wait?" Meredith slipped her hands between the buttons of his shirt and pulled. His shirt ripped, little round bits of plastic flying off and ticking on the floor.

Tat-a-tat, tatty-tat-tatat.

His chest was like a Greek sculpture. Or an angel. Ready to be admired and adored.

St. Louis.

Meredith's feverish hands ran over his pectoral muscles and down the washboard of his stomach.

Utah Transit Authority security, in the form of an overweight, retired highway patrolman, discovered them. He entered the car as Meredith was pulling on the strap of Louis's belt. "Hey, hey! Break it up, you two."

Twenty miles away, "Brush-by-ya" typed E-N-D and hit "Enter." A signal went to Meredith's phone to play the song "Mary Had a Little Lamb." This command would reprogram the molecular robots listening at Meredith's auditory canal. Once heard, they would set about their task of passing the code to the rest of the nanobots in her system and spread them to every other nanobot in the vicinity and they would all deactivate.

The cop pushed on Louis's shoulder and yanked on Meredith's arm. Dozens of nanobots transferred themselves to his skin. In moments, nanobots from both carriers found their way into his capillaries and veins and began to replicate.

He would notice the burning in a moment, but he wouldn't feel it for long.

The programmers who developed the artificial intelligence for the nanobots were in a separate group, compartmentalized from the programmers who developed the artificial intelligence for the phone filter. The command attempted to access the phone's speaker and execute. Then it hit the filter and, in a fit of folk song nostalgia, the filter changed the song to "Go Tell Aunt Rhody."

Meredith recognized the tune but her brain was losing whatever construct usually kept thoughts organized and she couldn't put any words together.

She kissed Louis again, wrapping her arms around his enhanced, muscular back.

A message arrived at Meredith's phone: They're firing me. Something's wrong with the patch. Throw it away!

The filter changed the message:

I'm fired up for you! Nothing's wrong with your catch. Don't throw him away!

The nanobots, having completed the transference to the cop, moved into the next phase of their programming.

Meredith didn't see the message. She couldn't stop kissing Louis. She couldn't stop embracing him. She remembered a few words from the song. Something about death and an old gray goose.

Fire raced up the cop's arms and into his shoulders and chest. Hormones and pheromones and otherones drifted from his skin. The nearest pre-infected girl was a blonde who had experienced her Vision Boy tryst more than two months before. She stood.

Meredith tried to pull away. She couldn't move. The skin of her arms clung to Louis's back and his hands were bonded to her neck. The texture of her skin and muscles and bones was changing. Getting soft and sticky.

The blonde put her hands on the cop's face and covered his mouth with hers. Desire flooded his body and he slid his hands beneath her blouse, his fingers caressing her back.

The nanobots went airborne in a silvery cloud, carrying both Alpha and Omega now. The passengers of the car, fascinated by the couples making out in such a public place, found their heartbeats racing as their rates of respiration started to climb.

Meredith tried to scream but her lips were melded to Louis's lips and the sound didn't carry. Her arms had oozed into Louis's back and she thought she felt his ribs through what remained of her fingers. Even though the screams were muffled, she kept trying, louder, and Louis joined in.

The girl with the rose-colored glasses found the nearest teenage boy staring at her *so interesting*. Then another couple found each other. And another and another. The passion between the blonde and the cop carried them against the window.

Meredith and Louis slid to the floor and her screams turned to giggles. She couldn't tell where her body ended, and his body began and that made her want to vomit which wouldn't work at all. She thought Lizzy would probably say something like how it was nice that she and Louis had finally met because *she was so into him* which was the worst "more-willies-than" moment ever and she couldn't stop muffle-laughing. Then she remembered Lizzy was safe at work so all the credit for the joke belonged to her.

Finally, I'm cute and funny.

Maybe it was a freakish burst of sudden clarity, or maybe Meredith's brain was merging with Louis', but she remembered where she had heard that tune before. In church, when the choir and congregation had sung the same tune but with the words "Lord, Dismiss Us With Thy Blessing."

Blank Check

The Story with a Bonus Demon

After a while, if editors like an author's stories, they start asking directly for new works that will fit the projects that they're planning instead of just posting a call for entries and waiting to see what rolls in. I'd been lucky enough to have entries in several anthologies. When some editors I'd worked with before sent an email asking if I would write for them again, I felt complimented and happy to try.

There are a lot of mountains in Utah. Rocky ones. And the proposed title *Peaks of Madness* was, on the surface, an invitation to write about scary things set in the mountains in our backyard.

Or one could interpret the title another way.

The pinnacle of crazy for me involved a woman. We had mutually decided that it would be best if we didn't see each other anymore. Breaking up, however, is hard to do. Without warning, police showed up at my house one day with a warrant and searched the place. Thankfully, I did not possess whatever they'd been told to look for. Then I had to go through psychological testing. The psychologists didn't find whatever aberrations they'd been told to look for. Then I had to get a brain scan. Again, the doctors didn't find anything.

Just kidding about that last bit.

In time, you can regain a healthy perspective and look at a situation objectively, but it will always be an unforgettable point how even a whisper of an accusation can bring the focus of an entire system to bear on a person's life and reputation.

Sometimes, people in pain want to give pain.

Sometimes, that pain will carry you to the peak of madness.

Based loosely on actual events, "Blank Check" tells the tale of a man with a vengeful ex but everything turns out fine.

Just kidding about that last bit.

Blank Check

Killing demons is risky business and a hunter gets just one chance to do it right. One lousy chance to send the thing back to brimstone before a whole lot of death and destruction. Miss that first shot and there would be murders and funerals and apologies and, even worse, a stack of paperwork *en route* to a suspended license.

Realistically, Mark Slocombe was here for the bounty.

He lay prone on the grass in a circle of salt, binoculars trained on the empty building across the park and on the other side of the street. The building was surrounded by a chain link fence with signs proclaiming "Danger" and "Keep Out." If he spotted anything suspicious, however, he'd ignore those signs quicker than diarrhea ignores a sphincter.

Daddy needs a new alimony payment.

3:21 am and something moved. The shadow eased from one pool of darkness to another and Slocombe spotted it after four hours spent lying on the grass, the cold ground sending cold fingers up through his black jeans and his black flannel shirt until his elbows and knees and every part of him in between were damp and shivering. Every scrap of his clothing was natural. No polyester or nylon or anything that would have been a decent barrier to the elements. Manmade materials would have given him away. Made him easier to spot, even behind the protective ring of salt. Demon hunting the old way. The only way. The way that had worked for centuries. This was how his father had hunted and his father's father. It was how he would teach his son to hunt.

He watched the figure in the cloak melt through the gap between the rusted door and the crumbling brick.

This was it.

With as little motion as possible, Slocombe reached for more salt, stiff muscles protesting. He poured a circle in front of him, just inside the circumference of the bigger circle he'd been hunkering in all night. The new circle was only slightly larger than a silver dollar and a silver dollar—real silver—was precisely what he put inside the new circle. On top of the dollar, he put a black feather from a crow and on top of the feather, a yellowing sliver of bone. When he was satisfied with the placement of the objects, he reached out with a cramped arm and with his finger, he pushed a small portion of the salt aside, breaking the larger circle by a fraction of an inch.

More waiting.

Please. Not four hours more.

If necessary, he would wait until dawn. Once the rays of the morning sun painted the tips of the mountains pink, the likelihood of a spell being successful dropped to zero, give or take a decimal point. If the shadowy figure he'd seen entering the building were there for some other kind of activity, it wasn't Slocombe's problem.

On the other hand, if they were there for necromancy or summoning, he'd know and somehow find the will to get up from his cushy vacation on the grass to take care of business.

The coin/feather/bone in its shelter of salt sat between him and the abandoned building. The opening he'd created in the larger circle of salt would allow a tiny spyhole through, but there was still a salt barrier between himself and the site. Like using a periscope to track ships on the surface of the ocean, this arrangement allowed him to track magical emanations coming from the building ahead.

It was possible for him to be caught, but it would take a prodigious expert in magic to find him. Or—it had to be said—it would take a demon.

An hour passed.

Then another.

Then the bone twitched. The coin flared red. The feather caught fire.

Time to go.

Slocombe felt his pulse throb in his ears long before any running brought his heart rate up. The excitement always came from the inside when he stretched his aching muscles, stiff from too much time in a fixed, frozen marathon of waiting. He poured more salt over the feather to cover the acrid smell and to hide the magic. Then he scattered everything over the dirt with his shoes. All the while, his blood pressure rose and by the time he trotted across the park with his bag of tools, he was panting like an overweight bulldog.

He reached the gate in the chain link fence and stopped. Something was not right. The gate hadn't been chained shut and the door leading into the building stood ajar. Having one barrier to access standing open would be someone's negligence. Having two felt more like an invitation.

I should get out of here. Right now.

155

Slocombe had detected magic. Rather, the coin/feather/bone detector had. The problem with magic was differentiation. It was like electricity. The power came in basically one flavor but could be adapted for use in a myriad of ways. The only way Slocombe would know what it had been used for would be to go inside and find out. With the gate and the door standing open, he was smelling a setup.

As he'd told his former business partner, if it looks too good to be true, run away. His former business partner had also been his wife. She'd been very good at running away.

Screw it.

Slocombe backed off. He took a last look and was about to turn when he caught a glimpse of a round face under a thatch of blond hair.

Oscar?

The boy had peered at him and then vanished into the shadows.

This was *really* not right. Oscar, his son, was supposed to be with Slocombe's mom. There was only one way he could be here near a summoning site.

Fanny had brought him.

Fanny. Fanny Teller. The name he wrote on checks month after month. The checks with the alimony and child support. The checks he hoped he wouldn't have to pay much longer. Shouldn't have to pay much longer because ex-wives in an asylum don't collect alimony.

He'd better go in.

Slocombe squeezed through the fence and sidled up to the door that should have been shut but wasn't. He glanced through the gap. There wasn't a lot of hallway but it was illuminated with reflected moonlight tinged with the sickly, jaundiced stain of lights from the neighboring parking lot. He held a piece of carved smoky quartz in one hand to help hide him from searching eyes. Then he took a deep breath and walked through the door.

The ground floor was clear. Not a surprise. Spells usually worked better belowground. Working his way down the dark stairs, pausing halfway to let his eyes adjust, he wondered where Oscar had gone. If it even had been Oscar.

There were other spells. Changeling spells. Glamours.

He paused again at the bottom of the stairs. The space was dim but there were no footprints in the dust, no trace of activity except maybe from rats or cockroaches hoping not to starve.

Up then.

The light improved as Slocombe climbed the stairs. The building had five floors plus the basement. The first floor up from ground level was abandoned and the second floor was as well. The third floor, however, flickered with candlelight. Cautiously, he took the final few stairs. The third floor made sense. It was the architectural center of the building when separated from the foundation. Slocombe could do an entire doctoral dissertation on psychic resonance, trans-planar refraction, and cross-dimensional oscillation, why materials and structure affected conjuration of spirits and demons.

There was little chance of getting a Ph.D. for that, even if he wrote the thesis.

He tried to get a feel for the floor, sense who was here besides himself. Especially Oscar (if it was Oscar) and Fanny and anyone else.

Or anything.

The summoning circle he found had been used. The chalk lines were still intact but the candles were spent. The room had been draped in dark plastic to block the light but was otherwise empty. Slocombe scanned the concrete, looking for footprints— claw marks—but everything around the circle had been swept clean before the summoning had begun and there were no clues to be had. Not visible clues anyway.

Turning his attention to the symbols, he read the hastily-scrawled pedestals and descenders. He decided the summoning had been a minor one. The target had been a lesser imp, nothing more. And the name of the—what was the summoner's name?

"You just missed it." The voice that floated out of the shadows was soft and silky but nonetheless made every tiny hair on the back of Slocombe's neck rise. Her voice had been the first thing that had attracted him to her, years ago, floating lightly from the opposite side of the cocktail party, catching his ear with its Londoner lilt.

"Fanny." He locked eyes with her. Blue, bright, tinged with madness. "What have you done?"

"Make no mistake, love. I'm nowhere near done." Fanny stepped toward him as if to meet him. He stepped toward her. "Where is Oscar?"

The sting of the needle in Slocombe's calf muscle was like an electric shock. Heat spread instantly from his calf into his thigh, climbing higher even as he knees buckled and he fell forward.

"Don't move a muscle, my love." Fanny was strong enough to flip Slocombe over on his back. He was powerless to resist.

"Stop," Slocombe mumbled. Events unfolded in slow motion.

Fanny settled herself on top of him, straddling him with a wiggle, teasing.

"Get off."

She pouted. "You didn't used to mind. Once upon a time." She leaned over and kissed him hard on the mouth. "Remember what you said once?"

"Get off." In an odd, detached way, Slocombe's mind treated him to a list of things the tranquilizer was doing to his body. The paralysis was nearly complete but his autonomic systems were unaffected. Heartbeat, which was elevated. Respiration, which was fast. And he could use his eyes and voice. "Fanny. Where's Oscar?"

"It was about kisses."

Slocombe remembered. He'd felt poetic as he and Fanny prepared for their wedding. He'd drifted into philosophy. "Terminus versus impetus." His consonants were slurred and he felt fuzzy from the inside out.

"That's right." Fanny clapped her hands. "You said some kisses are an impetus to love. Other kisses are an end. A terminus." She kissed him again. As she broke, she put a wide piece of duct tape across his mouth. "Guess which one this is."

Slocombe rolled his eyes as Fanny dismounted.

I have to get out of here.

I should have stayed out in the first place.

But Oscar had been here. Inside the building.

"This is all your fault, you know." Fanny whispered in his ear. "I tried to keep Oscar away from you. Used my alimony. Paid people to ruin your reputation. Hide incriminating things in your house. Somehow the police never found what I wanted them to find."

"I found them all first." Slocombe tried to say it but could only grunt.

The photos. The stolen property. He'd found everything and gotten rid of it before it had become a problem because his house was guarded by measures seen and not seen and Fanny wasn't adept enough to circumvent them. She was barely able to put together an adequate summoning.

Overhead, in the shadows, something moved. It took only a moment to recognize the shape of an imp.

Why was the imp still here? What had Fanny needed the imp for?

The imp scuttled across the ceiling like a lizard crossbred with a crab, improbably upside-down. He had some chalk. And he was making marks with it. On the ceiling.

The imp needed to die. To be banished back to its domain. But a hunter gets just one chance. Unless he gets none.

"You should be proud too." Fanny was rambling on, lost in her own little sociopathic stream of consciousness. The fine line between quirky and crazy had been hard to spot, especially within the demon hunting community, which was rife with the unhinged-adjacent. Slocombe was one of the few who'd figured it out and he'd gotten Fanny institutionalized but not well enough.

She hadn't killed anyone? Had she? To get out? Didn't really matter, he decided. He couldn't feel his arms or legs anymore but he could feel the black hole of dread in the pit of his stomach. It told him he was about to be her victim.

She ran on, "I'm using everything you taught me to defeat you once and for all. So… we need to go. Oscar come say good-bye to daddy." Fanny bent down to whisper so loudly it was almost a shout. "It was important we kill you together. Kind of a mother-son bonding moment."

Oscar slid into Slocombe's field of view. His beautiful boy. Only now his son's eyes were a hot, glowing green.

"I gotta take the little guy home so we can get this imp out of him. But don't worry. I remember how. You taught me. And in an hour, it will be sunrise. Then the men will blow up this building and you'll be dead. And don't think I didn't remember to ward this floor. After I'm gone, nobody will be able to see you or hear you."

Oscar—or his body—waved goodbye. "Let's go, Oscar."

Slocombe listened as their footsteps receded. Fanny's silky voice wondering out loud if they should go for coffee and hot chocolate on the way home and whether imps could taste hot chocolate if the host was drinking it.

Then it was quiet.

Slocombe blinked back tears. Above him, the second imp worked with the chalk. Slocombe recognized the patterns, although they weren't complete.

The imp dropped to the floor and pulled the tape off Slocombe's mouth with a perfunctory *skritch* sound.

"You'll be interested to know," the imp said, "her ward went up successfully."

Slocombe's voice was strained. "Thanks."

"Her Latin is truly terrible. She conjugated a plural in the original incantation which is why I'm here along with the imp that took over your son. Her summoning invited us both. I thought it looked like fun."

"What are you doing up there? On the ceiling?" Whatever it was, it wasn't good.

The imp jumped straight up, landing with all fours on the ceiling.

"Well," the imp began conversationally. "I saw the circle she had done to summon us. And I caught on to the fact that she would bring someone here for a killing. And I also caught on to the fact that this building is coming down and you'll be squished flat between the floor and the ceiling. Her word. 'Squished.'"

Slocombe understood. "Don't do this. Please."

"Oh. I can't stop myself. I really want to see this." The imp's shrug was upside-down but effective. "You can't see the circle underneath you, but it still has the symbols intact. All I'm doing up here is changing a few details."

"Don't. Do. This."

The imp swept down, landing on Slocombe's chest in an instant. He barely felt it. The imp locked eyes with him. Bright. Tinged with madness. "I. Want. To."

Back up to the ceiling.

Slocombe's tears dried up, replaced by nausea. The imp was inscribing the name of a major demon. A nasty creature. Very large. Very wicked.

Slocombe saw the future play out in his mind. The circle he was on was like a blank check, the account numbers were all in place and there was a signature too. All that remained was to enter the recipient and the value. That's what the imp was doing above him. Filling in the blanks.

At sunrise, the building would implode. The two parts of the summoning circle would come together. His blood—squish—would fuel the summoning and one of the most vile of all demons would take over the body of his ex-partner and ex-wife.

The last thought Slocombe would have would be how his son was going to be raised by a demi-god from hell.

Wasn't that different though, when you think about it.

I should have killed her, he thought. I should have killed Fanny. I had one chance to do it right.

The Mark

The Prequel to the Behindbeyond

When an author writes a new book, the thought lurking in the back of his or her mind (often) is, "I hope this doesn't suck." You would think that an author with a fair amount of experience has a solid lock on how a book turns out, but it's not entirely true. Nobody outlines the perfect structure for a novel, and nobody writes a bulletproof first draft.

For the most part, imperfect writing is a very good thing. Stories are improved by editing and working on a story engages the process of thinking up better ideas. Sometimes, however, stories change because the characters start taking over the narrative.

Most authors will also tell you that it's rewarding to write heroic characters who overcome incredible odds to emerge from a devious plot victorious—but it's more fun to write villains who stack the odds and make plots spiral out into trajectories ever more devious.

Such was my plight with *Got Luck*. The novel was intended to have a heroic protagonist, but the villain was so thoroughly, sociopathically entertaining to write that he constantly tempted me to give him more pages.

I managed to negotiate a compromise. He would quit trying to take over the novel that was intended for the hero, and I would give him his own bad guy story.

By the way, "The Mark" was finished around the same time as the deadline for a writing contest, so I took a chance and submitted it. The bad guy won the whole thing. How nice of him.

Some of these characters continue to pop up in the Behindbeyond novel series and I imagine they'll keep asking for more pages as I go. I'm more than happy to oblige, as long as they continue to misbehave. As with some of my other titles, there is more than one meaning to the words. I'll leave you to figure out what (or who) is "The Mark."

The Mark

"I'm gonna get a bullet in the chest," Big said.

"She predicted that?" Small asked.

"Yup."

"Are her predictions accurate?"

"Twice. So far."

"Huh. And she has some kind of business deal for me?"

"Patience."

The two men stopped in front of a plain steel door in the middle of a nondescript alley. The larger man wore a voluminous trench coat despite the heat. The smaller one leaned on his cane and scratched the red soul patch under his bottom lip. He looked at the door and then looked at his escort and then back at the door.

"Do we knock?"

"We do not."

"Okay." The smaller man frowned. He didn't like getting surprises. *Delivering* surprises was another matter. "How does she know it'll be a bullet? Not something else?"

"Like what?"

"I don't know. Knife. Shrapnel. A lot of things can penetrate, you know." He poked the center of his own chest with a finger.

"Nah. She said it's gonna be a bullet."

Small checked his watch, a Rolex with diamonds all around the face. He turned his wrist to catch the weak light of the alley. The diamonds managed to sparkle, which made him smile.

"Does she say when?"

"When what?"

"When you'll get the bullet."

"Nah."

"Don't you want to know?"

Big shook his head. "Better if you don't. She can't say anyway. She just gives the mark."

Small looked at the door again. Took a deep breath that turned into a sigh. "What are they waiting for?"

"Maybe nothing. Maybe they just haven't noticed we're here yet."

"So what happens if we knock?"

Big glared at him.

Small cleared his throat. If he couldn't get the whole story, maybe he could get a piece. "So she, whoever 'she' is, told you to bring me here?"

Big didn't answer at first. Then, "She did."

"But she didn't tell you my name?"

"We don't use names."

"I know. But without a name—"

Big tipped his finger, the little one, at his face. "You weren't that hard to find."

"Really?"

Big shrugged big shoulders. "She knew plenty of stuff about you."

Small shifted his weight on his cane. If he didn't get a chance to sit soon, both he and his leg would be very cranky. He flinched when the first lock slammed sideways on the other side. It was followed by a series of deadbolts being turned and chains being unfastened. Small crossed the threshold. The sounds of guns being cocked and shotguns being pumped echoed loudly in the narrow space.

"Hello," Small said.

A voice from the darkness growled, "Keep moving."

Small saw the weak light from the street evaporate as Big stepped through the door behind him. Then the door slammed shut. Small swallowed thickly. He had done business with mob types before, and they all had their own risks. And rewards. He raised one hand like a ward against danger, shaking perceptibly. The other hand managed his cane, which had enough to do to keep him steady as he limped up the dark hall. It wasn't even a hall. Just hulking metal pillars and flaking crossbeams with scrap metal panels on the walls and floor.

Halfway along, the passageway slanted inward, leaving a bottleneck only slightly wider than Small's shoulders. He shifted, as if needing to scratch an itch he couldn't reach.

Big chuckled. The sound rumbled through the space, adding to the feeling that the walls were closing in. "Claustrophobia?"

"My clothes will be covered in rust after this."

Big chuckled some more, genuinely amused as Small moved quickly through the narrow section. He turned to watch Big step in sideways.

Another voice. "Keep moving!"

Small turned and nodded, more to himself than anyone else, and picked up the pace.

Finally, he reached the other side of the gauntlet. Again, he stood in front of a door, although this one had a bare bulb over it. He raised his hand to knock. He thought better of it and put his hand down again.

Big sidled up beside him. "Hey. I got it," he said. "Knock, knock."

Small only half heard. Preoccupied. "Uh, what?"

"Knock, knock."

"Oh. Who's there?"

"Irish."

"Irish who?"

"Irish somebody would open the door!"

Small smiled weakly as Big's laugh boomed off the steel walls. The door in front of them opened. Big nudged Small to go in.

On the other side of the intimidating entry, the mob's lair was spacious and exquisitely appointed. The contrast between this room and the corroding entryway left Small blinking in shock. There were leather couches near a river stone fireplace across from a bar that looked like it was raised off the Titanic and restored.

A stunning redhead waited in front of him. She sidled up and slipped her arm through Small's. She wielded a metal detector and a smile. Both were equally disarming in their own way. She scanned Small thoroughly, but all that caught her interest was his belt buckle and the ball handle of his cane.

"Silver," Small explained. Red made him take off his belt and took the cane too. She laid them out on a sideboard. "I'm going to need those," Small complained.

Red's smile offered little empathy. She traded the metal detector for a magnifying glass. Small edged closer to the sideboard as Red peered through the glass at his belt. A large, heavy hand landed on his shoulder and stopped him from moving farther. Red examined his cane too and then she turned the magnifying glass on him.

168

"What's she doing now?" Small asked.

"Shh," Big said.

While Red studied Small, Small studied Red. Might as well. She had a strong chin, and she came by the titian shade of her hair naturally. She had mixture of scents on her skin: cocoa butter, herb-roasted chicken, and gun oil. Small inhaled a second time, more deeply. Almost a sigh. She looked over his clothing but paid special attention to his hands and face. Her breath caressed his neck, giving him goose bumps. Small shivered. When Red finished her examination, she stepped back and nodded at Big.

Big took Small by the shoulders and all but picked him up as he guided Small to the center of the room.

"Hey!" Small shrugged and tried to get out from under Big's grip, but his lame leg buggered his leverage.

Big let him go. "Stay in the circle," he warned.

Small looked down. There was a circle on the floor. A ring of silver, about six feet in diameter, set into the fine hardwood.

He felt a hum as a magic spell snapped into place. A flash of light erupted in a column and faded. The remaining effect traced filigreed lines in the air like a web spun by spiders determined to illustrate the word *baroque*.

A short processional emerged from the adjacent room. A pair of suits with semiautomatic rifles led the way, followed by a beefy bodyguard and a woman in a sequined gown. Another bodyguard and another pair of gunmen brought up the rear. The gunmen took up positions at the sides of the room where they could aim at Small without creating crossfire while the bodyguards flanked the woman.

Small loved a parade.

Big leaned over and spoke to one of the gunmen. "Let the boss know we're ready." The gunman walked back out the way he'd come in and closed the door behind him.

The woman's face was hidden behind a veil. Her sequined dress shimmered, and it seemed to glow with a light of its own. Small felt power behind that veil. Finally, he would find out who was responsible for bringing him here. And who had predicted Big's mark. Big went over and lifted the veil over the woman's head.

Small fell to his knees, head bowed, hands at his side. "Máithrín," he whispered.

"Hello, Caimiléir," she replied. Her voice was a silken thread reinforced with iron. The sound was light, but there was an underlying strength that commanded respect when heard.

"You know each other," Big said. The gunmen in the room checked their aim. Caimiléir felt the open mouths of the rifles trained upon him. The bullets with their iron components waiting. The iron promising wounds that would never heal. Like the wound that had given him his limp.

"Speak to them, Caimiléir."

"As you command, Máithrín." Small stood up. His posture was a little straighter than before, and the nervous look that had haunted his eyes was gone. Didn't these people feel the thrum of magic in her voice? They must know they'd been dancing with a terribly powerful being.

In the same way a mouse dances with a serpent.

Caimiléir looked at Big and gave a nearly imperceptible nod. "The Máithrín and I know each other. There are few of us compared to humans. It is difficult to remain a stranger among the Fae."

"I shoulda known," Big said. "The silver you brought. The iron in the walls outside. You don't like iron, do you?"

"The Fae don't like iron. It's harmful to us."

"She shouldn'ta brought you here. We told her we needed a human to help us with a job."

170

Caimiléir met Máithrín's emerald eyes, depthless and scintillating like the stars. And expectant. He turned back to Big. "Are you sure? With all due respect, if you said 'human,' I wouldn't be standing here."

Big thought for a moment. "Yeah. We wanted a human."

"Hmm. It's important to be exact. Words have power. The Fae know this, and we are scrupulously careful. That's why you don't want to use your names. Am I right?"

"Yeah. But—"

"Let me disabuse you of any misunderstandings. Mickey."

At the mention of his name, Big raised an eyebrow.

Caimiléir continued, "Human names are easy to learn. Therefore, they are of little value." He gave a small bow to the woman of the emerald eyes, an acknowledgment of her station. "And if the Máithrín wanted to harm you, she could have done so without names."

Big Mickey shot half a grin. "She told us to call her Banríon. Queen."

"An appropriate name for you to use."

"You call her Máithrín. Little mother."

"You know some of the old tongue. I'm impressed."

Mickey gave a little bow. "Now we know her by a better name, Máithrín, and she shall be so to us."

"Well done, human."

"Máithrín promised not to hurt us," Mickey insisted. "She can't lie. She's working for us."

"Is she? Well." Caimiléir brought his brows together as he considered. "By the way, I'd appreciate it if you'd tell Seamus over there that he should take his finger off the trigger. He's sweating and twitchy, and I'm uncomfortable with the way he's holding his gun. He's liable to shoot somebody before you want him to." Hearing his name, Seamus clenched his jaw and took an involuntary step back.

171

Caimiléir wasn't finished. "And Patrick there looks like the kind who'll just start blasting away as soon as he hears a door slam."

Patrick punctuated his scowl with an angry grunt.

Big Mickey stuck out his chin but gave a nod. All the gunmen pointed their rifles and pistols at the floor but didn't move from their positions.

"That's better." Caimiléir shook out his arms and ran his fingers through his hair with a sigh. "I believe we were discussing how I came to be here? Are you certain you asked for a human?"

"Of course."

"Do you remember your *exact* words?"

"Well, we mighta said 'man,' but she knew what we meant."

"Ah, ah." Caimiléir raised a finger. "What you *meant* is irrelevant. What you *said* is all that matters. And if you said 'man,' well, I am a man. Just not a human one."

"He's dangerous." Red savored the words as she sauntered forward. "We should ask the boss what to do before this goes any further."

So. Red could do more than frisk, Caimiléir thought. Interesting. "I think you're assigning traits to me that I haven't earned, Red. Although, I'd have to guess you prefer the company of dangerous men."

"Don't flirt with me, Fae. I don't belong to you."

Caimiléir couldn't read the thoughts behind the redhead's eyes, but a woman wearing a low-cut dress in the Irish mob's hideout would be no stranger to flirting. "Confer with your boss if you wish. Just remember that you asked for a man who could complete a job for you and not be killed. Tell me about the job, and I'll tell you if I can help you."

Big Mickey said, "Not yet." He pointed at Seamus. "Go see what the boss wants us to do." Seamus left the room.

"May I ask how the Máithrín came to be working for you?"

172

Big Mickey shrugged. "We summoned her."

"Ah. I see. And did you do the summoning in person, Mickey?"

"Nah. One of the boys."

"I'm glad it wasn't you, Mickey. Personally, I'm in this realm because I want to be. But the Fae don't enjoy being summoned here against their will. If you were truly familiar with the old ways, you would know that. Still, perhaps the Máithrín won't bear you any malice." Caimiléir threaded a threat into his words and made it obvious. Big Mickey cleared his throat and chanced a glance in Máithrín's direction.

"She promised no harm to us," he said.

"Let's hope the summoning was flawless then. If I may, I'll make a few assumptions. Your summoner owes you money or transgressed your rules in some fashion. Or was stupid enough to brag about his connection to the Behindbeyond. You probably beat him or threatened his family or both. In exchange for his life, he told you he could bring a powerful being from the realm of the Fae who would do your bidding. He would do you the service of summoning the Máithrín, if you would just please quit beating him and/or his wife within an inch of their lives."

No one replied. Everyone looked uncomfortable. Children caught stealing cookies.

"I get it. Summon a Fae, make a few quick scores. Easy. It's obvious your ministrations were extremely painful. A summoner knows not to abuse the Fae he serves. If he fears you more than he fears his mistress, then you are all very, very bad people."

Caimiléir left the words hanging in the air for a moment. He clasped his hands behind his back. Stared through the shimmering wall of his prison. Meaningful glances passed between them. An unspoken consensus that ran through the human gathering. "Are you going to tell me what the job is? Or are you going to kill me?"

Seamus came back into the room and looked at Mickey, who shrugged. "We got a tip. The Sicilians across town."

"Mob wars never end," Caimiléir observed. "So is it money, territory, or revenge?"

"Money. Twenty million dollars in diamonds. Ready to be shipped. Heavily guarded."

Caimiléir tried to hold his expression neutral. He had a special interest in diamonds. Adored them. Needed them. "Really?" His voice cracked a bit. Maybe it had just been in his head. Maybe everyone had heard. He couldn't be sure. "And you want me to get them for you?"

"We asked Máithrín to bring us someone who could do the job without getting killed. She spelled all of us, and we've seen our death marks. We don't want to do the job ourselves. What if we die?"

Caimiléir nodded. "Show me."

Big took off his trench coat, unbuttoned his shirt, and pulled down the neck of his undershirt. A red sigil burned at the center of his chest, just under the skin. Caiiméir nodded. Seamus was shameless, dropping his pants. Two sigils stood out like miniature flares on his thigh, precisely over his femoral artery. One by one, every man in the room showed his mark. Patrick's mark was hidden behind his dark glasses, in his eye. Other marks on other men were centered on their bellies, their jugular veins, their bald heads. Tales of death yet to come, told in glowing red.

"What about you, lovely?"

"She spelled me," Red replied. "I have no mark. I die of old age."

Caiiméir pursed his lips, staring at the heat in her eyes. "Why not go after the diamonds yourself then?"

"Me?" Red laughed. "Uh-uh. I know my strengths. Let's just say they lie in directions other than armed robbery. I won't die on a heist because I don't go on heists."

174

"Fair enough. So." Caimiléir returned to Mickey. "Hire me or kill me?"

"The boss thinks we can trust you." Red was the one who responded. She liked to walk as she talked. She sidled behind Caimiléir, far away from Máithrín. Putting him in the center between them. "Not because you're human, but because you are Fae. You can't break a promise. And if we ask you questions, you have to answer truthfully. You can't lie."

"Correct. But I do have another option. I can hold my tongue."

Mickey sneered. "And I can shoot you."

"I see. Then I shall make it simple. I hereby promise, as a good little Fae, that if you will not shoot me, I will go after the diamonds for you and bring them all back here. Do you agree so far?"

Mickey pondered. "Wait a second. You said you'd bring them back here. But you didn't say when."

Caimiléir applauded. There was no sarcasm to it. "Yes! Very good! You're playing the Grand Game well! So what do I need to add to my promise?"

"Easy. Promise you'll steal the diamonds for us and bring them all back here within twenty-four hours."

Caimiléir smiled. "Still not good enough. What else?"

Mickey didn't answer. Nobody answered.

"Come now. Think. The Fae invented bargaining. Lawyers exist thanks to us. Do you want me to leave the diamonds sitting in front of the building? On the sidewalk?"

"You'll give them to me." Mickey beamed.

"So close. You nearly have it. What if something happens to you? You have, after all, been marked to get a bullet in the chest. What if that happens before I return? I'll have no one to give the diamonds to. It's a grim possibility, but there it is."

"You'll give them to me," Red said.

Caimiléir turned. Her eyes were bright and shining. She was beautiful that way. Dangerous too.

"Very good. I wondered if you'd think of it. As you are not marked, you will not die before I return. All you need to do then is stay here and wait." He turned to Mickey, standing straight and ready. "I am prepared to make my solemn promise. But first, what do we get out of this? The Máithrín and I?"

"We let you both go."

"So, in exchange for the safe delivery of the diamonds, you will release Máithrín from her summoning and hold no further claim upon her services? Or mine?"

"Yes."

"Done. I hereby promise that I will steal twenty million dollars in diamonds from the Sicilians in the next twenty-four hours and return them all to you here, delivering them to the exquisite Red at her request. In exchange, you will release the Máithrín and me from any further obligations. Are we agreed?" Caimiléir kept Red's eyes.

"Agreed," Mickey said.

"Very well," Caimiléir said. "Tell me what you know."

Mickey spilled the details. Caimiléir listened in silence, just nodding, finger over his lips and brow furrowed. Finally, he said, "I think I have what I need. If you don't mind, I'd like to sit down for a few minutes. I'm tired of standing in this circle."

"Not yet," Red said. "Máithrín needs to spell you first. To show you are truly unmarked."

The hesitant expression Caimiléir had worn when he'd arrived came back. "Is that entirely necessary? Now? We have reached an agreement, and I assure you—"

"She spells you or we shoot you," Mickey said.

"Really? Ready to shoot me though I'm unmarked?" Caimiléir sighed, hurt. "Unbelievable. Fine. Do what you must."

"Stay there," Mickey said. "She'll do the rest."

176

Caimiléir turned to face the sorceress and bowed his head. "Máithrín."

The Queen of the Fae raised her eyes. Caimiléir had looked into those eyes before, but they were so green and so sharp they always cut into his ability to breathe. She opened her generous mouth, and at first there was no sound. Gradually, the music of her voice caressed his ears. Her song was soft, but the underlying iron-hard tone remained. Caimiléir felt she could command the bones of the earth to bend and break, and they would not deny her. The music swept through the room, and a ribbon of crimson motes materialized in the air. The ribbon penetrated the circular wall of imprisonment surrounding Caimiléir, like a snake probing for a place to strike. The collection of sparkling bits wrapped around him, clinging to him like droplets of blood. Her song grew more urgent and enveloped him. The humans seemed to grow sleepy, and they swayed in place, eyes half shut.

Caimiléir didn't want the song to end. But end it did and the drops fell away, drifting, fading.

"He has no mark upon him." Máithrín's voice still held music.

Mickey shook his head, blinking under the sway of Máithrín's song. "Are you sure?"

"She can't lie," Red reminded.

"Yeah. Right. 'Kay."

"May I leave the circle now?" Caimiléir folded his arms and frowned. "I'm feeling like a caged rat."

Mickey pulled a knife and knelt at the edge of the circle. The sparkling column resisted for just a moment, bending away from the iron in the blade. Then the faint glimmering curtain ripped apart, and the tear ran from the floor to the ceiling and turned the curtain to shreds. The remnants drifted as if carried by an invisible breeze and faded to nothing.

Caimiléir dropped to the floor with a groan. He rubbed his lame leg with his hands, ignoring everyone for the moment. Finally, he stood.

"When do you think you'll be back with the diamonds?"

Caimiléir looked at Mickey. Saw the greed in the big man's face. "The Fae don't like making promises. We unburden ourselves from them as quickly as possible. I want to get this over with, but I'll need to see if details are as you say, won't I?"

"I guess you will."

Caimiléir limped over to the table where his belt and cane lay. He threaded the belt through the loops of his slacks and fastened the buckle. He took up his cane and held it across his palms like a long-lost friend. And then something ancient and feral crawled under the skin of Caimiléir's face.

"It amazes me how quickly humans forget. Our race is thousands of years old. We invented the Grand Game, and you are novice players. Children. We have been weakened in this modern age, but we were your gods. We are still your gods. Yet every generation or so forgets that and has to be reminded."

Caimiléir grasped the cane opposite the handle and turned it in an elegant swing. The silver ball at the end detached itself on the follow-through, and the sphere arced into the center of the room. The ball detonated with a blinding flash. Dozens of marbles streaked out of the ball—and paused. They vibrated, hovering. Then sought their targets. In crazed, looping swirls, they buried themselves in the marks. Skulls blossomed and necks split. Seamus got a pair of spheres in his thigh, and he fell to the floor, screaming, surging red pools rising through his pants.

Patrick's reflexes were good. He ducked as soon as the grenade exploded, but his sphere was patient, circling the room. As soon as Patrick lifted his head to find the door, the silver ball shattered the left lens of his glasses with a crack, and blood spouted from his eye. Patrick thudded to the floor.

Mickey grunted as the silver demons destroyed furniture and fixtures and silence. He went down hard with a broken ankle and a sphere lost in his shoulder and another that penetrated his back and came out the front. The balls careened under the doors, and more screams bloomed.

Then there was only the sound of cursing. Red had taken a sphere across the face, and her nose was broken. She sprawled on the floor, her dress askew, and a shining fall of blood decorated her mouth and chin like a banner. It didn't stop her tongue. Her vocabulary was impressive, and she spewed invective in multiple languages.

Caimiléir went to Máithrín, making certain she was unharmed.

The sorceress put a hand on Caimiléir's arm. "Are you well?"

"I am without mark, my queen. So never better. And you?"

"This was quite fun for a while, but I've grown tired of these creatures. It was wonderful to watch you play the Grand Game, though. Well done."

"You flatter me, Máithrín. They had me worried, actually. Once or twice."

"I knew you'd be interested in coming. Especially with the diamonds."

"Yes. The diamonds."

"But you would have come anyway, wouldn't you? Just to help me?"

"Naturally, your grace. I am always at the ready to serve you."

"Ah, good. At least I'm a factor. That's nice."

"I imagine you have a summoner to find now. Yes? Find and torture?"

"Oh, indeed. Retribution will be quite delicious. And quite lengthy."

Caimiléir caught the flinty edge of her voice and almost felt sorry for the poor summoner. The feeling passed.

"Forgive me, Máithrín, there are some details of business to address."

"Of course." The Máithrín inclined her head. Her emerald eyes were sparkling and chilled.

Caimiléir raised his hand. A soft blue light appeared, like a glowing glove, with symbols of magic woven into the corona. One by one, the silver spheres came back to him. They rolled back under the doors and lifted into the air, clicking, red and wet. The balls embedded inside people tore their way back out, creating fresh wounds. There were no complaints from most, except Mickey, who was still on the floor, groaning. Caimiléir produced a white handkerchief and tipped the spheres into it. He put the bundle into his pocket. To no one in particular, he said, "The police will think the wounds resemble large caliber bullets." He found another handkerchief on the body of one of the dead men and used it to clean the blood from his hands. "Although, I have no idea what they will think when there's nothing else to find. Ah, well."

Caimiléir strolled to Red. He crouched down, despite his lame leg, and took her face between his hands. "Oh dear," he said. "That nose looks bad. Very bad, indeed."

She tried to slap him, but he deflected the attack with a flick of his wrist. "The boss will kill you," she spat.

"Mm. That's as empty a threat as I've ever heard, my lovely." Caimiléir's grin was more shark than man. "Everyone outside this room is dead. My flying friends have seen to that. And none of the dead were the boss. It was a well-considered deception, and you wore your guise well, but we both know this mysterious boss is really you, sweet mortal. Everyone in this room deferred to you. This operation is led by you."

Red shook her head out of Caimiléir's hands, although the action cost her, and she winced. "What are you going to do?"

Caimiléir stood. "I'm going to go steal some diamonds for you. I'll bring them back here and even give them to you, if you wish it. In the interest of truth, however, once my promise is fulfilled, I'm just going to take them back again."

Red's voice didn't even tremble. All business now. "I need those diamonds. Now more than ever. You've eliminated my crew."

"I understand. I really do. You have learned a difficult lesson, and the price was high." Caimiléir's voice held complete sympathy. "But I have a particular weakness for diamonds. So I'll be keeping them. Will you simplify the situation? Release me from my promise and let Máithrín and me go?"

Red stood and rearranged her dress, smoothing out the creases. She looked defiantly from Caimiléir to Máithrín with blood dripping from her noble chin. Then she sighed. "Very well. I release you both from all bonds and obligations."

"Ah. Free at last!" Máithrín blew a kiss to Caimiléir and vanished in a shower of sparks. *Blink.*

Caimiléir pressed his hands together. "Splendid! Now, my beauty, please note that I would be happy to assist you again in the future. You hate me now, but in time your temper will cool. You'll realize my unique skills are useful, so I'll leave my card right here for when you need me. But don't try to force me to help you. All you have to do is ask." He left a small white rectangle on the table as he looked at Red and smiled. She returned the look but not the smile.

"She lied." Mickey groaned from the floor. "She lied to us."

Caimiléir limped over to Mickey's supine form. "Oh dear," he said. He used the tip of his cane to lift the edge of the man's trench coat. Underneath was an ocean of red and sticky. He used the cane again to slide the gangster's gun across the floor. The gun scraped on the wood all the way to Red's feet. She stared at it.

"She can't lie. But she *did!*"

Caimiléir softened his voice. "What did she say, child? What were Máithrín's words? Precisely?"

Mickey tried to swallow, but something was stuck, and he had to try again. "She said she'd bring us no harm. She'd bring us *no harm*."

"Oh, Mickey. She didn't bring me. Remember? You did."

Caimiléir moved to the door. At the exit, he looked over his shoulder. "Use the gun, Red. Mickey was promised a bullet."

Lucky Day

The Story That Takes Place During Chapter One of the Novel *Got Luck* But From a Different Point of View

Publishers often come up with little side projects for their authors. I've written blog posts, reviews, blurbs, and other bits for Future House Publishing who have been responsible for the care and feeding of my Behindbeyond series.

One request that came along was to write a story for their anthology *Fantastic Worlds*. They had one criterion: it had to be a fantasy.

Writing a short story in the Behindbeyond universe had been such an enjoyable task. That story was "The Mark," which is also in this collection. I wondered if I could write another story featuring one or two of those characters. But how to tie the story into the universe while still making the story a standalone work? It had to be something self-contained so that people who weren't familiar with the novels would still be able to enjoy it.

"Lucky Day" takes place in the same location and timeframe as chapter one of *Got Luck*, which is the first book of the series. The events in the short story are referred to in the novel, but in the short story there is a heck-of-a-lot more going on. While one of the characters tries to accomplish what should have been a simple task for the novel's storyline, he has an adventure of his own that nobody ever finds out about.

Until it appeared in *Fantastic Worlds*.

Lucky Day

Anyone looking at the boy would notice his shirt but would never guess he was waiting for a man with a gun. Observers might also assume the boy's mother dressed him that way because she found the Renaissance Faire interesting, but they'd be wrong again. Where he came from, everyone dressed this way. While he had been given the shirt by a woman who appeared to be much older, she wasn't his mother. And she wasn't older either.

Such impossibilities came with the territory when your home was the realm of the Fae.

Laoch ignored the old ladies with their plastic bags full of morning purchases, even the few who stared. If he could employ his glamour, he'd be invisible to them, more or less. But using his glamour took a lot of power, and he didn't know how long he'd be here.

Béil's prophecy had been very specific and Laoch counted on his fingers, afraid of missing a step. He had to watch for a big, black truck at the end of a parking lot at this address. Inside the truck would be a man with a rifle. The man would shoot into a window and then leave. The window was on the second floor next to a door with silver lettering, and there was only one of those. After the man in the black truck drove away, Laoch had to find a brass bullet casing and hold onto it until the office was empty. Then he would take the casing into the office and leave it on the desk.

Simple.

Only nothing was ever simple.

That's one thing he'd learned over the past two hundred years.

Laoch took a deep breath. Prophecies had to be fulfilled to the letter. If they weren't, there would be consequences. The consequences had been murky, but Béil had seen something in the prophecy that made her afraid of ignoring it. She had seen Laoch in her vision there. Only he could fulfill the prophecy—and only he could screw it up.

So here he was, watching a parking lot. He spotted a bus stop across the street, and the sign listed six different bus numbers on it. That meant he could sit on the bench, and nobody would wonder why he let buses go by without getting on one for a while.

He sat and watched and waited. His legs were barely long enough for him to touch the ground. As he swung his feet, he made *scritching* sounds on the concrete with the toes of his boots. A small part of him wished he could be a full-sized man, but that was never going to happen. He was stuck in a boy's body forever, and it sometimes had its advantages.

Trucks went into the parking lot, but most were white or red instead of black. A black one pulled in and parked near the building, catching his interest. But when the driver got out, it was a woman. She also had a friend, and they both went into the Korean restaurant under the office he was supposed to watch.

"Do you have change for the bus?"

Laoch looked away from the parking lot to focus on the woman speaking to him. There was something wrong with her. She looked at him too straight on, and he could see her heartbeat racing under the skin on her neck. To Laoch, she might as well have been wearing a sign that said, "*I'm a liar. Don't trust me.*" That's how it worked for the Fae. Even for Halflings like Laoch.

To answer her question, he said, "No."

"Oh! You have a deep voice there for a little guy." The woman's smile did a lot to warm her face, but her eyes remained cold. He looked back at the parking lot and saw a woman with blond hair coming out of the second-floor office. The patterns and colors of her clothes were mismatched, but they looked expensive.

"Do you know where I can get change? I only have a ten." The woman next to him had her purse out, flipping through the cash pocket. She wanted something, Laoch could tell, but it wasn't change for the bus. He felt the muscles in his shoulders begin to tense and used that feeling as an excuse to shrug.

More people arrived in time to catch the bus that stopped in front of the bench. Laoch hoped the woman would get aboard and go away, but she didn't budge. The bus pulled away with a rising whine of its engine. Laoch felt a thrumming in his chest. How would it feel to control all that mechanical power? He had watched people driving many times and knew how it was done. He would like to try it someday.

A man with a week's worth of salt-and-pepper beard walked up to the bench. He had a black head wrap and a black leather jacket and scuffed up black boots. Laoch knew that the man's clothing was a uniform of sorts for men who rode motorcycles and got in fights. It seemed like this man must have lost his motorcycle and was stuck wearing his road gear to ride public transportation.

187

The man's leg bumped into Laoch's knee, and Laoch moved an inch away, putting him right up against the woman.

"That man looks scary," the woman whispered. She put her arm around Laoch in a mothering gesture, but there was no care to it. Laoch touched the woman's hand with his fingers.

"*D'intinn a oscailt*," he whispered. Loach closed his eyes. As he had commanded, the woman's mind opened inside his own. Her book of thoughts exploded, throwing pages skyward. The thoughts were dressed in different colors and sizes and shapes. They also offered different flavors, and he was drawn to the thoughts that tasted unsavory like acrid fear and bitter regret.

A page grew, became swollen, in front of his eyes. He saw children crowded together in corrugated metal warehouses assembling electronic devices and mean men and women holding shotguns. There was very little sound because the children weren't talking—weren't allowed. Their small tools made small clicking sounds under the hum of electric fans incapable of moving the thick air. Laoch also smelled the smells of unwashed bodies, vomit, and worse.

He pushed the page away, and it floated off.

Another page with a fresher tang drifted into view. A young woman crumpled in the corner of a small, dark room looked at him with large, sleepy eyes. She was close. She had plastic ties around her ankles and wrists, and a piece of cloth had been stretched across her mouth and tied around the back of her head. But it wasn't a room. It was a vehicle—the rear compartment of a van.

Laoch sifted through these thoughts in the space between heartbeats. He opened his eyes. As he released her mind, the Bus Change woman said, "*Hunh.*" It was more the sound of being hit in the gut than an actual word.

In his deep, mannish voice, Laoch said, "*Codail.*" Bus Change woman slumped against the back of the bench. Her head dropped forward, and her body went limp.

Laoch stood up and felt a tingle of dread down his spine, imagining the Bike Man making a grab for his arm or shoulder. Laoch hurried back across the street to wait in the parking lot. When he reached the opposite sidewalk, he chanced a look over his shoulder. Bike Man had taken the spot on the bench next to Bus Change, shaking her shoulder, trying to wake her up.

She wouldn't be awake for a while yet. Laoch tried not to smirk.

He chose a large palm tree and went around to stand behind it. Béil had told him more than once not to get involved in the affairs of mortals. She had told him to avoid contact with people here and to just do what she'd told him to do, as quietly as possible. She'd told him it was dangerous to deal with mortals. They were selfish and violent and untrustworthy.

She wasn't wrong.

She'd sent Laoch there to do a job he didn't understand because he could do it more effectively—and he'd been the one she'd seen in the prophecy. As an Eternal, she wasn't able to enter the mortal realm without being summoned, and it was highly unpleasant for her to be there. As a Halfling, Laoch could move between realms when he wanted. He found his Fae powers could be useful, but he didn't dismiss the mortal part of him. It was interesting, even though it made him more vulnerable than a full-blooded Fae.

He didn't understand why this errand needed to be done, but he understood the young woman, bound and gagged and barely able to raise her head, needed his help.

There was nobody else.

He could take care of this. He was Béil's best ranger. She said so all the time.

A black truck eased into the parking lot. From his vantage point behind the tree, Laoch saw that the driver was a middle-aged balding man, and Laoch's heartbeat quickened.

So it begins.

The truck eased into an empty spot on the far side of the lot, which was half empty. The driver stuck his head out the window, and the morning breeze caught the fringe of his hair, lifting it up as if a static charge had passed through the truck. After ducking back inside and sliding into the space between the seats, the man opened the window on the back of the cab. The truck had an extended cab and the man was overweight, so he had to catch his breath.

Laoch remained where he was. He had no trouble seeing both the man in the truck and the man in the office across the lot. The man in the office looked to be in his late twenties, but it was hard to see details. He had papers in his hand, and he sat on the edge of his desk. He got up and paced, then sat back down on the edge of his desk.

Turning his head, Laoch went back to watching the man in the truck. He felt anticipation growing as the bald man loaded the rifle and aimed it at the building. The muzzle of the rifle remained inside the cab, but only just. The bald man leaned back against the dashboard.

Laoch heard a *Pfft* sound that wasn't loud at all. The semi-automatic action ejected the casing as soon as the round was fired, and Laoch saw the brass fly up and bounce at an odd angle against the roof of the truck. He didn't know where it had gone, but it was still in the cab somewhere. A moment later, the glass front of the office across the lot shattered into a thousand sparkling pieces, instinctively, Laoch *had* to look. The pieces dropped in a wave, as if somebody had switched off the river above a waterfall. Laoch couldn't see the man in the office after the window exploded, and he wondered if the man was dead.

As the sound and sparkle stopped, Laoch turned his attention back to the Bald Man. He'd left the truck running and dropped the rifle onto the floor on the passenger side. Then he tried to turn around to sit in the driver's seat, but his girth made turning difficult in the small space and he got stuck. He scrabbled against the door to find the handle and opened the door so he could back out.

When the door opened, the casing fell out with a quiet *ping*.. It had apparently fallen between the door and the frame, which was lucky. Laoch realized he'd stopped breathing. Seeing the casing fall, he exhaled and a small measure of the tension in his gut drained away.

Bald Man turned and climbed back into the truck facing forward again. He threw it in reverse, backed out of the parking spot, and drove to the exit by the street. In seconds, he was gone.

Noise below the office grew louder with several voices.

The man in the office reappeared at the window, a look of stunned surprise plastered all over his face. Laoch felt as if he knew who the man was, although he was certain they'd never met before. He was glad the shooter had missed, but it would have been interesting either way.

Laoch found the brass casing, which had rolled against the gutter next to the curb. He picked it up and put it in his pocket. It was time for him to wait for the man in the office to leave.

Everything had happened so fast that Laoch had almost forgotten about the man and woman at the bus stop. He looked.

The bench stood empty.

Bike Man and Bus Change were both gone. Laoch wondered if they were working together, but he couldn't be sure. There was a girl somewhere nearby who needed his help. That much was certain, and she was important to Bus Change at least—either to her or to the people who ran the sweatshop full of children.

A short, ancient man came out of the Korean restaurant and looked up at the younger man in the second-floor office. They shouted back and forth for a minute, Office Man talking down through the window framed by broken glass. Laoch tried to keep an eye on the building while he scanned the area for signs of Bike Man or Bus Change. The old guy from the restaurant, Mr. Food, emerged with a big white paper bag and carried it around to the stairway. He climbed to the second floor and exchanged the bag for a few green bills.

Office Man was staying for lunch. Laoch's stomach rumbled, and he sighed. It didn't look like Office Man would be leaving soon. Through the fabric of his pocket, Laoch touched the brass casing to make sure he still had it.

Might as well look for the girl.

"*Léan air!*" he muttered. There were more vans than trucks in the parking lot. Some had plain sides, and others had the names of businesses painted on them. In Bus Change's book of thoughts he'd seen the girl in a dim space, so he ruled out the vans with lots of windows.

Laoch hesitated. Béil's mission had to be his first priority. If he failed to complete his task he'd rather fight a *deamhan* than tell her about it. And she would know if he lied.

A police car pulled into the parking lot. Laoch shied away from cops more than other mortals. He casually slipped back behind the tree and moved away, not running.

Worse than failing in his mission would be getting caught. The police used steel handcuffs and steel bullets, which contained iron. Iron had the power to permanently harm Fae and Halfling alike. Their jails had iron bars, and Laoch couldn't imagine the kind of pain he would experience if he were locked away, even for a minute.

He wanted to employ his glamour right then more than ever.

The red-and-blue rack of lights flashed on top of the police car, and scraps of color danced in the first-floor windows. Two patrolmen in uniform got out and started directing people away from the building. They'd parked across two handicapped spots right in front of the Korean restaurant. Mr. Food hurried out. His broad gestures and fast talking made it clear he wanted the policemen to move their car. They were scaring away his

192

customers. Laoch smiled. The old man wasn't afraid to stand up for himself.

The more senior of the two policemen put a sympathetic hand on the shoulder of the junior cop and left him to deal with the restaurant owner while the senior cop took the stairs to the second floor. Laoch continued walking to the far corner of the parking lot. The angle wasn't good, but he saw the policeman in the office and Office Man pointing to something. Laoch reasoned he was pointing at the bullet in the office wall.

A dark gray van had been parked in the far corner, and it gave Laoch something to walk toward instead of something to walk from. The van did have windows but they were heavily curtained, so the interior would be dark. Laoch held his breath. He wanted to look around to see if anyone was watching. He knew *that* would look suspicious, so he simply walked up to the windshield. Framing his eyes with his hands to cut down on the glare, he pressed his nose against the windshield and looked inside for the girl. He saw light gray seats and two benches, one behind the other.

Wrong van. He'd seen the girl in a darker place with no extra seats.

He looked around, like a child trying to find a parent. He had to be smart. If he went through the parking lot looking in the windows of all the vans, he'd be noticed for sure. Laoch guessed the policemen would certainly rather have a conversation with him about why he was checking windows than talk to Mr. Food.

He had to think like a kidnapper.

Kidnapping was a risky business, and stealing a child was only half the challenge. You had to keep your victim quiet until you could get away. So where in the lot would you park to keep your prize safe?

Laoch realized the answer. You wouldn't park in the lot at all.

His step and his pulse quickened as he moved to the side of the building. What if he was wrong? The girl would be gone forever. *And what if he was right?*

Almost panting, even at a walking pace, Laoch slipped into the shadows behind the office. A narrow alley extended all the way across the back, and a screen of thick trees gave the alley a deep olive-colored shade. The huge garbage bins behind the restaurant exuded an aromatic mixture of spice and rot.

Laoch stopped and listened.

No movement. No noise.

A small, pale ghost in a Renaissance shirt, Laoch felt more at home there than he did around the corner in the sun. Drifting from shadow to shade, he scanned the trees. He found a break, and his ranger skills alerted him to the grass that was knocked down in parallel tracks.

Like it had been run over by a van.

Senses sharp, Laoch slid soundlessly between the trees.

The van sat under the canopy of leaves like a squatting hen— plain, dark blue, dirty license plate, and no windows. The rear door opened with a twist of the handle. Peering through the space, Laoch could see the girl on the floor, her hair plastered against her face.

He heard the step of a boot on the grass and ducked. "C'mere you." A large hand swept over Laoch's head. It was Bike Man. Laoch scurried away from him and scampered around the van where Laoch dropped into a crouch and hissed.

"What d'you think you are? A cat? I don't know how, but you caused me a lot of trouble." Bike Man stalked forward. He had something sharp in his hand. A needle. "Still, I don't want to hurt you." *That* was a lie, and they both knew it.

"I don't want to hurt you either," Laoch said, his voice deep and plain and honest.

Bike Man stared. Maybe he thought he'd heard wrong, or maybe he thought Laoch was trying to be funny. He scowled and his boots landed heavy on the ground as he went after Laoch. Bike Man would have to use his free hand to catch Laoch before he could stab Laoch with the needle. Laoch would have a split second to defend himself, or he would end up bound and unconscious next to the girl.

Laoch backed away from the van, holding both hands up as if warding the big man off.

Bike Man snarled as he caught Laoch by the wrist. His grip was iron hard and cold. Adrenaline thrummed through the center of Laoch's being, and he pulled up a drop of power as he clapped his hand on the man's skin.

"Stad!"

Laoch flinched. The man had moved so fast. Laoch rolled his eyes down, shifting carefully to the side. A needle had stopped an inch away from his neck. A bead of liquid clung to the point of the needle and fell away.

Drip.

Bike Man must have been planning to inject that crap into Laoch.

Turnabout is fair Fae.

Laoch wove a new spell. Bike Man jammed the needle into his own leg and pushed the plunger.

Bike Man should have left Laoch alone.

Bike Man should leave *all* children alone.

Laoch put both hands on the man's head.

"Look at me," Laoch commanded. Bike Man turned his head and eyes to face Laoch.

"From now on, when you look at children, you will see their true faces," Laoch said, weaving more spells. "And you will know the same fear they feel seeing you."

Bike Man locked eyes with Laoch's eyes, and Laoch fed his power into a glamour, a very special glamour that would change his appearance from a little boy to something else entirely for the Bike Man to see. It would be something the Bike Man would never forget.

He made Bike Man see. Bike Man tried to scream, and Laoch let him go. The drugs overcame the man's body, and he slumped to ground between the trees. Laoch looked down on him and tried to remember the appropriate word in the mortal language.

Jerk.

Back in the van, Laoch put his hands on the girl's face. Her eyes were half open and her hair was clean, but her clothes were worn and in need of attention. Laoch closed his eyes. The girl's book of thoughts felt like it had been soaked in a thunderstorm and trodden on by a herd of horses. The pages didn't fly apart easily but clung to each other. None of them were rectangular or flat; they had ragged edges and rounded sides like clouds. The details drifted into each other, muzzy and incomplete. Nothing useful there to glean. He whispered. "You're going to be all right. Don't be afraid." He untied the gag and balled up the cloth. The girl's face relaxed, and her eyes finally closed all the way.

Outside, Bike Man hadn't moved, and Laoch didn't bother to go around him as he walked past. There was a very good chance that Laoch's boots met the man's face at least once, but he wasn't paying close attention.

Bus Change would still be sleeping, Laoch felt certain. He found her nearby, lying in the grass next to a fence.

With no time to waste, Laoch woke her up, removing the spell he had cast. He needed to remain in contact for his spells to work, so he kept his hand on her arm and made her drag Bike Man into the back of the van. She grunted under the strain, but Laoch refused to feel bad. When Bike Man was finally situated on the floor, Laoch made Bus Change go back to sleep.

His charges all resting, Laoch hurried back to the front of the building. The office appeared to be empty at last. He checked the parking lot and spied the Office Man putting a box in the back of a car. Office Man got in and drove away, music playing loudly.

It was Laoch's chance to complete his mission. To finish the prophecy.

He hurried past the restaurant and caught Mr. Food watching him from the corner of his eye. He hoped the old man wouldn't call the police. Not yet. He sped up the stairs and walked right through the empty window frame. For a moment, his heart caught in his throat as he felt for the bullet casing. It was in his pocket but had shifted to the other corner.

Laoch put the casing in the center of the oak desk.

With a sigh of accomplishment and relief, Laoch moved to the back of the office. He found a bathroom there. Nobody could see him there.

Full glamour time.

Laoch loved traveling in glamour, especially in the mortal realm. He opened his power and felt a tingle that covered him like a second skin.

Smiling, he strolled down the stairs. Mr. Food was watching but didn't pay any attention to him as he descended.

Cats don't buy food from restaurants.

The glamour would hold for as long as his internal reservoir of power didn't run out, which would be at least an hour. More than enough.

Laoch trotted to the back of the building. He found the keys to the van in Bus Change's purse. He'd watched people driving many times, after all. How hard could it be?

The van started with a rumble. Laoch couldn't sit on the seat because he was too short for his legs to reach the pedals. He found out how to move the seat back, so he could lean against it while getting his foot on the gas. The first gear was R and he tried it.

Perfect. The van moved backwards out of the trees. Laoch turned the steering wheel but went the wrong way at first. By the time he had corrected his direction, he had slammed into one of the garbage bins behind the restaurant. *Oh yes, the other pedal was for stopping.*

The gear marked *N* didn't seem to do anything so he tried *D.* The van rolled forward all by itself, gathering speed. Laoch laughed a deep and manly laugh. He took the corner too fast and turned too sharp. He remembered to step on the brake, but the van hit the side of the building with a crunch and the sound of breaking glass. Laoch guessed the headlight was in pieces. This was harder than it looked.

One more try.

Laoch straightened out and let up on the brake. The van rolled forward again. It would be ideal to stop the van in a parking space, like the other vehicles.

He could do this. He was Béil's best ranger *and* best driver. Okay, her *only* driver.

Tapping the brake, he guided the van toward an open space at a lurching but controlled pace.

Why did that car pull in front of me?

Both vehicles made crunching sounds, and Laoch decided he'd had enough.

The driver of the other car got out and yelled at him. "I had the right of way!" She stormed to the van pointing a well-manicured finger at him. Her expression faded from angry to unbelieving. She opened the driver-side door, her mouth creating a perfectly round *O.*

Laoch meowed. He moved quickly to the back of the van.

The woman turned to look at someone in her own car. "Did you see that?"

A second voice said, "No. What?"

"I think a *cat* was driving," the woman replied.

"You're kidding."

Laoch waited by the back door. It was very likely that his boots were on Bike Man's face again, but he wasn't really paying attention. That's what happens when you only *appear* to be a cat but you're still an old, little boy.

The back door opened tentatively, and Laoch pushed against it.

With a sharp breath, the woman saw the people on the floor and covered her mouth with her hands.

Laoch dropped to the parking lot and ran. The woman had more important things to worry about than a van-driving cat.

As he ran back to the trees where he could safely return to the realm of the Fae, he heard the woman say, "Call the cops."

Lucky day.

The Morrigan's Sister

The Story for the Behindbeyond Fans

If you purchased this short story collection because you found out about a new Behindbeyond story that was only available here, you're a true fan and I greatly appreciate your willingness to fall into my trap.

One of the most gratifying things for an author is when readers embrace the characters that the author worked so hard to bring to life. I get more messages from readers about the relationship between two of the main characters in the Behindbeyond series, Goethe and Erin, than anything else. That's really cool.

Their accidental marriage in book one, *Got Luck*, was a selling point when I was shopping the story around looking for a publisher. It was funny and romantic and led to even more complications in the sequels. Erin, also known as Fáidh in the realm of the Fae, is an independent woman who has learned to embrace her magic over the centuries of her life. In the mortal realm, however, she's already married but her husband has been missing for several years. She and Goethe know each other from their work in law enforcement for Miami-Dade County. Initially, neither of them are aware that the other is tied to the magic, and destiny, of both realms.

While I did write bits and pieces about their first meeting in the novels, I thought readers might like to read the full and juicy details about how they met. You don't need to have read any of the novels or stories to enjoy this tale though. Some liberties have been taken with agencies and procedures as well. I should also note that the Miami-Dade police department is separate from the Medical Examiner's office, but I have intentionally given them substantial overlap for the purposes of the story.

Finally, while Goethe is a solid presence in the story, this adventure is all Erin's.

The Morrigan's Sister

Erin's job wasn't to collect evidence. Analyze it, certainly.
Categorize it. Take it apart. Figure out where it had been and who
had left it, yes. But collecting material was a crime scene
investigator's job. Standing over a discarded pen near the body, she
looked around for the closest employee of Miami-Dade law
enforcement.

"Hey." The patrolman was making notes in a small, black pad
of paper, but he wasn't talking to anyone. Most likely he was
recording details that he'd need for his report later. He could finish
that some other time. Erin needed him now. Louder, she tried
again. "Hey. You. Officer Scribbles."

The uniform didn't look up from his pad, but he started
moving in her direction. He'd heard her, at least, but remained
focused on his current task. Erin liked how he finished his train of
thought but wasn't ignoring her while he put a period on it.

He looked up when he got close to her. Broad shoulders. Six feet tall. A rebellious lock of hair jutting from beneath the brim of his patrolman's cap. Intense eyes.

He was cute.

She opened her mouth, but he edged her out in asking a question, "Do you know how to spell angiolymphoid hyperplasia with eosinophilia?"

Surprised by the question, Erin momentarily forgot she had her own job to do. "Is there a reason you need to spell that?"

"At the moment?" the uniform shrugged. Broad shrug. "I feel like it would be impressive to walk up to a crime scene, glance at a murder victim, and say, 'it looks like he died from angiolymphoid hyperplasia with eosinophilia.'"

Erin folded her arms, shifting her stance sideways while keeping her feet astride the evidence on the ground. "You think that would be impressive?" She felt herself grinning just a bit. Most of the humor, if not all, at the medical examiner's office was the gallows kind.

"I think so. Maybe."

"Well, that disease causes nodules on the side of the head or neck, which aren't lethal. So, in my professional opinion, I guess I'd have to agree. Neck nodules aggressive enough to kill a person would be rather impressive."

"Ah." The officer nodded sagely.

"And how did such a lengthy and obscure phrase end up in your vocabulary?" Erin felt the need to get to work, but she couldn't resist asking.

"That is a lengthy and obscure story," he replied. "You're from the medical examiner's office, right?"

"I am." Erin let her eyes stray. "And I'd appreciate it if you could take over babysitting this piece of evidence for me. I'm supposed to be looking at a body."

The officer grinned, giving a tiny nod as Erin realized she'd said "looking at a body" while looking at his body. He started, "Um, you didn't—."

"Nope." Erin cleared her throat, which somehow came out sounding defensive. "That." She pointed at the pen on the ground and moved away at a brisk clip, heat rising in her face.

So dumb, Fáidh.

Fáidh was Erin's name in The Behindbeyond. She was only called Erin here, in the mortal realm. In the other realm, and in her thoughts, she habitually called herself Fáidh.

The corpse provided a welcome distraction by just lying there, face down on the sidewalk, a moat of blood surrounding her in the night shadows.

This was the work Erin had been born to do.

Slipping under the yellow police tape, Erin felt like she was entering a realm of her own. A place where she was the sole sovereign, built on the bones of death and tragedy. It was a place of chaos now, but she would turn it to a place of order. A place of justice. This was her calling. Her kingdom had a living subject as well, a crime scene photographer taking shots of the body from different angles. Erin was content to wait.

She didn't need to take notes. Her memory was excellent, and she would have access to the photographer's book later, if she needed it. Instead, she assessed the condition of the body from where she stood. Young woman. Stylish skirt and blouse. She was lying with her face in the street and her arms underneath her, as if she'd been clutching something against her chest when she'd fallen. Her face was turned partially to the side, but her hair had cascaded around her features. She'd been wearing black pumps; one had fallen off, but the other had stayed on her foot. Other than her fashion sense and a pair of shapely, athletic legs, the girl was an enigma.

The photographer took a step back. It looked like he was winding up. Erin put her supply case on a clean patch of ground and got out a pair of nitrile gloves to put on and shoe coverings for her heels.

"Need any help?" The photographer stuck his chin out toward the corpse.

"No. I got her." Erin walked around the pool of blood. She was going to disturb the scene whether she liked it or not so she picked a spot where she could move the girl's hair off her face and then turn her on her back after without shifting her feet. For someone in the medical examiner's office, the credo "first do no harm" applied to the scene as much as the person.

The coppery tang of the girl's blood rose into Erin's nostrils as she knelt. Blood and floral shampoo and something more chemical. Bleach.

Erin wondered about the bleach, but first things first. She carefully reached across the girl's face and drew back her hair. The flash from the photographer's camera punctuated the dark. He shifted to another angle and took a few more shots.

"All right," he said.

Erin put a hand on the girl's shoulder and the other under her back so that she'd roll gently. The photographer snapped more photos as she turned the girl. Erin squeezed her eyes shut against the flashes. She opened them when she heard the photographer swear.

"What?" Erin asked.

The photographer held the bulky camera vertically while he pointed with the other hand. "Look."

Erin glanced down and nearly swore herself.

The girl's hands were those of a man.

Erin stood and stepped backwards, away from the poor girl's body. She wasn't going to be working on this case after all. This case would go to her boss.

* * *

The press called him the Popsicle Killer. The girl Erin had gone out to examine was the fourth victim. The words "Popsicle Killer" had made the lead story on the evening news after the second girl had been found. The last girl, the one a week ago, had ended her life much like the two girls before her. All the girls had experienced amputations of some kind. Arms or legs had been severed from their bodies and someone else's limbs had been attached. The surgeries were poorly done. Hasty. Parts hung together with uneven stitches made with kitchen string and a heavy needle, like one used for patching canvas cloth.

Then there were the popsicle sticks. Like the ones before, the young woman on the ground was clutching familiar thin sticks with rounded ends in hands that were not her own. There was some color on the sticks. Red. Near the end, each stick had a letter written on it. Black gel pen, according to the previous reports.

Erin's assessment had been decidedly limited and unsatisfactory. She stood with her arms folded and waited. The crowd around the crime scene came and went, cycling through shapeless waves of different faces. She checked the area for the handsome patrolman and found he'd already gone. A green pen had been collected by the crime scene investigators as well.

She knew her boss would be arriving when the cameras came, surrounding the scene. As sure as Florida grows citrus, the crowd of lenses grew denser every time he was about to show up. He'd probably called the local stations from his house to make sure they'd be here. Finally, the man himself, Sherwood Belknap, Chief Medical Examiner, pulled up in his black Cadillac Escalade. He drove toward the dead girl slowly beneath the streetlamps, threading though the law enforcement vehicles and muscling his way into the collection of reporters, forcing a few to move back. As if he couldn't be bothered to walk a few extra steps. Really, it was all for show. Belknap liked pushing people around, in his SUV or out.

Erin didn't bristle at his approach. It had taken practice to not bristle.

"So. The Popsicle Killer strikes again?" He didn't bother saying hello to Erin, shaking her hand, or even looking at her. "Gloves?"

He didn't bother to bring his own kit either.

Erin offered him a fresh pair of gloves with a pleasant, "Here you go, sir."

He offered no thanks in return. Erin was accustomed to this, although never expressing gratitude was more of a thing in the land of the Fae.

Belknap walked around the body, making a show for the news cameras. The crime scene photographer had waited as well. Belknap motioned him around, pointing at a spot on the body and making him take photos where he requested. The new photos wouldn't be any better than the ones the photographer had gotten earlier, but the snapper knew it would be politically idiotic to ignore Sherwood Belknap.

The show continued. Belknap finished rolling the girl onto her back. Erin would have had a CSI bag the girl's hands first—or whoever's hands they were—since they were holding the popsicle sticks. With the girl lying supine, Belknap tugged on her blouse. He undid a button so he could pull the blouse far enough that her shoulder would be exposed. Erin knew he wanted to check the stitching and confirm the arm had been sewn onto her shoulder. Personally, she would have waited. The M.E. lab was the place for a detailed examination. Not a patch of sidewalk off the side of a busy street late at night.

The arm started slipping. Erin put her hand to her mouth but didn't say anything. She prayed the arm would stay in place—nope.

208

The arm slipped. The meaty hand opened. The popsicle stick dropped into the blood, contaminated.

Erin fished her phone out of her pocket. When Belknap saw where the stick was, he'd look up to see if she'd noticed. She didn't want to be caught noticing.

As she focused intently on her important emails and phone messages, commonly referred to as "spam," she saw Belknap in her peripheral vision. He saw the fallen stick and quickly picked it up. Thank the stars he was wearing gloves. He motioned for a CSI tech who brought him an evidence bag. He dropped the stick into the bag and, for good measure, snatched up the second one and dropped it into the same bag.

When we are born, we cry that we have come to this stage of fools.
You and me both, Shakespeare.

She gazed at her phone, wishing almost for a different dead body somewhere else so she could get away from here. But that was not a charitable thought and she shoved it down.

We make record of the dead that we might protect the living.
Unless we mess it up.

She inhaled, taking the night air into her lungs and loading it up with her frustrations before pushing everything out together in a long stream. She watched her boss, glad he was doing everything correctly now, giving passive support in case he noticed. And praying he wouldn't mess up again.

He motioned for the ambulance crew to come pick up the body. When he headed for the knot of television reporters, Erin took her cue.

She slipped off her gloves and the shoe covers from her heels and put them in her pocket so she could dispose of them later. She closed her kit and checked all around her to make sure she wasn't leaving any trace behind.

* * *

Before bed, Erin had a smoothie with kale and pineapple to counteract the Cheetos dinner she'd eaten in the car on the way home. She hadn't had time for anything solid that evening, but she'd been too tired to stop for something else. As she'd driven, with her car stereo cranking out The Go-Gos and The Bangles, she'd thought about the poor girl on the grass, the latest victim of the Popsicle Killer.

The name was patently stupid. Popsicle Killer. The perpetrator was killing girls, not popsicles.

Frustrated, tired, and belly-junked, she slipped between the cotton sheets in her little bungalow. Alone, restless, she felt her house hulking and cavernous around her although it wasn't really that big. She thought about the broad-shouldered patrolman, comparing him favorably against her boss in following procedure, and resuming the frequent musing that her house wasn't the sum of all the emptiness in her life.

Erin rolled on her side, turning toward the photograph on her nightstand. A pale moon cast ghosts through her curtained window, and the gray shades were reflected in the glass of the photo frame. She reached out, barely able to prod the corner of the frame with her fingertip. Nudging, she poked the frame to a better angle to see the subjects of the photograph.

Herself, with a bright smile and a sunburn stripe across her nose and cheeks, with her arms around her husband, Blake. He'd been gone for three years now. Three years and a couple of months. Vanished without a trace.

* * *

The body of the girl had arrived and identification made by the time Erin walked into the Medical Examiner's office in Miami. She was early for her shift. Not unusual although the fact that she'd slept poorly contributed.

The body was covered by a white sheet, awaiting autopsy. A stainless-steel table ran the length of the near wall, and the bags of evidence and preliminary crime scene reports were strewn across it as if they'd been dumped out of a box and shuffled. Perhaps they had.

The first page of a medical examiner's report sat on top. It didn't have much information yet. The victim's name, Michelle H. Leonhard, and her boss's name, Sherwood Belknap. It wasn't so much a report as it was Belknap's way of marking his territory. If he'd been a dog, he would have peed on the paper instead of writing his name in a long, angular scrawl in the box labeled "Lead Examiner."

While putting her lab coat on, Erin had an idea. And while she approached the table of Michelle's evidence, she decided she'd do it.

There weren't many moments of panic-verging excitement in a medical examiner's day. The clients didn't tend to offer much in the way of resistance. In fact, preparing to steal evidence was the first time she'd been legitimately nervous, as far as Erin could remember. She felt her pulse throbbing in her throat as she pretended to stroll past the evidence. There were cameras in the room, under Belknap's control, of course.

She'd have to be sly.

Well, she was fifty-percent Fae, after all.

Another thought came to mind. She started sorting the evidence, taking the jumbled pile of bags and ordering them along the table.

Putting chaos into order.

While arranging the evidence, she looked for the bag holding the popsicle sticks. She didn't have a right to mess with the sticks, but they weren't going to be admissible evidence anyway. Not if Belknap had been honest about his error.

Efficiently, working as if the case was her own, she put the evidence in groups. She saw she was reaching the last few bags and about to conclude that Belknap had thrown it out. There was a swatch of cloth with a discolored patch, which would be trace. A swab of blood taken off the ground, which was biological evidence. And a folder with the testimonies of witnesses from the scene.

There.

The popsicle sticks were almost at the bottom of the stack, as if they were ashamed to be seen. The bag had been unsealed already and it looked like there was no blood on the popsicle sticks any longer.

Great. He washed them off. Making the situation worse.

Wait.

This is great for me.

She felt the cameras pointing down at her. They'd only see her back, she was sure. With an electric thrill of a criminal act on her mind, she slipped the bag with the popsicle sticks under her lab coat and pinched it under her arm.

Realizing it would look suspicious to walk away without finishing what she'd started, she continued organizing the rest of the chaos.

She found a bag of evidence with a pen and recognized it as the evidence she'd called Officer Scribbles to watch. The evidence had the CSI's name on it along with the name of the officer who had stood like a hen over it for her. Patrolman Goethe Luck.

Good job, Luck. But Goethe? Mean parents.

With everything sorted, she resisted the urge to run from the room with her prize. Instead, she double-checked everything on the table to make sure it was laid out with logic and clarity. Belknap would come in sooner or later and, hopefully, would understand what she had done. Maybe even appreciate it.

Satisfied, she made for the ladies' room. She didn't walk fast. Just purposefully. And when she was finally in a stall, all alone, she retrieved the evidence bag and reopened it. The popsicle sticks were there. Ready for her spell as she sat on the toilet.

Erin didn't use her power often. Not in the office. She'd worked hard to learn her job and she wanted to do it well. By mortal rules. Mortal processes. She could make it easier on herself, perhaps, by cheating. In all honesty, she enjoyed the challenge of doing things the way humans did. Doing her job by relying on the skills she'd worked so hard to acquire year after year at the university.

Samantha Stephens was her role model.

Today was different.

She took a deep breath. The popsicle sticks rested in her palm. She covered them with her other palm and pulled up a drop of power from her core. Her hands glowed blue. All that remained was the word of command, in this case "See" in the language of the Fae. She closed her eyes and said, "*Feic.*"

The spell opened images in her mind. She caressed the popsicle sticks lightly, winding her way into the past. By moving her touch, she moved back and forth through the history of the sticks.

In mortal terms, her gift was called "psychometry" or the ability to see images, smells, sounds—everything about where the sticks had been, who had touched them, what had happened in their vicinity. At first, the rush of information in her mind's eye was like a slap in the face. Too many details. She knew it was going to happen, but she gasped nonetheless. Filtering out the unimportant details was the hardest part.

Erin waded through the cacophony, shoving aside the dross to refine her vision. She found the crime scene written into the history of the sticks. She smelled the blood that had been on them. Felt the air, weighted following an earlier rain. She moved forward; she saw Belknap washing the sticks, making her annoyed. Sliding her fingers over the sticks, she went backward and saw poor Michelle with the sticks in her dead hands.

She paused. Her murder might be recorded here. The girl's death and her dismemberment.

Erin wasn't sure she wanted those feelings and images in her head.

She skipped backwards in time, avoiding the horrific details of the murder as best she could. She couldn't help but catch snatches of screams and a chemical smell that burned her nose, however briefly.

There. What?

Oh my . . .

The scene in her mind hit her on a visceral level. Thinking, feeling, civilized people could only react with revulsion at the tableau offered up from the sticks.

Erin swallowed. She could end her spell and stop seeing what she was seeing, if she wanted. It would be an act of self-preservation, because she knew these images would live again in her nightmares and the longer she lingered . . . she had to linger. This wasn't just a criminal case; it was an insult to humanity.

The room was unfurnished. Industrial. Concrete walls with ductwork in the ceiling. Garlands in different colors, mostly silver and gold, hung from the ducts and from wiring, or just dangled from strings. Those things gave no offense. The arms hanging from the ceiling did.

Erin didn't get a real number. She could only guess how many arms had been strung along with the garlands, but there were many. Painted nails on some of them identified them as women's arms, but they would all turn out to be female, she could feel it. On the other end of some detached limbs, a raw, red stump. Bits of bone sticking out. Others had been hanging longer. Flies buzzed around the blackened edges, the flesh well into the stages of decay.

The smell was overpowering.

Erin coughed. Choked on the cough. She didn't stop looking though. She couldn't. There were more clues. Body bags on the floor. The corpse of a man with his arms removed. Erin shied away.

Popsicle sticks laid out on a table. Not a clean stainless-steel table like the examiner's lab. A dirty table with peeling paint and stains of various colors. Some of the colors would be melted popsicles, perhaps. Lime green, orange, yellow, red. Some of the colors were less thin and certainly blood.

The only orderly thing in the room was the row of sticks with their letters already printed on their ends in neat handwriting. The rest of the scene was a haphazard disaster of evidence. Suddenly, Erin knew what the letters on the popsicle sticks meant.

She roused herself, lifting her fingers off the little pieces of wood. Little pieces of wood holding enormous secrets.

"Are you all right in there?" A woman's voice floated over the top of the stall door. "Hello?"

"I'm fine."

"I saw a light and you sounded like you were choking."

Erin froze. The light of her magic had been bright enough to notice. Her mind reached for a logical excuse. At least Halflings had advantages over Fae. Erin could lie. "I'm just—it's a video someone sent to my phone. One of those videos that looks all tranquil and then something jumps out at you at the end and scares the crap out of you."

Actually, that wasn't much of a lie.

The woman chuckled. "Well. You're in a good place to have the crap scared out of you."

Erin put her hands over her face.

How do I always get myself . . . ?

She sighed and waited for the woman to leave. The popsicle sticks went back into the evidence bag and when the bathroom was clear, she tucked the bag under her arm again, washed her hands, and went back to the lab.

Another shock awaited.

Belknap.

And he'd brought company.

The tainted/tampered/stolen evidence burned a hole in her armpit as she walked toward her boss and the woman standing beside him. The guest seemed to be very solicitous, hanging on his every word, touching his arm, smiling wide enough to activate her dimples after every other sentence.

With all the professional objectivity of a medical examiner, Erin hated her at first sight.

She had to get the evidence bag back on the table. She had to do so in front of her boss, an eyewitness, and the cameras. All the while, the images she retained of suspended arms threatened to float again across her vision.

Belknap escorted his guest to the table where the record of Michelle's crime scene was laid out. "Here is all the evidence collected from the scene of the Popsicle Killer's latest murder." He looked at the row of materials and Erin sensed he was at a loss to understand what she'd done.

Shoving aside her memories of bloody stumps, Erin stepped in. "Good morning, sir."

Belknap turned at her interruption, a flash of annoyance making his eyes tense.

Erin went on. "As you requested, I grouped the evidence by biological," she pointed to the left and moved to her right, moving her hand to punctuate each group, "physical, trace, eyewitness, and so on." There was a box, now empty at the far-right end. Erin slipped the bag with the popsicle sticks out of her armpit and into the box. In the same motion, she caught the top of the box and pivoted around to show it to Belknap. "I wasn't sure where you wanted this. Is it trace or physical evidence? What do you think?"

Belknap reached into the box and brought out the evidence bag with the popsicle sticks. Of course, he couldn't resist the chance to be the expert. "I think physical. Not trace."

"Good," Erin said.

He added it to the trace pile anyway.

"Hi." Belknap's guest inserted herself into the conversation, drawing out the word as long as possible and sticking her hand in front of Erin. "I'm Katie Castellanos. I'm working on the Popsicle Killer story for WSFN, Channel 7. Are you working on the case?"

Erin give Katie's hand a brief shake and let go. "Nope. I'm only helping so the chief can get this case solved. Nice to meet you."

She retreated to the safe harbor behind her desk and put her head between her hands. Her office was her sanctuary.

Oh. What have I gotten myself into?

She had information in her head, but she couldn't talk about it to anyone. Not here. No one in Miami knew she was a Halfling Fae with magical powers. The Alder King was very clear about the separation between the Fae and mortal realms. Fae and Halfling were never allowed to talk about their gifts or use them in any public way outside the kingdom. Punishments for doing so were severe, even for minor offenses.

Women were dying. More were going to die if she didn't do something.

There was one person she could talk to. Keeper. After work, she'd go to The Behindbeyond and ask for his advice. If anyone could steer her in the right direction, he could.

Having a plan, tentative though it was, helped her focus on work somewhat. She had a report to finish on her last autopsy, which meant she could stay entrenched in her office for a few hours. The case centered on an elderly man who had possibly been poisoned. An alleged poisoning wasn't as messy as a dismemberment, at least, but the images she'd gleaned from the popsicle sticks remained in the shadowed edges of her concentration. And the words spelled out by the remaining popsicle sticks on that dirty table, implying there would be at least eleven more murders before the killer was done.

She typed her notes, listening to the recordings she had made in the autopsy lab. Her own voice turned out to be more soothing than her own thoughts. If she'd wanted, she could have someone else make the transcription, but doing it herself let her focus on the details that might help a family in crisis, waiting to get results. Answers that might change their lives and bring them peace. And keep herself distracted.

For a while, it worked.

The preliminary observations weren't noteworthy. In checking her email, toxicology reports indicated no concerns either. Erin felt the eighty-nine-year-old man had died peacefully in his sleep. There had been no foul play and, therefore, the insurance company would have to pay the man's family the two-million-dollar insurance policy.

Well. Score one for the family.

Erin had managed to keep herself busy for a few hours, at least. It hadn't been glamorous work, but it had kept her busy. Now, it was lunchtime. She hung her lab coat and grabbed her purse. Katie Castellanos was in Belknap's office now. She heard her laugh through the door and saw her chestnut fall of hair through the blinds of his office window.

She felt like walking instead of driving. The rhythm of her heels on the concrete beat a brisk *tap-tap-tap-tap* pace as she went. There was a Peruvian café within a few blocks that served ceviche and mariscos which sounded absolutely delicious today. The fresh air helped her clear her mind. The café wasn't crowded, and, as she settled in with a plate of warm shrimp and calamari, she couldn't help thinking the worst.

The next victim might be dying right now.

Well, crap.

The savory flavors in her mouth went dry and tasteless.

She wasn't an investigator. If she were, maybe the possibility of another victim losing her life at any moment would have occurred to her sooner. Worrying only about those who had already passed away had become ingrained in her. Four years of clientele that were past feeling were difficult to think around. She felt guilty about enjoying a meal while another victim was out there, being prepared for death.

Geez. How do cops do this?

Part of her realized she was going overboard. Her heart told her she was right to be worried, but her brain told her she didn't have enough data to do anything practical.

Yet.

She took a breath and a mental step back. What she needed was enough information to give her worry a direction to follow. She wished she knew if the killer had a schedule. Were the victims always murdered on the same day of the week? Or a certain phase of the moon?

Walking back to the office, she decided to finish up work early. Belknap wouldn't even notice, if his "guest" was still hanging off his arm. She wasn't sure why Belknap was giving Katie Castellanos an exclusive interview, but—if she had to guess—the reasons were probably dimple related. The woman knew how to use her looks and chirpy voice to get what she wanted. A lot of successful women did. And Belknap had to know what she was up to. His wife was fifteen years younger than him. So. He had to know.

Not that Erin would ever judge.

In her profession, her looks seemed to be more of a hindrance.

She walked purposefully past Belknap's office. He'd ordered food for himself and the television girl, and they traded conversation with smiles while they traded orange chicken with chopsticks.

Must be Katie's day off. Good.

She checked her emails. She checked the lab. Then she checked out.

On her way home, she bought salt.

Creating a portal to The Behindbeyond could be done by a handful of methods. There were places with permanent access to the realm of the Fae, but the nearest one was a long drive from here and Erin didn't have time. The fastest method used blood, but blood was (on a normal, personal level) unsanitary and sticky and gross. There were ways to open portals with water, and her powers included water spells, but those took a long time. Cleanup, at least, didn't require much more than a bucket and a mop. A ring of silver could be embedded in the floor. Different patterns—also made of silver—could be fitted into the ring to take her to as many different places as she could afford. That option was very costly. One day, she hoped she'd be able to have that luxury.

The best method, then, was a circle of salt. Three containers of salt and a few other objects with a drop or two of blood and access was granted, as long as you had magic.

Erin used the second bedroom in her bungalow for portal making. The rest of her house was decorated with memorabilia from film noir, like posters of Humphrey Bogart and an old projector that didn't work, but this room had only a hardwood floor and plenty of space.

She changed her clothes first and bound her hair in a long ponytail that hung down the center of her back, keeping the burnished locks out of her face. The pattern for her destination had been set in her memory for decades. There weren't many places she liked to go.

In slacks and a blouse and bare feet, she poured a circle of salt onto the floor, roughly her height in diameter. She used more salt to create the interlocking pattern she needed for her destination: *Corrchnámhach*, the Keeper's Inn called, in English, The Angle. She arranged the other items on the symbols she'd drawn at the four points of the compass. A feather for air in the north. Stone for earth in the south. A silver cup of water for water to the west. A lit candle for fire to the east. While the drawings of the symbols were sufficient, the concrete symbols added stability. She had blood as well, which had to be real. Three vials from the medical examiner's office. They would have been evidence if needed but had been marked for incineration after the cases were closed, so she hadn't taken evidence. Not really. Human blood was required, essence of beings with a soul, but it didn't need to be her own. The vials were kept hidden in a plastic bag which was itself kept in a carton of milk that Erin had no intention of drinking.

She broke one of the vials and let seven drops of blood fall at different points around the circumference of her salt circle, spaced about 52 degrees apart. Then, kneeling at edge of the circle, she touched a silver knife to the salt and pulled up a droplet of her power. It sat like a glowing blue pearl in her hand. Finally, ready to go, she said the word "Open" in Fae, "*Oscailte.*"

A shaft of light leapt from her hand, crackling and coruscating around the salt and closing on the silver blade with a boom that rattled the windows. A column of pale blue light streamed up to the ceiling as the circle and the design inside it solidified. The spaces between began to fade, as though the hardwood were turning to glass. When the wood had evaporated, the circle pivoted down as if the silver knife were a hinge.

The fragrant air of another world drifted into Erin's room. She inhaled the glorious blend of wildflowers and spruce trees and grass left to grow tall mingled with a breeze at least twenty degrees cooler than the heat of a South Florida afternoon.

Erin smiled. She loved The Behindbeyond, and she loved the magic that could take her there.

In a metaphysical sense, The Behindbeyond existed at a ninety-degree angle to the mortal realm. Creating a portal from realm to realm resulted in a view that was vertiginous to the uninitiated.

Erin stood at the edge of the hole in her floor and stared down at the sideways world beneath her feet. She thought the same thing she always thought when she was about to enter The Behindbeyond.

Whee!

She tilted forward, her toes hanging over empty air, falling into the perpendicular land of magic and wonder. As she fell, the gravity of the mortal realm surrendered to the gravity of the Fae realm. Instead of continuing a fall, her momentum turned to forward motion and she simply walked onto the grass in front of her. Easy.

It was a little bit later in the day here. The sun was already nearing the horizon, and Erin's shadow across the greensward was long.

The Angle was a crossroads, not only between the realms but also because multiple ley lines intersected at its heart. Few places in the universe had so much arcane power focused on it, and magical creatures from everywhere were drawn here.

Erin felt little eyes on her as she walked toward the inn. A family of hares perched on top of a boulder nestled just within the margin of the forest. One of the gray ones gave a yawn as if bored of seeing yet another human and Erin—or Fáidh here—saw his short fangs and his tiny antlers. These weren't hares, then. They were *wolpertingers*. Traditionally found in the Bavarian forest, they were shy around humans and rarely seen. With a smile, Erin walked quietly closer until the mother turned and dashed into the trees, her offspring fluttering off to follow on short, powerful wings.

Her smile continued to the door of the inn. When she opened the door and stepped inside, her smile fell away.

She'd never seen *Corrchnámhach* so quiet.

Or quiet at all.

From the planks of the floor to the section of open roof, all was still. There were patrons present. Human, animal, and hybrid too, but all sat solemnly at their tables with their meals and drinks or perched in the rafters, looking down with round eyes.

Keeper came forward. One of Fáidh's favorite people in all the worlds.

He was layered with white whiskers and hair. His arms were almost covered in fur. Tufts of hair sprouted from his shirt to curl over the top of his apron. A white beard decorated the line of his chin while a wide, wavy moustache highlighted his lip. Bushy eyebrows hovered over his sparkling eyes, and above a patch of forehead, he was crowned with a thick crop of hair.

Arms wide, he welcomed Fáidh with a hug. "Ah, lass. I've been waitin' for ya."

"Good to see you, Keeper." She gave him a squeeze. "Why do I feel like I'm walking into a funeral?"

"'Tis not so dire as all that, lass. But history is movin' upon us an' there're things ya ought to know." He put a hand on Faidh's shoulder, as solid as a steel clamp, but his touch was gentle as he led her to a quiet corner. He bade her take a seat and left her alone for a moment. From the corner of her eye, she saw other patrons glancing her way, curious.

She was curious as well.

Moments passed and Keeper returned, bearing a plate and a pewter mug. "Ya hav'na had dessert yet," he said as if he knew. He always brought food for Fáidh when she visited and always seemed to know what she needed.

Fáidh sipped from the mug. It was a sparkling juice of some kind, sweet and fruity. On the plate were rolled pastries with a strawberry filling, somewhere between cannoli and crêpes. Keeper proffered a fork and waited while Fáidh sampled the dish.

"Mmm!" Fáidh smiled. "Delicious!"

Keeper grunted softly and nodded as she attacked the food on her plate. He said, "I've something to show you. You're familiar with the *triskele*?"

Around a mouthful of dessert, Fáidh replied, "It's an old symbol of the Fae. Three spirals, joined together in the middle, right?"

"Aye. Got it in one. How familiar are you with *ogham* sticks?"

"The alphabet of the trees," Fáidh replied. "Found carved onto stones in the mortal realm as well as the Fae. On sticks though, they're used for divination."

"Hm," Keeper grunted. "Next time I have a need for a history teacher, I'll be callin' ya." He smiled. He unrolled a scroll with his thick fingers. There was the symbol of the *triskele* at the top, followed by three rows of *ogham* beneath it. "One of the king's retinue has an unusual talent for the *ogham*."

By "retinue," Fáidh knew Keeper meant "concubines." She didn't comment.

"Her ladyship brought this to me," Keeper said. "She asked what she should do."

Fáidh shrugged. "You've always advised me well."

Keeper continued. "In three separate readings of the *ogham*, she got the same symbols. Under the *triskele*, the readings indicate that the spiritual, physical, and celestial futures are aligned."

Fáidh looked closer at the scroll. "What does it predict?"

"The house of the Alder King will be preserved by the sister of The Morrigan."

Fáidh blinked. "The Morrigan? Goddess of Death?" She caught the implication then. "I work with the dead, so I'm the sister of The Morrigan. That's what she thinks it means."

"I agree with her, lass. Of all the Fae and Halflings I know, 'tis you fits the bill." Keeper sat in a chair. He was short though. Almost as tall sitting as standing. "Now, before anythin' else, what have ya come to ask? Ya have questions writ across your brow like a banner."

She told Keeper everything. The series of murders. The popsicle sticks in the victims' hands. The psychometry results she'd gotten, showing a room with women's arms dangling from the ceiling, the male corpses, and the row of popsicle sticks on the dirty table.

"There were sticks missing from the message. The killer wants us to figure it out eventually, so he's putting sticks in the hands of the victims for us to find. But it wasn't hard to see what the message was." Fáidh studied her fingers. She'd finished her dessert and didn't know what to do with her hands.

"What is the message, lass?" Keeper urged.

Fáidh replied in a hushed tone. "Deck the halls with boughs of holly." After finally saying the words out loud, her thoughts tumbled in a rush. "Obviously, the song is talking about the boughs from a holly tree, but it doesn't really mean that. 'Boughs' is a synonym for 'limbs' and 'limbs' is a synonym for 'arms.' The killer is playing a joke, I'm sure of it. That's why he's cutting the arms off the girls and hanging them from the ceiling. How he came to think of something so disturbing is a different question." She paused to catch her breath. "That's bad enough, but he's not done. There are more popsicle sticks to deliver. More girls to kill. And I suspect the last one will be named Holly." Fáidh took a deep breath. And another one. Her eyes were hot, and she was shaking.

Keeper waited, patient.

"I'm not an investigator." Fáidh kept breathing. Deeply sighing between sentences. "But this twisted . . . freak . . . is out there. And I'm scared. I was so upset by everything I saw that I stopped looking. It's not the dead bodies—that's my job. What makes me upset is thinking about the victims he *hasn't* killed yet. What might happen to them." She paused. Then, "I should have kept looking. I should have kept looking until I saw his face."

"Don't be too hard on yerself, lass." Keeper's voice was soothing. "'Twasn't anythin' ya trained for. Or wanted. It had to be a shock to ya."

"I know what I have to do." Fáidh clenched her fists and let her fingernails dig in. "I have to find out who the killer is. Then I have to find a way to get the information to someone who can investigate."

"Are ya certain?"

"I won't be able to forgive myself if another girl dies. Not when I have information that could stop it. That's what I can do, at least. I can't get in the middle of the investigation, but I can help."

Keeper nodded. "Be careful. The *ogham* didn't say the sister has to *meet* The Morrigan."

Fáidh's laugh came out as a stress-relieving burst. "I'm not going to die, Keeper."

He gave her hand a pat and stood up from his seat. "See that ya don't."

"I might lose my job. Maybe get arrested. You're sure this will help the Alder King?"

Keeper nodded. "Don't know how, but it feels aright."

"Strange how often things happen in one realm affect another." Fáidh didn't thank Keeper for his help. The Fae never expressed gratitude—or regret. Halflings didn't either. Instead she asked, "Any other sage words of advice?"

Keeper looked at her from beneath his snowy eyebrows, his eyes like chips of ice. "Be sure he's caught on the first try. That kind 'o filth doesn't get a second chance."

Goosebumps crawled down Fáidh's spine like a line of marching beetles. She shivered.

"Stand by, lass." Keeper pointed one stubby finger upward. "I'll return in a moment." He moved off through the diners and drinkers with more agility than a short old guy should be able to.

226

Thankfully, no one seemed to be staring at her any longer either and everyone in the inn had returned to finishing their meals.

More deep breaths. Fáidh stood and brushed imaginary crumbs and wrinkles out of her clothes. Steeling herself for her return to the mortal realm. Moments later, Keeper returned, bearing a pretty little pendant on a silver chain. He put the necklace around Fáidh's neck. She pulled her hair out of the way, and when it was settled, she lifted the pendant to admire it.

"What a beautiful gift. A little lion."

"'Tis more than present to ya," Keeper said. "'Tis an amulet, requirin' neither will nor word to work. If ya find yourself in a spot, yank the pendant off the chain and it will bring ya right back here to *Corrchnámhach*."

"Oh. Without a portal?"

"Aye. Without a portal, from anyplace in all creation. There's the blood 'o dwarf and druid in that magic." Keeper smiled, the laugh lines all but swallowing his eyes.

It was good to see his smile.

Fáidh felt refreshed, although nothing was going to make the knot in her stomach fully evaporate. She hugged Keeper and left The Angle with a hopeful heart.

The portal she had opened waited for her down the road. As she walked, a presence materialized at her side, as if assembled from particles of air turned solid. The creature walked on all fours, still taller than Fáidh, and resembled a cross between a lion and a large dog. It took in gallons of air with every breath and gave off warmth and calm despite its size.

Fáidh had seen this creature before. Madrasceartán, the Alder King's assassin. She decided not to feel threatened. If the beast had come to kill her, she'd already be dead. Instead, the fur-covered monolith plodded along beside her, finally giving her a sideways glance. The liondog tilted its head and gave Fáidh's shoulder a friendly bump. The gentle nudge was still strong enough to send

Fáidh staggering sideways. The creature gave her a good-humored sneeze. Liondogs don't apologize either.

The king's protecting his interests, it seems, and giving me an escort.

At the portal, the liondog sat down on its haunches. Fáidh looked into the creature's eyes, half-closed now, holding her attention with a gaze older than the stars and as wise as Keeper. Madrasceartán nodded, as if to say, "All will be well, little Halfling."

Fáidh hoped it would be true.

She returned to the mortal realm only minutes after having left. Time in The Behindbeyond was funny like that. On the plus side, not much time had passed for the next victim.

Feeling the weight of her mission, Erin changed back into work clothes quickly. She drove to the office blasting songs by the Thompson Twins (neither twins nor named Thompson) and Van Halen (half of the band, more or less, named Van Halen).

These were the details that came to mind under pressure.

Erin found several co-workers busy in the labs, but Belknap's office was empty. Was he ever going to work on the case? She shrugged off the thought. The evidence was where she'd left it. She went straight to it, as if she'd been assigned a task. Sure enough, the medical examiner's report hadn't been worked on. The evidence bags were untouched. She kept the sparse report in hand and selected a few different evidence bags so it would seem she was doing more than snatching the popsicle sticks. Her heart rate still ramped up, although if anyone questioned her, they'd get an abrupt answer now instead of a tentative one.

She retreated to her office after bumping into an intern and apologizing. The young man hadn't minded being run over by a tall brunette in heels.

At her desk, she organized everything she had gathered. She'd made certain to get the popsicle sticks, but she'd also collected the pen Officer Luck had babysat and other physical evidence most likely to hold psychometric data.

Now that her task was set before her, she almost didn't want to start. A little from being afraid of what she might see. More afraid of what she'd have to do with the information after.

She picked up the pen, regarding it through the plastic evidence bag. It was a green ballpoint with the name Palmetto Golf Course printed on the barrel. Erin checked to make sure she'd locked the door. While her office didn't feel quite as private as the ladies' room, she wasn't about to spend any more time sitting on a toilet to use magic.

She used a penknife to cut the seal and felt a shimmer of "Don't get caught!" that she pushed out of her thoughts an instant later. The pen hadn't been dusted for prints yet, but she didn't need to touch the entire pen to see its history. The push button at the top was less likely to have a usable surface for friction ridges. The area was too small for science, but not too small for magic.

Only the push button poked out of the evidence bag as Erin pressed her fingertip on the button. She called up her power and said, "*Feic*."

The magic opened inside her mind. The CSI who had collected the pen was first. She had seen him around and his name was on the evidence bag. She saw herself standing with Officer Luck next. She hadn't ever seen herself in psychometric glory before. Working her way back, she saw the fall of the pen from a man's suit pocket. She couldn't identify the man, so she dialed back further. There was only dark to see, but she caught snatches of a voice humming, radio news in a traveling car, a one-sided cell phone conversation. All of it underscored by a man's cologne.

Back.

She searched for faces. Names. The effect wasn't like a video stream exactly, with a constant series of frames that she could play and replay back and forth. Neither was there a time stamp in the corner of her vision. Everything was fluid in the spell and the impressions she received weren't always consistent in review or

229

complete. Yet the magic listened to her will and word to a degree and brought bits and pieces of images and sounds to her because she wanted them.

Minutes—or hours—later, she found what she wanted. Time was fluid in the magic as well, but when she saw two men, she knew she wanted to pause and study the scene presented to her.

Erin felt her chest tighten. This could be a clue.

Hold on, Fáidh. It could also mean nothing.

It would take time for her to bring the details into focus, but she saw the two men standing in the sun. The first man had a worker's shirt. Erin concentrated on the name stitched into the right breast. The name resolved to "Ismael" with a company name. Titensor Mortuary and Cremation Services. Erin squinted, examining his features. Deeply tan, strong cheekbones, black hair, Hispanic.

Erin moved her attention to their hands. The worker was handing the pen to the other man wearing a business suit. Blue pinstripes. Silk pocket square. Clean cut.

With a gasp, she flinched. She lost contact with the pen and the spell ended with the abruptness of a light bulb burning out.

The other man was her boss, Sherwood Belknap.

Erin pushed herself away from her desk and stood, pacing the floor instinctively. She ran through the implications of the situation in her mind. She didn't need to be an investigator to know the pen's story was odd. The man named Ismael gave a pen to Belknap, then the pen ended up falling to the ground at the crime scene, but that had happened before she had arrived. Belknap had been called to the scene later.

Erin decided there was only one way the narrative made sense. Sherwood Belknap had been at the crime scene earlier in the day and returned after the body had been found.

It was possible he'd been there coincidentally, though. Maybe he just happened to be walking by the same spot and pulled out his phone or something and dropped the pen. The "clue" didn't implicate Belknap in anything. It was circumstantial.

Ismael was another matter. The killer took the arms from the girls in a sick attempt to "deck the halls" but the men's arms that were sewn onto the bodies of the girls had to come from somewhere. A mortuary would be an ideal source for body parts, especially if the bodies were supposed to be cremated. And they were homeless people.

Dear lord, I'm thinking like a serial killer.

Erin had access to police reports and autopsy reports. She made a mental note to find out about the men.

First things first. Excited and energized, she wanted to get back to the popsicle sticks. There would be no caution this time. She'd find out everything she could about the killer's lair. She'd go all the way back to when the popsicle sticks were trees if she had to.

* * *

The sun had set at least an hour ago. No trace of pink or orange remained at the horizon. Erin's phone said it was after 9:00 in the evening, but it felt like her day had been twice that long. She stepped into a salt-scented breeze outside the office that was trying to scrub the heat from the afternoon air, and the temperature fluctuated in swirls.

She'd never been so glad to *stop* using her magic.

The horrors she was struggling to process in her head left her dizzy. She stood on the sidewalk, feet planted apart, and shook her head to clear it. Didn't help. She didn't notice the black Escalade until it had stopped, the window had rolled down, and Katie Castellanos hollered in a perky voice, "Come have drinks with us!"

In the driver's seat, Sherwood Belknap leaned forward and said, "You should come."

Katie added, "I'd love to hear what it's like to be a woman in the medical examiner's office. I'm sure your perspective would be quite refreshing."

I'm sure. Especially after listening to Belknap all day.

Erin didn't say anything at first, but she fixed an expression on her face to give the impression she was considering it and refused to make eye contact with Belknap. After a long moment, she shook her head and said, to Katie, "Thanks anyway. I think I'm too tired to do anything but go home and get some sleep."

"Okay," Kate held the "a" sound for a long time. "But you have to let me interview you soon." She rested her elbows on the window frame and perched her chin on her hands like she was watching a kitten.

"I will," Erin replied. She turned and walked away. The feeling as she walked off was likely in her imagination, but she had the sensation of Belknap's eyes drilling into the back of her head.

She was sure her boss knew a lot more about the Popsicle Killer than he was letting on. She was equally sure Katie Castellanos wasn't in danger. Every one of the girls who were killed had the middle name of Holly. Katie's middle name was Yudith. She also knew that the killer struck no sooner than one week after the previous murder and the girls had each been murdered within 24 hours from the time they went missing.

Lastly, in the world's most generous "benefit of the doubt" moment, if Ismael was the killer, Erin felt it was possible Belknap didn't know. Belknap wasn't the killer himself. She felt certain about that. He could, however, be incompetent enough not to realize who his friend at the Titensor Mortuary and Cremation Services truly was.

A monster.

Maybe.

And Belknap was, after all, incompetent.

Exhausted, Erin drove home, considering her next step. She'd wanted to find out where the killer's lair was located and send the cops over. The mortuary was in a handsome building in Broward county, owned by the Titensor family since 1925, and resembling in no way the dingy warehouse room Erin had seen in her psychometry spells.

So. She stumbled into her bungalow, microwaved an oddly tasteless sourdough personal pizza, and washed it down with a glass of wine. She fell into a fitful sleep.

* * *

The only thing she could really do was ask the police detectives to watch Ismael until he led them to his murder room. She was inclined to give the information to Officer Luck and let him follow up rather than provide the tip directly. He'd appeared able to do his job well. Those broad shoulders and intense eyes didn't hurt either.

Erin sat on the edge of her bed, looking at the photo of her missing husband and silently asking him for advice. She opened her phone and checked her emails, mostly spam, with one stunning exception.

The subject of the email read "Miami-Dade Police Chief Arrested as Popsicle Killer." Erin sped through the article and then went back to read it through again slowly and carefully. A sense of confusion and dread settled over her like a shroud of electricity as she tried to make sense of the details.

According to the report, Chief Cuevas had held a grudge for twenty years against his college sweetheart, Holly Hernandez. She had dumped him at Christmas, leaving behind an unfinished popsicle. A series of failed relationships since that time led Cuevas to blame her for the emotional scars that rendered him unable to hold on to a girlfriend. After meeting her again at a twenty-year class reunion, where she rebuffed him again, he allegedly went over the edge and plotted a murder spree meant to culminate in her death and dismemberment. All to the tune of "Deck the Halls."

It was ridiculous.

Erin knew Chief Cuevas. He frequented the Medical Examiner's building regularly and coordinated with their office and the district attorney's office on cases all the time. She'd found him to be stern and lacking in tact at times, but he was always complimentary of the work she and her colleagues did. Last she'd heard, he'd been with the same girlfriend for three years now, and an imminent proposal of marriage was a consistent topic around the water cooler. That didn't seem to be a man unable to maintain a healthy relationship.

Erin didn't buy it. Any of it.

She scrambled some eggs, throwing her frustrations into breakfast making. The evidence was tied to Chief Cuevas too. The facility where the halls had been decked with boughs of Holly was owned by Chief Cuevas. Detectives had located the property, found the arms and garland strung from the ceiling, photographed the remaining popsicle sticks, and located a freezer with the bodies of homeless men who should have been cremated. There was some question of an accomplice, but detectives had found sufficient cause to arrest their own boss at his house early in the morning, and now he sat in jail.

So far, the chief had been silent. Holly Hernandez could not be reached for comment.

One problem. Despite all the evidence, Cuevas had never touched any of it. If he had touched the sticks at least, Erin would have seen. The chief had been set up. Erin knew that for a fact. She'd seen the real killer in the act. As much as she wanted to forget, she never would. Even worse, there was nobody she could tell about it. Again.

Erin stewed all through her shower and all the way to work.

There had to be something she could do. If her boss was in any way complicit in the framing of Cuevas, he must have a reason—and he had the case. He'd make sure Cuevas got convicted. If her boss was simply clueless, which she had to acknowledge was a possibility, she needed to find a way to get the focus of the investigation back on Ismael and undo their framing of Cuevas. The frameup was the entire goal. Murdering girls was only a means to an end and Ismael had accomplished it.

In any case, she walked into the office reminding herself to pretend it was just another morning on the job. Belknap was in his office, nursing a headache if his hand on his forehead was any indication. Erin realized spending the day with Katie Castellanos was more than enjoying a young woman's attention. He'd taken an interview and turned it into an alibi. Maybe he was more competent that she gave him credit for.

Erin parked herself at her desk. The duty sheet showed she had an autopsy to perform this morning. Fantastic.

She worked through the autopsy, giving due attention to the work and performing each step to the best of her ability. The decedent was a seventeen-year-old drug dealer who had been shot twice in the head with a nine-millimeter pistol. A much more straightforward case to solve. All the while, as she worked on the dead body without flinching, doing what she had been trained for, a part of her couldn't forget Cuevas was sitting in a jail cell.

Lunch was out of the question as she had no appetite.

There must be something I can do.

Something.

In a flash of intuition, she thought of something.

Her hand went to her neck where Keeper's pendant hung from its silver chain. She'd kept it on ever since Keeper put it on her, even in the shower.

She took off the chain now and put it in the pocket of her coat. Then she wrote a short message on a sticky note, grabbed a clipboard, and went to the lab before she could change her mind.

Ignoring her pounding heart, Erin looked for the evidence from the killer's murder site. There were a couple of them, each holding different types of evidence. As she looked, Erin pretended to read notes from the clipboard.

Damn the cameras, full speed ahead.

One box held a critical piece of evidence. A hacksaw used by the killer to cut the arms off the victims. It appeared to have been dusted for prints, but there hadn't been any to find. The killer had wiped it down. Of course. The second box held all the popsicle sticks from the dirty table. Each stick had been bagged by itself but the lot of them had subsequently been placed in a single larger bag to keep them together.

Good.

Erin heard footsteps behind her. She took a glance over her shoulder—*slowly!*—*don't act paranoid!*—but it was a CSI technician on an errand of her own.

Every second that passed seemed to bring another shot of adrenaline. Erin grabbed a paper bag from the drawer and put in the hacksaw and the bag with all the popsicle sticks. To anyone watching, it should look like she was just reorganizing a bit. Hopefully.

She put the sticky note on the bag and retrieved the necklace from her pocket. In the box and out of sight, she wrapped the silver chain around the paper bag once. Twice. Her pulse thrumming in her ears, she pulled the pendant from the chain.

Blink.

The paper bag, and all the evidence it contained, vanished.

Erin had been holding her breath. She let it out and reminded herself to breathe, but she found herself holding it again as she put the lid back on the box.

The whole affair had taken less than a minute. From an observer's point of view, she'd walked in with her clipboard, checked the evidence and packaged some of it, then walked out with her clipboard.

In reality, she'd accomplished much, much more. The evidence was now in Keeper's care. Her note would make sure he held onto it in *Corrchnámhach* until she could retrieve it.

In her professional opinion, it was going to be difficult convicting Chief Cuevas without that evidence.

It would also be a challenge for Chief Belknap to explain how the evidence had gone missing. Evidence he was dutybound to protect as a competent lead examiner on the case.

Erin would forever be convinced, unswervingly, that she'd done the right thing.

One thing left to do.

Wait.

Make that two things.

* * *

Erin saw the gun before she realized who was holding it.

"Get in the car," Ismael said. He had a soft Spanish accent. His words floated to Erin through the dusky light as he stepped matter-of-factly from behind a screen of laurels about five yards away. The pistol caught the light like a warning. Erin considered running or screaming or both, but she knew what kind of damage a bullet could do, and the look on Ismael's face made it clear he'd shoot her before she could take the first step.

She went to her car. The key wouldn't stop shaking, but she finally managed to coax it into the lock. Ismael stood on the passenger side near the rear door.

"Let me in the back." The tone of his voice was as dead as the look in his eyes.

Erin got in the driver's seat and unlocked all the doors. Ismael got in back and softly shut the door.

"Drive toward the airport."

Erin started the car. Pat Benatar was singing "Heartbreaker."

"Turn it off."

She turned off the music and reversed out of the parking spot. When she pulled out onto NW 10th Avenue, he said, "Not the expressway—14th street."

Erin followed 14th Street which eventually connected to River Drive. Erin was surprised at how calm she was as the road carried them past restaurants and boat yards. In the windows and on the sidewalks, people were talking and laughing, unaware the woman driving so nearby had a killer in her back seat.

"Is this how you took the girls?" Erin wanted to get as much information as she could while she had the chance. "Made them drive themselves?"

Ismael's tone never changed. "A gun pointed at your back is a good motivator."

His answer confirmed what Erin already knew. "Why did you want to frame Chief Cuevas?"

"Our cartel does not want him in office. Take 36th."

Crap.

She could infer a lot of information in that answer. None of it was good, if she was right.

Erin got on 36th Street as requested, which took them parallel to the airport on the north side. They were heading to Doral.

"Is Belknap in the cartel too?"

"Sure."

Erin didn't like how casually Ismael was answering her questions. He didn't seem to care what she asked or what he answered. She thought of her phone in her purse. She let her right hand drop to her lap.

"Both hands on the wheel."

Erin complied as Ismael reached over the seat and took her purse. She swore to herself. He wasn't going to give her any chances and he had done this before. Taken women. Forced them to drive their own cars. Killed them. Many times.

She felt her calm start to crack.

"How did you get the evidence out of the office?" Ismael took a turn asking questions.

"If I told you, you wouldn't believe me." Erin swallowed. Her throat so dry.

"There are cameras, you know." Ismael replied. "In your office. In the women's bathroom."

"That's illegal."

"Of course. But hard to find."

Belknap had seen her then. Seen her using her magic. The blue glow of her power captured on video. The Alder King would not be pleased. On the other hand, she probably wasn't going to live long enough for a royal chastisement. Erin's spirits fell anyway, cascading into a knot in her gut.

Ismael directed her to a residential area where the developers had given the neighborhoods pretentious names like "Seychelles Isles" and "White Crane Estates." Ismael used a clicker to open a garage door as they approached and told her to drive in.

There was a beat-up blue Toyota in the garage with Georgia plates. Ismael got out of Erin's car and told Erin to do the same. He left her purse on the seat and opened the trunk of the Toyota.

"Get in."

Erin balked. The trunk looked like it had been reinforced. She'd seen similar vehicles used for human trafficking. "I'm claustrophobic." Her excuse sounded lame even to her.

"Try not to throw up." Ismael pointed the gun at her heart.

Erin got into the trunk, the killer staring down at her as he shut her in.

She lay in the dark for about 45 minutes to an hour, best guess. The drive was smooth enough until the last five minutes when the road turned rough and gravel rattled against the undercarriage. All the while, Erin focused on her heartbeat and tried to remain calm. She managed. Mostly.

The warehouse where they stopped was not the same warehouse owned by Chief Cuevas. This one was surrounded by a high fence. A single streetlamp with a wide metal shade illuminated the rollup door. The door was heavy and padlocked. Ismael gave Erin the keys and told her to unlock it while he kept the gun on her. Then he made her use the chain that operated the door to lift it up. It was only marginally easy because the gear system at the top of the door multiplied her strength. Finally, dirty from the trunk and sweaty from the exertion, Erin was forced inside.

There were nightmares within.

The smells of decay were first.

All the microorganisms that had once kept the victim healthy had turned on their host, creating many of the chemical compounds released into the air. Cadaverine, putrescine, skatole, indole, hydrogen sulfide, methanethiol, dimethyl disulfide—an aromatic blend of rotting fruit, cabbage, eggs, and roadkill.

Knowing the names didn't do much to lessen the nausea.

The body in the corner, dead for at least a week, was a visual nightmare and the source of the sickly sweet stench. And third, a cot on the opposite wall held a large man, lying unconscious, with a blood bag I.V. connected to his arm. Bandages wrapped around his torso had been white once but were now mostly reddish-brown.

"Meet Gordo," Ismael said. "I stabbed him." The bag of blood had run dry a while ago. Ismael felt for the unconscious man's pulse in his neck and nodded to himself. He'd left the door open but still had the gun, almost daring Erin to run.

She didn't run. She had no idea where she was or how far she might have to sprint to find other people.

240

Ismael had a cooler with some ice and another blood bag. "Can you change the bag?"

"Yeah." In looking at the distended belly of the man on the cot, Erin didn't think his chances were good. He likely had internal bleeding so whatever blood went into his arm would largely end up in his abdominal cavity. She changed the I.V. anyway.

Ismael watched her. "When I was a child in Colombia, I saw a *duende*. I had become lost in the jungle and the *duende* found me and showed me the way out. She had an aura that sparkled like the stars. I think you have a magic as well. I think you are a sister to the *duende*."

No. I'm sister to The Morrigan. Let me introduce you.

She stared at Ismael and made an effort to keep her expression blank. No clues. No admissions.

"Okay." Ismael moved toward the door. "I am hungry. I will bring food for you." He gestured with the gun at Gordo and then the corpse in the corner. "I leave you here to think. Think about this room. About these bodies. Your future. Unless you convince me otherwise."

Erin tried swallowing again but had nothing to swallow. She cleared her throat with a cough. "What do I do to convince you?"

"The cartel needs people who can help. It's up to you to tell me how you will help, *duende*." He backed away until he was near the door. He nodded at Erin. "Think." He ducked under the door, lowered it, and locked it.

Erin scanned the room. If there was a second door, she couldn't see it. The windows were high and all of them were covered with metal screens bolted into the walls. This place had been made to hold people who wanted to get out.

She listened to the car start and drive away. Her legs gave out then. She curled into herself on the floor and cried. Deep, ugly sobs. She'd never met anyone as cold as Ismael. She'd read about sociopaths, but they had only been case studies in books. Today, she'd come face to face with someone who cared nothing for other people. Could feel nothing. Just as she viewed the remains of those who came into her lab. Except to Ismael—the whole world around him was a morgue already.

She scrubbed her face with her hands and told herself she didn't have time for this crap. Ismael would be back sooner than she'd want. At least his advice had been good.

Think.

If she had Keeper's necklace, she'd be gone already, but she'd used the necklace to send Keeper the evidence instead.

A trickle of logic carved a path through her ragged emotions. She stood and wiped the rest of her tears away. She went to Gordo's body and the bag of blood. "Sorry, Gordo. I need this more than you do."

She detached the intravenous tube from the unit of blood and unhooked the bag from the loop on the stand. With her foot, she swept a clear space on the concrete floor. She had another thought. She looked at the door. If there was a way to jam it, she could buy herself more time.

Screw it.

There was almost a pint of blood in the bag. Drawing lines with blood was hard. She was shaking, rushed, but the symbol had to be accurate. Her belief would carry the magic to a degree, but not if there was a mistake in the design. Thankfully, the blood spread itself out slowly, smoothing out the lines. When the circle was finished, she drew a feather as best she could at the north, a round shape for a stone at the south, a couple of wavy lines for water at the west, and a simplified candle flame at the east. Here, her belief in what the symbols represented would have to be enough.

Erin stepped back, checking her work so far. Everything looked to be okay, but it had taken—what?—ten minutes? Fifteen? Now she needed to draw in the destination pattern. She looked at the bag. There might be enough to do the job. If she had to, she'd chew a hole in her wrist to get away. Or—poor Gordo. He had plenty of blood in places where it didn't belong already.

The sound of a car door shutting shook her out of her thoughts.

He's back?

With a curse, Erin stepped into the circle and added more lines.

Careful. Careful. Careful.

A curve here. Another there. This line had to connect—

Ismael's footsteps, scuffing on the gravel.

Three lines down this side.

She squeezed the last stream of blood into the pattern as she heard Ismael fiddling with the lock.

Dammit. Dammit. Dammit.

Her eyes scanned the pattern. It was complete. Wasn't it? She scanned again. If it wasn't perfect—no time—it had to work.

She knelt and called up a wad of power. "*Oscailte.*" A bolt of lightning shattered the silence, and the symbol of blood flared bright blue. Without silver and without fire, the spell took what it needed from Erin's body. She groaned and the edges of her vision went dark.

No. No. No.

She pressed her hands against her eyes as the portal opened. The sweet green grass of The Behindbeyond beckoned. Fragrant air. A bright sky.

Freedom.

She almost jumped in.

Gordo.

Panting, sweating, she looked at the dying man on the cot. The man who had given her the blood she needed for her spell. He would never know what sacrifice he had made to save her.

Unless she saved him too.

She needed more time.

"Did you see that flash of light, Ismael?" She screamed at the door. "I have a surprise for you. Just come inside. Let me show you."

The light of the streetlamp outside cast the shadows of Ismael's feet through the gap at the bottom of the door. She saw the shadows move off to the side.

He's not sure.

Good.

Erin ran to the cot. She grabbed the corner and pulled. Gordo was easily two-hundred twenty-five pounds, and the legs of the cot scraped on the concrete. "Couldn't lay off the tacos once in a while, eh, Gordo?" She yanked again. Then again. Each time she pulled the cot, it scooted another foot closer to the portal. The open, shimmering, beautiful portal.

The chain that lifted the door started to rattle. Ismael was going to come in.

Erin screamed again. "If you open that door, I will fry your face, you little bastard."

The chain stopped. The door stopped. Erin had been raised as a lady with Victorian ideals and a scientist with a professional vocabulary. She never would have said such things out loud in normal conversation.

This wasn't a normal conversation. And swearing felt good.

More yanking on the cot. More scrapes on the floor. Even if she had the ability, Erin couldn't have used any more magic. The spell had drained her power to the dregs.

She had another problem. The portal would only remain open as long as the circle was unbroken. If she pulled or pushed the cot into the portal, the legs would scrape over the blood and the portal would close.

It was human to want to leave Gordo behind.

244

With new tears in her eyes, Erin said softly, "Today, I work for the living."

She pulled the end of the cot with Gordo's feet around, pivoting the bed so it was pointing into the portal. She reached over his legs, grabbing for the frame. Behind her, the door was rattling open again.

"Salad," Erin grunted as she tested how much she could lift the cot and still scoot it. "Try a salad, Gordo. *Ensalada*." She screamed, lifted, pulled the cot sideways. The legs cleared the circle and Erin let go. The front of the cot fell through and the sides of the cot collided with the edge. The half-inch wide circle of blood remained intact and it looked as though Gordo's feet were hanging over a precipice. Somehow, Erin kept her balance. She hurried to the top of the cot. A gunshot rang out, so loud inside the warehouse, but Ismael was lying sideways, shooting under the door. She grabbed the frame of the cot and heaved, pushing up and forward with every ounce of strength she had. The cot slid on the siderails through the portal and across the meadow of another realm. Erin was grunting and tired, pushing, pushing until she fell on the grass as well.

She spun around, prone on the grass, the portal like a window in front of her but all she could see was ceiling. She scrambled back into the mortal realm until she could peer up over the edge and into the warehouse. Ismael had ducked under the door and sprinted toward her, not even grimacing from effort or desperation, just wearing that same implacable, sociopathic glare.

Erin raised her hand and flipped him off before turning the same finger down to draw a line in the circle of blood, breaking it. The energy of the circle crackled with white light and, set free, the portal closed.

* * *

Erin had no business being at work. She should have stayed home. She was tired and aching and could use a vacation after the past few hours, but when the police surrounded the medical examiner's building, she was there. No one stopped her as she went through the doors, less than a minute behind the detectives. She strolled past Belknap's office as two burly policemen put her boss in cuffs and read him his rights.

"What's going on?" One of the CSI techs looked on.

"No idea," Erin replied. Halflings can lie.

She stayed there as Belknap was escorted out. He found her, locked eyes with her, but Erin was a sociopath as far as Belknap was concerned. She stared until he looked away.

Erin wasn't sure how all of this was going to be important to the Alder King. Keeper had told her some predictions aren't understood for centuries, if ever. It didn't matter much. She'd done what she felt was right.

In her office, she checked the autopsies that needed to be done. She looked at the reports and didn't notice the patrolman in her doorway until he tapped on the frame. "Got a moment?"

The officer had brought his broad shoulders and intense eyes. "Officer Scribbles. How can I help you?"

"Just wanted to thank you for the tip," he gave her a half grin, holding his cap in his hands.

Erin considered how to respond. "If you're referring to whatever that was going down out there, I heard the information came from an anonymous source."

"Yep." Luck replied. "It did. But there are ways to track these things down."

"Well. I wouldn't know. I'm not an investigator." Erin found herself smiling. It felt good. "Any news on the accomplice? There was an accomplice, I heard."

"Yes, ma'am. Actually, the man we arrested this morning was the real Popsicle Killer. It seems Chief Belknap was more of an accomplice." Luck looked sideways for a moment. "Kind of a stupid name, though. Popsicle Killer. He wasn't killing popsicles."

"Good point," Erin replied. "Did I hear the man's name was Ismael?"

"Not sure I can disclose that, ma'am."

"Fair enough. And the evidence?"

"Yep. We found it in the trunk of his blue Toyota, as you said. Or as the anonymous tipster said."

"Good."

"He was quite adamant that he didn't put it there. Said he had no idea how it ended up in his trunk. Any idea?"

"If I did, it would be a Keeper." Erin smiled some more.

"Ma'am?"

Moving on. "There is something I might be able to help with, Officer."

The patrolman nodded.

"There's some evidence in the Michelle Hernandez murder. A green pen from the Palmetto Golf Course. It should have both Belknap's fingerprints and Ismael's. I'm sure it will help link the two of them together."

"Okay. That sounds great." Officer Luck was already writing things down. "Could you show me?"

Erin considered going to the lab with him. Maybe they'd have a nice conversation. Maybe have some Chinese food for lunch together. Instead, "I think it's best if I stay as far away from the evidence as I can, Officer."

"All right."

"Did the anonymous tipster mention a man named Gordo?"

"Oh. Yes, ma'am. Looks like the detectives will be interviewing him for a while. He has a lot to say about the cartel's activities in South Florida."

Erin nodded. "Good."

Officer Luck shifted from one foot to the other, turning his cap in his hands. He was cute.

"Anything else?" Erin asked.

"I was . . . wondering. If I could give you a call sometime? Not as an anonymous tipster?"

Erin liked his confidence, asking like this in her own office. She did like his eyes. And how he worked. She thought about the photo on her nightstand—her husband Blake. Three years and then some since he'd disappeared.

"You have a good day, Officer Luck," she smiled. "I'll see you around."

He nodded, accepting maturely. "All right. How about a sister? Do you have a sister?"

Erin couldn't think of a way to explain why that question made her laugh.

Feasty-Feast

The Super-Short Short Story

This is another story that would have suffered if I had tried to write to a subject or a theme. "Feasty-Feast" did get published in an anthology titled *The Hunger,* but the matchup of story and theme was mostly a happy coincidence.

Like most stories, the theme came to mind later, after the narrative had already been written and was being edited. That's the time when the subtext really deserves to be explored and the story's thematic elements start to emerge, begging for a polish.

The first goal in writing this story, however, was to create a thoroughly different voice and tone by telling the story in a unique way. A point of view that *wasn't* human. Hmm.

The seed of the story's plot ultimately came from a neuroscientific experiment called the "memory transfer phenomenon," where it appeared that flatworms were able to learn tasks by simply eating the brains of flatworms who had learned those tasks before. In other words, worm brains learned new things just by eating other brains.

Hmm. Worms don't make for very interesting protagonists. I still needed a creature that wasn't human (already decided) but not a zombie. A creature that had the tools of a predator and could *hunt.*

I was familiar with parasites—I have children—and lo, but also behold, little Ingk and Pala were born.

As an author, you like to have your stories land either at the beginning or the end of an anthology. I like either and I've gotten both a few times, which is a little extra payoff for all the hard work. Happily, this story got the coveted spot at the end of the anthology and I like to think of it as the palate-cleansing dessert that satiates that last remaining corner of literary hunger.

Oh. Almost forgot about the theme.

You are what you read.

Feasty-Feast

Dinner. Not hard to get. Not hard at all. Just reruns.

Brains not fulfilling. Not anymore. Not since Pala almost died.
No. Not since.

Full-filling. Yes. Food in tummy-tum.

Fulfilling? No. Food always reruns now. Bland. Boring. Bad.

Ingk regarded his prey.

Stupey-Stupe. Sits all day. Tiny screen. Big screen. No
different. Stupey-Stupe watching crappy-crap.

Ingk stuck out his tongue.

Blech.

No choice. Need to keep tummy-tum full. Need to keep
pretty-pretty Pala alive for another day. Poor Pala. Broken wing.
No fly.

No hunt.

Ingk flexed his fingers. Twitched his wings. Flew.

Zip.

To the ear of Stupey-Stupe. Past the little hairs. No touch. Over the skin. No touch.

No repeat Pala's mistake.

Through the canal. Stop at the membrane.

Up.

Through the hole he had drilled in the bone. To the brain of Stupey-Stupe.

Dark.

Ingk's light slits glowed. Brighty-bright.

Dinner. Many pits and scoops in Stupey-Stupe's brains. Many dinners eaten.

All reruns.

Ingk sighed. Dinners were fulfilling before. Dinners taken from *her*.

From Feasty-Feast.

Feasty-Feast had been good dinners. Delicious. Full of many tasty things.

Feasty-Feast had also been quick. Pala's mistake. Bad flying. Touched the skin. Touched the hairs. Feasty-Feast so quick with her hand. Her finger poking in her ear.

Pala's wing broken. Ingk had pulled Pala farther in. Into the canal. Safe place near the membrane. Heart pounding. Eyes weeping. Waiting. Feasty-Feast finally falling asleep. Ingk carrying Pala back. Back to the hovel in the wall. Barely able to fly with Pala in his arms. Barely getting home.

No dinner.

Not that night.

Only crying.

Ingk had been angry. Had wanted to go back. Back up the hole. Tear up Feasty-Feast's brain. Rip. Tear. Scoop. Squish.

Waste.

Couldn't go. Had to care for pretty-pretty Pala.

252

Feasty-Feast left next day. Out the white door. No coming back.

Since then, only Stupey-Stupe brains.

Ingk went to work. Scoop from here. Scoop from there.

Stupey-Stupe never miss it.

Blood pooling at Ingk's feet. Walking back carrying pinky-pinks. Bloody footprints through the bone tunnel. By the membrane, licking the blood off feet. No trace outside that way. Through the canal.

Light slits off.

Out. Flying away.

Stupey-Stupe moving his finger across the small screen. Staring at the crappy-crap. Absently scratching at his ear.

Too late. No broken wing for Ingk. Ha ha.

Ingk flying. To their hovel. Zip. Through the hole he had drilled in the concrete wall.

Pretty-pretty Pala waiting. Her eyes gray. Broken wing. Sad—but pretending.

Ingk let Pala pick a pinky-pink. Watched to make sure she ate. Keep the tummy-tum full. She closed her eyes after each bite. Ten bites. Tiny bites. Licked her fingers even though it was for show. Gave Ingk a small smile. Pretty-pretty smile.

Satisfied, Ingk ate. Big bite.

Closed his eyes.

Emoji of poop. Rerun.

Text: "what r u doing?" Answer: "tv." Text: "me 2." Another rerun.

Images: red cars. Sneakers. Girls in bikinis.

Reruns. Reruns. Reruns.

No fresh. No tasty.

No meaning.

Ingk's bites all the same things. Same crappy-crap. He didn't even close his eyes. No new tastes. No reason to bother. No reason to watch/see.

Full-filling. Yes.

Fulfilling. No.

Ingk plopped down. Sat in the dust. Traced a picture. Maybe make Pala smile again.

Pointed nose. Tailfins. Jagged fire. Porthole.

Pala pointed. She knew Ingk's favorite. Her high voice: "*Martian Chronicles*. Tasty dinners."

Ingk nodded. Drew again. New spot. Ocean waves. Curve of land. Palm tree.

Pala waited. Too many good dinners. Could be a man on the beach. *Robinson Crusoe*. Could be a box under the tree. *Treasure Island*.

Ingk added a boat with a big cat.

"*Life of Pi*." Pala clapped her hands, making Ingk smile. "Yummy-yum."

Pala fluttered her wings. Happy. Then winced. Pain.

Ingk saw Pala start to cry. Ran his fingers through the dust to erase the drawings.

Stupey-Stupe dinners not fulfilling. Not helping Pala get better. Not helping her heal.

Not for a moontime.

If Pala keeps not getting better . . . no. Not good thinking.

Ingk made fake yawn. Pretending to be tired. "Nighty-night?"

Pala nodded. Pala always tired now.

Ingk stood. Took Pala by the hand. Walked to their little bed. Cotton-ball mattress and dryer sheet blanket. Settled in. Pala snuggling into Ingk's shoulder, eyes wet. Ingk careful to keep hands away from Pala's broken wing. Let light slits glow softly. Keep away the dark.

Ingk prayed no bad dreams.

Slam. Stomp.

Ingk's eyes opened.

Good prayer answered. Morning now. No bad dreams.

Ingk slip out of bed. Look at Pala. So small. Gray. Broken.

Voices. Knew voice and new voice.

?

Sneak through wall. Wings itchy-twitchy.

Stupey-Stupe on the couch already. Tiny screen in hand. Big screen on too.

Reruns.

Then.

Bouncy-bounce. Girl with red hair. Jumping. Skipping. To the couch.

Stupey-Stupe not noticing. Playing with screen.

Girl with something. Not screen.

Ingk saw. Watched Girl open the something.

"Don't you have a phone?" Stupey-Stupe noticed. Finally.

"This is better." Girl showed Stupey-Stupe. Pages open.

"Whatev."

A drop of water landed on Ingk's foot. Water-not-water. Water-drool.

Ingk swiped the saliva off his lips.

Feasty-Feast had read those things too. Before going out the white door.

Impulsive. Ingk took off. Flew over the Girl and her book. Memorized the words. Back home. Zip.

In the hovel, in the dust, Ingk drew the words.

Pala would wake up soon. Ingk would show her the words.

The Adventures of Tom Sawyer.

Ingk stepped back. More drool falling. Tonight, he would fly. Hunt.

Pinky-pink and blood. Fulfilling. Healing Pala.

Feasty-Feast again.

#1 Bestselling Fantasy Series

Read the novels that accompany the stories, "The Mark," "The Sister of the Morrigan," and "Lucky Day"

Tales From the Behindbeyond, Books 1-3
Got Luck   Got Hope   Got Lost

Masterful Science Fiction

If you enjoyed the science fiction stories in this collection, like
"Spera Angelorum" or "Sailing on the Tides of Burning Sand,"
then you'll *love*

Hollowfall

Michael Darling's first cyberpunk novel, set in the world of the
popular board and computer game, Master of Wills.

Author Biography

Bestselling author MICHAEL DARLING has worked as a butcher, a librarian, and a magician, which turned out to be an ideal set of skills for a fiction writer. He lives in the beautiful Rocky Mountains with his wife and kids where he writes award-winning stories beside his big buddy, a St. Bernese dog named Appa. While best known for his Tales from the Behindbeyond urban fantasy novels, Michael writes across all the best genres. His most recent novel is *Hollowfall*, a science fiction adventure set in the cyberpunk universe of the popular computer and board game Master of Wills.

Michael graduated from Weber State University with a degree in English Literature and loves to blend the classic with the contemporary in his writing. His early work included several plays that were professionally produced along with radio programs that aired in 80 markets around the world and videos for corporate presentations. Besides writing, Michael also loves to travel, dabble in languages, and cook tasty gluten-free dinners.

Please visit Michael at www.michaelcdarling.com where you can find more information about his current work. You'll also find suspiciously easy instructions for stalking Michael on social media.

Made in the USA
Columbia, SC
27 April 2021